Cannibal-King
City of the Watcher III

Volume Three of the
City of the Watcher trilogy
Andrew M. Reichart

ARGA
WARGA
PRESS

Weird Books for Weird People

Also by Andrew M. Reichart from Argawarga Press:

Wallflower Assassin

Weird Luck in the City of the Watcher

Time Traveling Blues in the City of the Watcher

Argawarga Press is an imprint of Autonomous Press that publishes strange fantasy, horror, and science fiction.

Autonomous Press is an independent publisher focusing on works about neurodivergence, queerness, and the various ways they can intersect with each other and with other aspects of identity and lived experience. We are a partnership including writers, poets, artists, musicians, community scholars, and professors. Each partner takes on a share of the work of managing the press and production, and all of our workers are co-owners.

Front Cover by Mike Bennewitz @sonofwitz

Interior by Casandra Johns

Originally published in 2015 by Argawarga Press

ISBN-13: 978-1-945955-35-8
E-ISBN-13: 978-1-945955-57-0

Argawarga Press • argawarga.com

BEING A THIRD ACCOUNT OF THE BATTLE OF MELKHAIOS

edited by Alexander Woad,
Acting Archivist

First person text recited by Jack Waghalter in paratheatrical 'memory rant' monologue-trance, during a series of sessions conducted and recorded by Alexander Woad at the Archive of Thoth in Ohlone City, California, Earth-X00023.

Dialogues transmitted by spy Crow Terminal via stolen Reality Patrol telepaphone implant; recorded and transcribed by Alexander Woad.

All other text compiled by Alexander Woad.

for Joy

"He can transport himself, in no time at all, to any place that he can visualize. And he has a very vivid imagination. Granting that any place you can think of exists somewhere in infinity, if the Prince can think of it too, he is able to visit it. Now, a few theorists claim that the Prince's visualizing a place and willing himself into it is actually an act of creation. No one knew about the place before, and if the Prince can find it, then perhaps what he really did was make it happen. However—positing infinity, the rest is easy."

— *Roger Zelazny, Creatures of Light and Darkness*

"Bring war material with you from home; but forage on the enemy. Thus the army will have food enough for its needs."

— *Sun Tzu, The Art of War*

Contents

Intro

I am nothing. I am no thing. The self is an illusion, just a confluence of forces, a set of predispositions and acquired inclinations. Predispositions: genetic and epigenetic, and other things inherent to the material world, such as the shape of my body, the law of gravity, the law of solid objects. Inclinations: acquired by trauma, or hormones, or self-actualization, or reason (should such a thing actually exist), or will (should such a thing actually exist). Blend in with these forces the thing called memory; though I've heard that we don't keep memories in a storehouse, but remake each anew every time it is reaccessed—and thereby even memory is fleeting, circumstantial, malleable, organic, ephemeral, and subject to compound error.

I am things such as these, and I am the thing that perceives them from within. I am an animal with a monkey mind, having a moment of awareness at a given time or place, being where I am, doing what I am doing, thinking what I am thinking, or thinking nothing. This is what "I" am and so are you, but the point is that it's thoughts like these that enabled me to endure the days of torture at the hands of the Feds. Thoughts like these, plus self-hypnotic meditation and lots of practice from getting tattooed.

Unfortunately, how I got in such a predicament is another story, and I apologize for not telling it here. My wife Beth and I got up to a whole sequence of revolutionary antics. This particular story is about what happened after I escaped, out of one frying pan and into a sort of fire, and traveled knowingly for the first time from Earth to another world.

I guess the last thing you need to know is my superpowers, aside from the prone-to-interdimensional-travel thing. Just three minor ones: *Weird Luck*, a *Sovereign Shield*, and the so-called *Power to Clear Men's Minds*. Back on Earth I knew I was weird, and that I had a way with words; but although I was frankly at a loss to explain the phenomenon I jokingly called my Sovereign Shield (cf. its initial gradual manifestation during my seventh grade dodge ball championship, and numerous odd events thereafter), I didn't truly know I was outright magic till I went to a magical world. That's this story.

Prologue Outside City Gardens, Trenton

CHESTER and OLDER ALECK lean back against a concrete wall. The low gray overcast glows with light from the city beneath it. Loud music booms from the other side of the wall.

CHESTER: Do these guys even play here this year?

OLDER ALECK: Obviously.

CHESTER: You know what I mean, dude, on Earth-Prime. I thought they played CB's.

OLDER ALECK: There is no "Earth-Prime."

CHESTER: Whatever, dude.

OLDER ALECK: Some Earths they played CBGB on this tour, on some they played here, sometimes both, none more real than the other.

CHESTER: Whatever, gimme the thing.

OLDER ALECK: On what basis would you even judge that one world is more—

CHESTER: Gimme the thing.

Older Aleck hands Chester an inch-thick stack of paper bradded together, and a short, wide metal cylinder like a smallish hockey puck. Chester waggles the puck.

CHESTER: *(cont'd.)* Where's this go?

OLDER ALECK: Nowhere.

CHESTER: What's 'nowhere,' Antarctica? Deep space? Post-Giuliani Times Square?

OLDER ALECK: No, I mean it's empty.

CHESTER: The heck I need this for then? I got a warehouse fulla these things.

Tries to hand it back. Older Aleck refuses it.

OLDER ALECK: It's clean. Jailbroken and stripped of quantum history.

CHESTER: Yeah, like I said, I got a sub-dimensional warehouse with thousands o' these of all shapes and sizes and whaddayacall providences—

OLDER ALECK: I think you mean "provenances."

CHESTER: —and a drone that drops the one I want into my hand one point five secs after I think it. All stripped, natch, you think I carry hot Patrol gear?

OLDER ALECK: Chester.

CHESTER: Yes, Aleck fuckin' Woad who thinks I'm stupid, how may I help you?

OLDER ALECK: Stop talking.

CHESTER: Why would I stop talking.

OLDER ALECK: So I can tell you the plan.

CHESTER: Go. Not sayin' a word. Zip. Silent. Mmm.

OLDER ALECK: You bring them the book as a peace offering, they incidentally find the disk on you and confiscate it. You ask for amnesty, Xax grants it because you're an asset and he needs you for the next step.

CHESTER: Oh. *(pause)* Bonus. Why didn't you mention the amnesty thing before?

OLDER ALECK: Because you never stop talking. So you tell Xax about Clark, Xax codes this handy empty gate disc with the code I got him, he gives it to Clark to tempt me, and he also tricks Clark into stealing the manuscript.

CHESTER: Wait, what?

OLDER ALECK: Trust me. This is how it happens.

CHESTER: How the fuck so?

OLDER ALECK: It just does. It happened this way in my past. And all this leads up to how we lure Xax into our trap.

CHESTER: Easy on that 'we,' man.

OLDER ALECK: And not before he gets the Reality Patrol to grant you amnesty.

CHESTER: Right. Okay. Hmm.

Chester nods in time with the music.

CHESTER: *(cont'd.)* Okay, I'm in.

OLDER ALECK: Fucking finally.

They both nod in time.

CHESTER: This 1986?

OLDER ALECK: 1985.

CHESTER: Oh, ohhh—that makes sense. It was *'86* they
played CB's.

Older Aleck sighs and shakes his head.

Prologue in the Palace-Temple of Goromath

Night. Topmost floor of the Palace-Temple. GENERAL GOROMATH stands at the east window of his chamber, gazing out over the Herax Zone at the titanic stone face on the mountain.

He has removed his "Cannibal-King" eyepatch, revealing the golden orb of one of the Eyes of Kaios. It glitters in the starlight.

AKAZ, the God-Dog, the Wolf of Kaios, etc., bursts forth from
   the crackling fire of wood and bones in the fireplace.
AKAZ: Ahem.

Goromath turns and beholds him.

GOROMATH: Ah. Perfect timing. Good dog.

AKAZ: Fuck you.

GOROMATH: Be that as it may, thanks for coming.

AKAZ: I'm only entertaining these shenanigans 'cause it seems like this'll up the odds of you dying in the process at some point.

GOROMATH: Ah, Akaz. No one else among our peers offers such candor.

AKAZ: Yay.

GOROMATH: Perhaps upon the death of Apraxos you might even forgive me, haha.

AKAZ: I'm so sure.

GOROMATH: You must admit, all the discord between us has fed us both, just as the discord around us has. Me feeding on Strife, you feeding on Chaos; we're not unalike, you and I.

AKAZ: Ugh, puke. Can we just get on with it?

GOROMATH: Very well. Promise me the Fifth Sphere and jump in my mouth.

AKAZ: Whut.

GOROMATH: Promise me that when Melkhaios falls, you will allow me to retain the Circus of Burnt Skulls, uncontested; and with it, mastery over the Fifth Sphere of the cosmos. You keep the Spiral Ride, and the corresponding cycles of Death and Rebirth that wind between the Sixth and Seventh Spheres; that is rightly your realm of dominion, without question. But cede to me the Fifth Sphere, for once and for all.

AKAZ: Nope.

GOROMATH: Swear it and I will give you an army able to overcome even the Herax.

AKAZ: What army.

GOROMATH: The army of the Cannibal-King.

AKAZ: Bullshit. Even if they got it together, which they won't, they'd destroy your whole damn racket.

GOROMATH: Nay, they would destroy the machinery of *Apraxos*; but I long for such destruction. This drudgery of institutional suffering feeds Apraxos well—but to me it is insufferable monotony. I long to restore the world to its natural disorder of, as it is said in scripture, "shouting and killing and reveling in joy."

AKAZ: Even if it destroys your Herax army.

GOROMATH: A small price to pay for my own deliverance. Now swear, and jump in my mouth.

AKAZ: You're gonna just let me jump into yer mouth.

GOROMATH: We must. I have someone for us to speak to. *(He taps his golden eye.)* Possess me and we will speak with him together.

Akaz stares at him in silence.

GOROMATH: *(cont'd.)* Swear.

AKAZ: And you propose to make me keep my word how?

GOROMATH: I trust that circumstances will unfold to reveal that I am your truest ally, and that the world will prove much more to your liking with me holding the Circus.

AKAZ: And then what? Apraxos gone, what's to keep the Witch-Queen of Gomothrax from crossing the bay and taking his place? Nice little poetic sequel to how she took Gomothrax from him, way back when she first came here. Heh.

GOROMATH: Our world will be far too wild for her tastes.

Goromath smiles down at Akaz.

Akaz leaps into Goromath's mouth.

GOROMATH: Blood Eagle! We wish to speak with you.

Far beyond the mountain, in featureless flat desert, BLOOD EAGLE stands staring into the distance. At his feet lies a dead Herax soldier.

BLOOD EAGLE: Who.

GOROMATH: Enshroud yourself in prayer and speak to us with your thoughts. Behold: with me is Great Akaz.

BLOOD EAGLE: Akaz? *(Blood Eagle looks within. Falls to his knees. Bows his head to the ground.)* Great Akaz, I behold now your sacred majesty. Who is this minion whom you now possess, who speaks into my mind?

AKAZ: Heh.

GOROMATH: I am General Goromath.

Blood Eagle sits up.

BLOOD EAGLE: Goromath—!

GOROMATH: And now you have killed at my behest. Rendering you *my* minion.

BLOOD EAGLE: You talk nonsense.

GOROMATH: Wrong. I possess one of the Eyes of Kaios. Just as Apraxos binds his minions to his Eye of Kaios through the medium of a contract signed in blood, I bind my minions to me through the eternal bond of having spilled blood at my behest.

AKAZ: Fucking creepy.

BLOOD EAGLE: I would never kill at your behest.

GOROMATH: But you have done so; and the proof is that we converse now.

BLOOD EAGLE: Impossible. Whom?

GOROMATH: The Herax captive at your feet.

BLOOD EAGLE: That cannot be.

GOROMATH: I let him be captured. The plot he described, to raise the Cannibal-King and unite the Givers, is mine. And his final blasphemy that provoked you into killing him—such was my intention all along. All to the dual end of inspiring you in your dream to unite the Givers, while conscripting you into the body of my minions.

BLOOD EAGLE: You have tricked and trapped me.

GOROMATH: Coercion was needed to ensnare you into your own destiny. But I will deliver unto you the conquerors of the Herax. And I will feed through you and your minions upon the souls of the Herax.

BLOOD EAGLE: And obliterate your own army?

GOROMATH: With you leading the destruction, and killing my old expendables, any and all killers who slay at my behest shall join my new dominion. Even if this does not result in a net growth of my army, I will far prefer to preside over diversified chaos than the blank, lockstep Herax. And the slaughter will be, for me, a feast unlike any I've had for centuries.

AKAZ: That's fucked up.

BLOOD EAGLE: How can you hold dominion over both enemy armies at once?

GOROMATH: *(Laughs.)* Given the opportunity, how could I possibly resist?

BLOOD EAGLE: So the union of the Givers under the true Cannibal-King is not your dreaded nightmare, as your agent told me.

GOROMATH: It is, on the contrary, my dearest wish.

BLOOD EAGLE: Does that not endanger the myth that you are the Cannibal-King? Undermining the very basis of your Palace-Temple?

GOROMATH: Yes, and joyous to me is the destruction of the propaganda strewn by Apraxos. Damn his false myths! He must die!

BLOOD EAGLE: How can any of this be?

AKAZ: The world is fucked up, man.

GOROMATH: I feed on Strife! This world is for wild fighting, not the homeostasis of grinding despair.

BLOOD EAGLE: Great Akaz, how can you be in league with your foe Goromath?

AKAZ: I'm not. Let's kill him as soon as we're done with Apraxos.

GOROMATH: I promise you, once Apraxos is out of the way, you will both see fit to let me live.

AKAZ: Fat fuckin' chance.

GOROMATH: This world will be renewed in conflict. Wait and see. Meanwhile, kill Apraxos with me. With the aid of the real Cannibal-King.

BLOOD EAGLE: What can the likes of you mean by "real Cannibal-King"?

GOROMATH: I mean the man himself, as actually prophesied. Not the mockery of mutilated scripture that

Apraxos made of me. The real King. Kaios reborn. Incarnation of the Sun Dragon.

BLOOD EAGLE: And all this will come to pass as your dead
minion told me?

GOROMATH: Aye.

BLOOD EAGLE: You will capture me, but only to bring me
into Melkhaios? And when I am freed within the city, I
will rob Apraxos of the Skull of Kaios? Which can then be
used to summon the Cannibal-King?

GOROMATH: Aye.

AKAZ: Remember to act surprised.

BLOOD EAGLE: What?

AKAZ: When you see us. Act surprised. So Apraxos doesn't
suspect what we're up to.

BLOOD EAGLE: Ah.

Prologue in the Ruins of the Vast Festival

It's 1999 on Earth-X00023 and Senior Special Agent BELI-AL XAX and Special Agent MAX WARLOCK, Reality Patrol operatives in black suits and black ties, stand inside a dimly-lit RV. They loom over Agent NED WINGS, a black bag man for the United State Security Agency, lying on the floor with a gruesome compound forearm fracture.

WINGS: Please... medic....
XAX: Quick question.
WINGS: Not... telling you... shit.
XAX: Now now, that's no way to elicit a favor.
WINGS: Favor...? Look at my arm! Where's your decency?
WARLOCK: Doubt there's a medic left.
WINGS: Fuck. Fuck.
XAX: We just need to know who rescued Waghalter.
WINGS: Please....

Agent Xax grabs the broken arm. Agent Wings screams. Agent Xax looks at it.

XAX: This isn't from a wrist-lock. This is from a weapon.

Agent Wings screams more. Agent Xax lets go of his arm.

WARLOCK: *(to Xax)* I'm betting hatchet wound, sir. Or kukri.
XAX: Waghalter's handiwork?

Agent Wings just pants and whimpers.

Someone tries the door. It's locked. Agent Warlock opens it a crack and displays a badge reading 'United State Security Agency' and 'Inter-Dimensional Council.'

WARLOCK: IDC.

He slams the door and locks it.

XAX: Who chopped your arm? Waghalter himself?
WINGS: Please....
WARLOCK: Just answer the question, Wings, what's your problem?
WINGS: My problem? Waghalter's been right all along, that's my problem! We've been the bad guys ever since we started hunting him.

Agent Wings spits weakly at them.

XAX: Ha. Hahaha.

WARLOCK: Oh. He converted you.

WINGS: You don't get it.

XAX: I'm impressed.

WARLOCK: Even while you were torturing him, he was able to use his mind control.

XAX: I would love to see his psi ratings.

WINGS: Not mind control. He's just... *right*. He didn't control my mind. He... opened it.

XAX: Sure sure sure. So who was with him? His wife?

WARLOCK: I bet she's the one who hit him.

Agent Wings glowers up at Agent Warlock and says nothing.

XAX: Who else was with them, Wings? Jack's Brother? Doomer Kelso?

WARLOCK: Picture it: Mrs. Waghalter busts in, hatchet in hand for stealth instead of a gun, and when she sees the state of her man she takes a swing, which Wings cleverly blocks with his forearm. But Jack stops her from taking the followup swing at Wings' head.

Agent Wings clenches his teeth.

XAX: You're saying Waghalter actually spared his own torturer? He's not a saint, Max.

WARLOCK: Didn't just spare him. Planned to use him as an ally.

XAX: Ah. Of course. Devious. I keep thinking of Waghalter as a hothead.

WARLOCK: Yes and no.

WINGS: Even you bastards won't stop him.

WARLOCK: Shut up, Wings.

WINGS: *(to Xax)* Even when you cut out his eye....

XAX: My previous visit here was entertaining, I admit.

WINGS: Everything we did to him... it all just made him stronger.

XAX: Poor Wings, clueless to the last. *(nose to nose, whispering)* That's. Been. My. Plan. All. Along.

Agent Xax places a small device against Agent Wings' temple and presses a button. A blue spark. Wings jolts and falls over dead.

Agent Warlock unlocks the door, speaks to people outside.

WARLOCK: Back up.

He and Agent Xax leave, shoving their way between USSA agents.

Later, Agents Xax and Warlock speed in a black sedan across sunbaked salt flat, Warlock driving. Following fresh tracks of several vehicles toward a column of smoke.

They drive past an acre of burned-out cars and scattered remnants of burned wooden structures. The wrecks all look like they've been in the desert for months or years; whatever's burning now is something else, beyond.

Agent Xax has a small glass jar containing an eyeball. He holds it up to one eye, squints his other eye shut, as though looking through the severed eye.

WARLOCK: Festival looks more or less as we left it.

XAX: I did not care for the way folks made fun of our RV. I have no desire to sleep in the dirt. I'm glad this stupid, stupid festival got shut down after the fire riot.

WARLOCK: Acid in the desert is good. The openness. The featurelessness of the vast plain.

XAX: Even the minds of mundanes can fray the surrounding reality, however slightly. I'm sure the tripping hordes that night helped to thin the membrane between the worlds.

WARLOCK: Plus Waghalter himself on 7g of psilocybin by his own account, walking in a circle around the fallen wicker man in the center of town all night till dawn. You think he just drove up this morning and finished opening the portal?

XAX: But how, though.

WARLOCK: The IDC did say it looked like it was opened from the Kaios side.

XAX: Tsk. I'm afraid I can't credit them, or any Earthlings for that matter, with having all that much of a clue. With those clunky sensors back at IDC HQ? No offense.

WARLOCK: None taken. This isn't my Earth.

XAX: Are they all that different, really?

WARLOCK: *(shrugs)* I have little in common with Earthlings of any version.

XAX: Let's wait for the real report, from our real analysts at the Reality Patrol, before we speculate how it opened.

WARLOCK: Yes, sir.

At the base of the column of smoke, a burning black heli-copter lies upside-down atop a smashed black sedan. An-other sedan, also burning, rests smashed nose-first into the side of the double wreck. More sedans are parked nearby; USSA agents in suits swarm around. Agent War-lock parks a few dozen yards away. He and Agent Xax step out of their car and lean against it. Xax consults a small handheld gizmo.

XAX: Okay, Waghalter's gate shut itself. Whew. Hopefully no one else got through.

WARLOCK: That triple crash looks improbable.

XAX: That's Waghalter's Extreme Chronic Synchronicity Syndrome.

WARLOCK: It could be someone else's. Could even be mere standard CSS. It's not even entirely impossible for a mundane crash to look like that.

XAX: With a bonus interdimensional portal conveniently in your path? That's textbook Weird Luck, Max.

WARLOCK: Ah, but—

XAX: Portal to a world where you happen to be convenient-ly prophesied as a god?

WARLOCK: Still, considered as a distinct element, the crash—

XAX: You can't separate them.

WARLOCK: Yes and no.

XAX: I'm saying, if there's even a hint of ECSS, then any-thing weird in the vicinity becomes ECSS.

WARLOCK: That's an oversimplification. For example, someone else's CSS can set off a minor coincidence in the vicinity, at the same moment a major one, such as the portal, is set off by Waghalter's ECSS....

XAX: This isn't mechanical engineering, Max. Forces in the Luck Plane can't be teased out like that. It's a web o' chaos.

WARLOCK: Agree to disagree. I consider the research on that topic inconclusive.

XAX: Eh.

Warlock withholds any mention of his own first-hand experience with Weird Luck.

They look on.

XAX: If the USSA finds anything uncooked enough to autopsy for ballistics, I betcha they'll find the old "inexplicable characteristic pattern" of men killed by slugs from their own guns—but without powder burns, ha ha.

WARLOCK: I frankly don't look forward to facing Waghalter's Sovereign Shield.

XAX: Yeah, you're probably gonna wanna avoid shooting at him. *(winks)*

WARLOCK: Probably so.

XAX: C'mon.

Agent Xax pulls a silver disc out of his pocket. Flicks it tumbling through the air. It splits into four slim discs, which arrange themselves in a square and hang there in space. Through the square can be seen a dim stone hallway.

XAX: Shall we?

They walk through.

Escape from the Ruins of the Vast Festival

Any mortal would fragment under the treatment I've received, but I am become Odin at the Well of Mimir. Ordeal brings wisdom. Every stab and pulse of pain only cements my fearlessness. These bunglers should know that their neuroelectric agony machine serves only as a meditation tool, pushing me into deeper equanimity. They should know that the only way to terrorize me is with actual bodily harm, not mere pain. Perhaps they do know, and just need me mostly intact. Or perhaps they have only begun, the removal of my eye only the first maiming in a series of nightmares. But even so, ordeal brings wisdom. And power. What did Odin gain from the Well in exchange for his eye? No one knows, reports vary, but something magnificent, surely. And I have traded my eye for—what? What new worlds will unfold before my phantom eye?

Please pardon the *in medias res*; it's possible you haven't read *The Argus MacWargus Show*, which tells the tale of the events leading up to this one. (In my timestream it isn't even written yet, but who knows when you'll see this.)

Beth and I frankly dislike being apart much. You know how young children sometimes pair up, inseparable BFFs holding hands on the playground, going everywhere together, synced-up in a cute little dyadic micro-universe? It's not *saccharine*, at least I think not, but we're that kinda couple, I'm afraid. One side effect: if we're apart for over a day, when we find ourselves back in each other's company we find it surreal and disorienting for a bit, as if it's too good to be true. Giddy. Don't hate on us for it; our romance has proven an especially helpful foundation to help us through the collapse of 'democratic' 'civilization.' To understand my mood when she arrives, remember this side effect.

After being kidnapped by the Feds, transported to a secret torture site, and interrogated for days by Agent Wings, Agent Xax, and others—including the agonizing surgical removal of my left eye—life prior to my capture had faded to something as unreal as a dream that has vanished upon waking. So you can imagine not only my surprise and relief, but also the incomprehensible romantic surrealness of seeing her, *her*, out of nowhere, busting into my trailer swinging a hatchet. At the moment I behold this heavenly vision through my one remaining eye, it renders me almost dizzy enough to faint.

There's another layer of incongruity making this moment all the more confusing. It so happens that, after exhausting strain and under horrifically challenging conditions, I've *just* finished convincing my torturer, Wings, Ned, to help me escape. So much for that plan. Too bad for the guy, but sometimes you reap what you sow, I guess. Truth be told I can't feel too sad for him given the oceans of harm he's inflicted over his career to me, my people, the world. Serial killer? Mass murderer? Serial mass murderer, technically, for decades before we ever met him, all over the world; and that's only literal body count. Oceans of harm beyond that. I'd been debating whether or not to kill him anyway once he let me go, for vengeance and spite and perhaps some form of justice. Been pretty well on the fence. But the ethical way to do that is in cold blood, after careful consideration. Not like this, mistaking him for a combatant when he's surrendered.

I shout "Beth!" by reflex, as if that could stop her in her wrath. My voice seems to echo in a featureless void of infinite distance between us. Unfortunately for Agent Ned, his illumination via my 'power to clear men's minds' (as it's been called) has dazed him. A paradigm shift such as he's just gone through can trip you out pretty good in the moment, with cognitive-perceptual aftereffects lasting months or even forever. Ned finally realized I was actually the good guy, he'd been the monster all along, hunting us, harassing us, killing our loved ones, kidnapping and torturing me. I liked how he squirmed when I gave it to him about letting that bugfucker Xax cut out my eye. Like most such folks, Ned always knew that his work was evil, he just thought it was justified. And as with any episode of *The Argus MacWargus Show*, I truly enjoyed watching him struggle with the horrifying realization that his justifications actually, nope, did not suffice. For Ned it shook not only his ego and identity, but his sense of purpose and self-worth: all his dedication, bravery, cunning, and willingness to go to extremes in the name of what was right—every bit of it now rang false, retroactively condemning his entire past. A genuine villain, pursuing extremes of human excellence at being a brutal tool of oppression.

Undermining even, at least for the moment, and here is the point, his sense of self-preservation, apparently; since despite his years of training and field experience, all poor dazed Ned can muster just now is to block her swing with his forearm. Her strike lands perpendicular to his ulna, chopping it in half. He shrieks, but in an instant she's on him, hand shoving his mouth shut and head back, twisting the axe-head still wedged between broken bone-halves, saying over her shoulder at Doomer: "Get him outta there!" with a nod in my direction. Ned proceeds to scream muffled screams through his nose, flailing at her with his three free limbs to no substantive effect.

Doomer slides in and shuts the door. He hurries to my chair and starts cutting cords.

"Don't kill him," I say.

"Not yet," says Beth.

"Happy to see you, hon," I tell her.

"I'd kill the fuckin' world for you," she replies, snarling the words into Ned's face, levering the hatchet again. He nose-screams at a higher pitch.

"He's on our side now," I say.

"Prolly not anymore." Doomer laughs, helping me to my feet. "He fucked you up good. What's with the eye?"

It's too much to explain. Not just the details of the removal process, which I can't even think about, but the fucked up machine that healed my eye socket, and the weird little ritual around the eyepatch. So I just say, "Gone."

Beth wrenches the hatchet out of Ned's arm and raises it to chop his forehead.

"Beth, don't." I reach for her, losing my balance, and falling on my ass next to Ned. Her eyes get weepy. She places the hatchet on the floor. Touches the pirate eyepatch. Starts to raise it, thinks better of it, touches her fingertips to it again.

"It's okay. They healed the socket."

She sobs. Doomer kneels down and takes over holding Ned's mouth shut. "Hi," he says to him. "Shush or else."

Beth and I hold each other and sob a bit. I can dimly hear Ned moaning along with us, half from grievous injury and half from deepest regret.

"We should get outta here," says Doomer after a couple of moments. "Bring him or kill him?"

"Neither." I struggle to my feet with Beth's help. "You're on your own," I say to Ned. "Don't kid yourself that you can un-know what you now know. If you try to keep working for the Agency, the cognitive dissonance will probably make you shoot yourself."

Beth spits in his face. "Count to a thousand before you call for help," she growls. Then kicks him in the face with her boot.

"Beth." I put my hand on her arm.

"He cut your fucking eye out!"

"Not him." I'm glad she's focused on that, and not the million other evils he actually has perpetrated.

"He didn't exactly stop it from happening." She looks down at him. He's curled up weeping, blubbering something that might be *I'm sorry*. She kicks him in the back, hard, and he yelps.

"He's redeemed. And you've already hurt him, bad."

"Repenting doesn't lead to instant absolution," she says, echoing my thought of vengeance from moments ago. She spits on him again.

"Best of luck," I say to him, rather hollowly. We leave him crying in the RV and shut the door. I hate that the world has made us this cruel. I know Beth does too. I know Doomer couldn't care less, and the idea makes me laugh with a combination of relief and horror.

The van sits right outside. The sun rises over the craggy black horizon. We look around warily as they help me in the passenger side door. I fall into the seat, finding it infinitely more comfortable than the metal folding chair in which I've spent the past several days, and I sink instantly into a vertiginous reverie. "Safe," I sigh—out loud, I think. I lie there in faint bedspins for a timeless moment. But a soft wet cold thing shoves at my temple, sniffing like the inhale of a bellows at the edge of my eyepatch.

It's Akaz, my enormous shaggy galoot of a mutt, great dane, german shepherd, wolf, who-knows-what, pitch black and with irises so dark brown they seem black as well. "I'm okay," I assure him, throwing my arms around his neck and bonking my forehead against his sledgehammer-like forehead, third eye to third eye, communing mutely.

"You up for manning the MG?" Doomer nods up at the ring-mounted M240 machine gun overhead.

"Uh," I reply, hard pressed to imagine standing up.

"Your Brother has most of them occupied a few miles east of here," says Beth. "Just a dozen or so are still scattered around the compound—we were planning on splitting up, someone on the MG and someone else on my bike. Give them multiple targets to deal with so they can't coordinate. Then we regroup in a minute on the west side of the compound."

Doomer unhitches the motorcycle from the jury-rig on back of the van, his crosswise-slung machine pistol repeatedly swinging into his way. "I've got speed if you need it," he says. "Or just coke."

"Uh, no."

"Good for pain."

"Maybe later." There's nothing I'd rather do than elevate my mood—except making sure to avoid the sort of unimaginable crash I'd surely fall into when it wears off.

"You and I can just get the fuck out of here," says Beth, "let Doomer be decoy. But if you can manage the MG, it'd be some insurance."

"Uh, okay," I say, then black out for a second. I awake to Beth kissing me. She reaches across me and straps on my seat belt.

"You stay put," she whispers, kissing me again. "We'll sneak out."

Beth starts the van's engine. As Doomer revvs the roaring motorcycle, we drive off quietly. We hear the bike zoom away, followed momentarily by sounds of Doomer whooping and hollering and firing the machine pistol in short bursts.

Cannibal-King II

The real terror comes from the sound of the helicopters. Gunfire from the cars behind us is barely audible over our engines and the wind; barely frightening, they firing essentially blind and at high speed. How about fear of crashing? Well, impossible to maneuver on this surface at this speed, even for Beth, but we're just driving in a straight line indefinitely. Kinetically it is a bit anxiety-enhancing, but rationally it's not a terrifying risk just now. Two helicopters approach, though, painfully loud, their soulless roars echoing off the featureless vast plain, beating our ears with dizzying intersecting polyrhythms. The noise alone is overwhelming. The complexity of the sound is further disorienting. Most of all, though, the sensation commands our unceasing awareness of the fact that no matter what we do, no matter where we go, we are visible to the maker of that sound and entirely at the mercy of whatever weapons they might have aboard.

We speed at dawn across open salt flat, our tires leaving big plumes of dust behind us. Dark craggy horizon lies a couple miles away, or a couple dozen, no way to know. Beth drives the van. Doomer, burly and shaggy, rides Beth's

998cc Vincent alongside us. I crouch on the passenger seat with my head edged up through the ring mount, still dazed from the unreality of my escape, doing my best to aim the belt-fed M240 machine gun at anything that might come in sight. Goddamn Akaz crowds me on the passenger seat, black-furred head out the window watching the cars chasing us, tongue lolling. I keep snapping at him, "Dude! Dude! Get in the car! Get your head in the fucking car!" To which he eventually responds by rolling his big black dog-eyes. I'm worried sick that he'll take an unlucky bullet in the head from the Feds behind us, unlikely though it may be. Sonofabitch routinely obeys like a Prussian soldier when it doesn't matter at all; but when something actually dangerous is going on, there's no talking to him. I push my leg against his flank in hopes that'll make my *Sovereign Shield* cover him. He shrugs around resentfully into a different position.

These worries for my dog's well-being are emphatically eclipsed by my first visual contact with the helicopters: holy shit, if I do not shoot them, we are dead. It's that simple. The mental and emotional defenses I'd kept up throughout my captivity feel gone without a trace, leaving me paralyzed with panic. My one remaining eye is raw and wet from bawling—head in Beth's lap as she sped away from camp, nose dripping, drooling on her jeans—so now the dust and wind blinds me.

And yet—is this Weird Luck? I shoot something on one of the helicopters and it plummets, a thunderous kerrang lost in the cloud of dust. The other peels away to get out of range.

I can't see the cars behind us at all through the dust, can barely hear the occasional pistol-fire. One pulls up beside us.

I wipe crust from my eye with a dusty knuckle and see what must normally be a shiny black Crown Vic, now dusted to a dull beige by the desert, one black window smoothly sliding down to expose a black pistol held by a black-suited white man. He fires true, despite the speed and dust, and thanks to my Sovereign Shield his bullet rebounds upon him and I see blood as his car swerves away. A couple other cars I scare off with some bursts from the MG. Hot shell casings and belt links fall on Akaz but he doesn't seem to notice.

Then the other helicopter comes in straight for us, Vulcans blazing.

I wheel the machine gun frontwards as best I can, ring mount dragging and catching from the dust, cursing myself for not having greased it better. And what the fuck, Weird Luck is with me today or my Sovereign Shield is covering the whole van, 'cause the main rotor shears off and away, and the helicopter slowly noses down toward us, tail arcing diagonally over and around.

Then there's a flash-bang of lightning? Or I see stars? I feel sure that helicopter passed over us, didn't hit us, but where is it—

—then Akaz, he having been a somewhat eccentric but otherwise mundane dog for all the years I'd known him, clear as day says the words, "What the fuck?"

I gawk down at him, only to behold that things are far stranger than I could possibly have expected: for his eyes have turned to orbs of flame, and his tongue to blazing fire.

Following his gaze behind us in the dust cloud, I watch the helicopter crash on its back more or less directly on top of one Fed car and in the path of another, destroying both.

The pileup vanishes in the dust. Two, three, four other cars keep after us.

And in the following instant, obscuring our pursuers even more fully than any dust: a volcano appears behind us out of nowhere, vomiting a column of black smoke.

The remaining cop cars speed out of the side of the volcano as though it were a 3-D projection. Is it a *real* volcano at all? So small and symmetrical.... I hear a high-pitched rattling, like a crowd of percussion at some kind of festival or ritual.

My vision clears, the dust and wind inexplicably having no effect at all. Beth, who could be a stunt driver, slows the van to a stop as quickly as could be done on this surface without flipping it. I spin around forward to see a couple dozen huge naked bald dudes standing in our way, arranged equidistant a few paces apart from one another, tapping on awesomely loud little finger drums at their belts. They make a terrifying cacophony. Doomer skids to a stop, hovers a moment, and ends up dumping the bike in slo-mo on its side, hopping awkwardly away and then falling on his ass.

"Hey!" Beth hollers at him. "My bike!"

"Sorry!" says Doomer, staying seated on the ground.

The cop cars pursuing us brake and skid, one coming to rest right behind us. I look the driver in the eye down the barrel of the M240. He keeps his pistol trained on me. We stare at each other. I fire in through the windshield at him. Somewhat contrary to expectation, he explodes in a bloody fireball, filling the car's interior, blowing out the windows, immolating his partner. The stump of his arm, still clutching his pistol, flies to the sand nearby.

My dog says, "Fucking awesome."

The mysterious desert men cheer.

Pistol-fire erupts on both sides of me, swiftly followed by grunts or screams and then silence.

"You see?" roars a voice among the desert men. "He bears the Sovereign Shield!"

I look around. Dead Feds in their cars. Thirty or so nightmare humanoids standing in the settling dust. Completely hairless, muscles rippling beneath bone-white skin, crisscrossed head to toe with raised pink keloid scars. Blood-red eyes, pointed ears, and wide, lantern-jawed mouths full of shark's teeth. Naked but for harnesses, butch but sexless (crotches even more heavily scarred than the rest of their bodies). They all brandish terrifying implements of jagged glass.

Akaz jumps out the passenger window and paces across in front of the van, as if sizing up the group, his eyes blazing like bonfires. The biggest of the desert men says, "And behold! He comes accompanied by Great Akaz himself!" And they all, including the speaker, fall to their knees and bow repeatedly, chanting, "Akaz! Akaz! Akaz!" Praying to my dog.

Then the speaker proclaims: "The Cannibal-King has come!" Which inspires more bowing and chanting: "Cannibal-King! Cannibal-King! Cannibal-King!" Then they all jump up and run to the cop cars, haul out the corpses, tear them apart and devour them.

All of which is uncanny enough in its own right, but their use of the name Akaz adds rather a strange slant. See, when this huge black super-smart dog strayed its way into my life a decade or so ago, I was still strongly under the influence of the Dungeons & Dragons game I'd run in junior high and high school. As Dungeon Master I hadn't been inclined to set my game in the world of Greyhawk or the City-State of the Invincible Overlord or Middle-Earth or whatever; I wanted to create my own world, with my own monsters, my own maps, even my own pantheon. My god of death and chaos and whatnot, my version of Shiva or Nyarlathotep or Arioch, was a big black wolf with fires for eyes. I had named him "Great Akaz," words that came to me out of nowhere like so many ideas for my game world. Many years later, I named my adopted stray galoot after him. Later still, my and Beth's band even had an anthem for our mutt called "God-Dog," partly to the tune of "Gor-Gor" by Gwar.

Oh and in my game, among the tribes who worshiped Great Akaz were semi-mortal humanoid fire-and-earth elemental beings of the wasteland, who breathed fire, and used glass swords, and ate people with their rows and rows of big shark's teeth.

All around us they continue devouring, chanting between bites: "Cannibal-King! Cannibal-King! Cannibal-King!"

Blood Eagle II

I sit there amid brass and belt links, holding hands with a rather dazed Beth, together silently staring out at Doomer as he pushes the motorcycle upright. Akaz sniffs the air whilst the speaker of the humanoids bows and speaks to him. Now and then we glance at the blood-covered man-eaters around us, snarling and rending, and quickly look away, clenching our hands together.

"The dog's on fire," says Beth.

"I think he's a god here," I reply hollowly.

"That makes sense," she says.

"Remember where I got his name from?" I ask her.

"Some demon lord from the *Lord of the Rings* books or some shit."

"From my D&D game. I made him up."

"Right."

"That's what he looked like. In the game. Black as night, flames for eyes."

"Tell me you didn't turn our dog into a demon," she says.

"One of the monsters that worshipped Akaz in my game was a species of cannibal supernatural warriors called 'The

Givers of Fire and Flame.' Half human, half fire elemental, half earth elemental."

"That's three halves," she says.

"Armor Class 5 from their semi-elemental flesh and magically scarified hide, same as chainmail. Four hit dice, tougher than a goddamn bugbear. Bite for 2-7, and those glass weapons got up to 2-12 and even 3-18. We're talking first edition, this is like 1980 or '81."

"I have little to no idea what any of that means," she says.

"I made these guys up."

"So you're saying this is not a clan of Nevada mutants like *The Hills Have Eyes*."

"I don't know."

"You're saying, 'I've a feeling we're not in Nevada anymore.'"

"Did you notice the volcano?" I ask.

"What?"

"Behind us."

"Wha—" she repeats, almost, stopping short as she glances in the side mirror. She looks at me, eyes wide. I raise my eyebrows. Not taking her eyes off my eye, gripping my hand even tighter in hers, she fumbles with her free hand for the window-crank and jerkily rolls it down, letting in more sounds of cannibal devourment. Then she cranes her head out. Her hand goes clammy in mine.

After a long look she falls back in her chair. She slowly rolls her window back up as though nearly daunted by the effort. A moment later she takes a deep breath, then looks at me once more.

"As I recall, that would be the Seat of Shamash, volcano-god of the Givers."

"So you're saying that we're in your D&D world."

"I don't know."

"Tell me it's better than the USA." She looks heavenward.

A pallid, scarred, shark-toothed face appears beside me, making us both jump. The speaker of the Givers leans up to my window. "Cannibal-King," he says, addressing me, apparently. "Cannibal-Queen," he continues, to Beth. We gape at him.

"My name is Blood Eagle." He reaches his hand in the window. I recoil, groping with my free hand for the pistol at my hip. His hand hovers in front of me. "I am prophet of the Givers of Fire and Flame; I have dreamed long of your arrival." He pulls his hand back slightly. "Do you not do the Clasp in your world?"

I release my pistol-grips and warily shake Blood Eagle's hand. He reaches in across me to offer his hand to Beth. He smells like sunbaked sand, not like a human or any animal I've smelled. Keeping her fingers of one hand tightly interlocked with mine, she releases the hilt of my Grandfather's bayonet hidden in the dashboard and reaches over to shake him lefty.

"Although there are those who believe my dreams and visions," says Blood Eagle, "the Givers tend toward skepticism; and most of my people openly doubt me. Therefore you may be called upon to perform certain miracles to convince the various Giver tribes to join our army."

Someone taps on Beth's window, causing us both to jump again and grab ahold of our respective weapons. It's

Doomer. Ahead of us Beth's motorcycle stands upright on its kickstand. Beth rolls her window back down, jerkily.

"You see that fuckin' volcano?" Doomer shook his head. "Trippy."

Beth and I nod weakly.

"Look, gimme the keys a sec," he says. "I'm-a get a scrap of plywood out the back to put under the kickstand. Dirt's pretty hard packed but I don't trust it. That bike's gonna fall over again sooner or later." He socks Beth lightly on the shoulder. "Sorry 'bout that, by the way. Portal got me light-headed goin' through. Bike's fine."

"Uh, Doomer," says Beth.

"Yeah, Miz Waghalter?"

"That can wait," she says.

"Two minutes," he says.

"Doomer," says Beth, "we're surrounded by combatants." To Blood Eagle, she adds, "No offense, but I'll tell you to your face: the way things are lookin' right about now, you're gonna have to perform certain miracles to not get filled fulla lead. You guys are fucking terrifying. And this situation is beyond fucked," she concludes, gesturing toward the volcano, then around at the carnage.

Blood Eagle cocks a hairless, scarred eyebrow.

"Fucked?" asks Doomer. "Whaddayamean fucked? We not only escaped, we escaped offa the damn *planet*. Perfecto!" He makes the sign of the heavy metal horns with his leather-gloved hand.

"What do *you* mean," I ask him, "'*going through that portal*.'"

"Sorry! Sometimes I get fuckin' lightheaded crossing through, dammit. Happens to the best of us, hell gimme a break, you puke half the time, and her bike's the fuck fine! Keys please."

"I'm not handing you the keys to this van!" says Beth. "We should be guns drawn, engines on, Jack on the ring mount!"

"Naw, these guys are cool, Akaz totally vouches for them." Doomer nods across the van to the other window, at Blood Eagle. "That dude's like totally Akaz's henchman."

Beth and I look at Blood Eagle. He bows his head solemnly.

"And the rest of these dudes straight-up worship him."

"Worship Blood Eagle," I look back and forth between Blood Eagle's creepy inhuman eyes.

"Worship Akaz, man," says Doomer.

"There are a few who worship me," says Blood Eagle, "though even so, they view it as worshiping Akaz and Shamash *through* me. I strive to dissuade them, to teach them this is idolatry, with mixed success. According to principle and tradition, we worship only Akaz; our reverence for Great Shamash, Lord of the Volcano, is not as a god but as our patriarch. For we are his spawn sired upon Shub the Earth Dragon, and are thus among her Ten Thousand Young. Also we revere him as our high priest: Shamash himself worships Akaz with us. And although we follow the Cannibal-King as our monarch, even he worships Akaz. Do you not?"

"That shit-headed galoot?" I say, incredulous, glancing around for him. Where the hell is he?

"Finally, of course," continues Blood Eagle without blinking, "we utterly revere the Sun Dragon and Earth Dragon. But our prayers are for Akaz, only Akaz, according to ancient principle. Of course we fall short at times, and fall into idolatries large and small; we all have foibles and illusions. Even Akaz Himself."

Beth says to Doomer, "*Akaz vouches.*"

"Totally," he responds.

"*Akaz's henchman.*"

"Pretty much."

"*Worship Akaz.*"

"Yup."

"You hear this?" Beth asks me.

"Loud and clear," I say, staring at Doomer. "Clear as mud."

Akaz leaps up onto the hood, startling me, Beth, and Doomer. Blood Eagle doesn't flinch. "What'cha talkin' 'bout?" asks Akaz. His rumbling voice sounds like a furnace, resonating through the windshield.

Another Bone Council

Overhead the sky has turned a deep electric blue. On the horizon rises a bright, too-large crescent moon. Waxing, assuming the same rotations and revolutions as Earth.

Beth and I sit in the dust of the desert, holding hands again, or perhaps still. She wears the bayonet on one hip and her pistol on the other; I've got my bandolier of rifle bullets, my pistol, and my Grandfather's kukri. At Akaz's request I also have my hatchet, again from my Grandfather, resting on the ground before me.

"Why did the dog ask you to bring that?" Beth indicates the hatchet.

"He goes, 'Bring it to the meeting, it'll look good,' whatever the hell that means. Followed by something something, 'Axe in the prophecy.'"

"Glad I brought it to the jailbreak," she says. "Figured we'd need it in California."

I shudder at that, remembering Ned Wings, my maimed torturer. The antique axe-blade has been wiped but not cleaned, and still has his blood in its pitted face.

Blood Eagle kneels in the center of the circle—me, Beth, Doomer, and twenty-five Givers sitting knee to knee on the hard, parched, dusty ground. Beside Blood Eagle, Akaz lies on his side, limbs stuck out like the legs of a fallen table, snoring. His eyes and mouth are shut, but tiny wisps of flame dance in and out of his nostrils.

Blood Eagle rattles what looks like a life-size human spine cast in gold—the vertebrae from neckbone to tailbone must be strung on some metal shaft, just loosely enough to clack a little against one another. It sounds oddly mechanical and inorganic. He shakes the spine-rattle around at us one by one, five clacks at each of us, turning slowly around on his knees to cover the entire perimeter. Then he intones, "By the power of the Spine of Kaios, I declare this Bone Council open. All righteous questions shall be answered."

There follows a moment of deep silence, the Givers so motionless it's as if the ground beneath is reaching up through them to radiate stillness in the air, tangibly insisting the silence persist.

"*'Why do you all speak English?'*" whispers Beth to me.

"I got one," Doomer blurts out, loud, making me and Beth both jump. Murmurings from the Givers give me the distinct impression that he is speaking out of turn, and perhaps perilously so. Doomer continues, heedless, turning to address me and Beth directly, in his loud-ass voice: "I wanna know how come everything outta your mouth since we got here is looking this total gift horse in the mouth. 'Oh but this momentary digression en route to California that just totally saved our lives is so darn inconvenient.' Can we just enjoy the fact that we just dodged a dozen armed Feds out for blood and traded them in for a cargo cult of warrior-monks who frickin' worship you like *literally?*"

"They worship *me*." Akaz spits out a puff of flame, his body otherwise unmoving. He smacks his lips and resumes snoring.

"Whatever," says Doomer. "Shit, bring these guys to California as like your elite guard or whatever."

"'Inconvenient'?" I ask.

"Doomer," says Beth.

"What," says Doomer.

She and I proceed in unison. "What the fuck are you talking about."

"Whaddaya mean? I thought you wanted to go conquer California or whatever."

"*Conquer?*" I say.

"We've got friends on Ohlone Island," says Beth.

"We're gonna help them *defend* themselves," I say. "On their terms."

"Semantics," says Doomer, waving it away. He gestures at the Givers. "Bring these guys. Give 'em guns. They'll kick ass. And I bet they'd jump at the chance."

"Quite probably," says Blood Eagle, "most of us here would follow you anywhere, Cannibal-King. I cannot promise how many hundreds more would join us, however. A few."

"A few *hundreds*," Me breaking into a quick sweat now at the thought of having a battalion of fiercely loyal supernatural cannibal superhumans at my disposal back on Earth. Terrifying. Horrifying. The antithesis of the world we want to build. Utterly tempting.

Blood Eagle nods. "At least a few."

"Sweet," says Doomer.

"No way," says Beth.

"Why!" asks Doomer.

I look at her, kinda wondering myself for the moment whether it's quite so cut and dried.

"We're going there," says Beth, "to teach martial arts and guerilla tactics to the people who live there *now*. We're not colonizing them with our garrison in order to fend off an invading colonial garrison from the United State of America, goddamn it."

I feel *mostly* convinced.

"And if those people aren't tough enough to defend themselves," asks Doomer, "you're gonna deprive them of an *army* that could save their bacon?"

"Or an army that could eat them, maybe?" she says.

"Touché," says Doomer, "but still."

But still.

Blood Eagle resumes his intonation. "First, however, before we follow you anywhere else, Cannibal-King, we must follow you in our march on the City of the Watcher." He rattles the spine.

"Nope," I manage to say, before Doomer cuts me off.

"What," asks Doomer, "you mean march on it again? Why?"

"We have waited over four hundred years for him, Earth-man," says Blood Eagle. "Waited for our march on the city, as prophesied."

"Wait wait wait," Doomer says to him. Givers murmur and shuffle in place, clearly unhappy with his tone toward their prophet and/or his breach of Bone Council protocol. "You haven't toppled Whatshisname yet, the Watcher?"

Blood Eagle frowns and shakes his head. "Four hundred years have we waited."

"It's now," says Akaz.

"What?" asks Doomer. No response. He turns to me and Beth. "What does that sonofabitch mean by that?"

"Dude," I say, "all I know is my dog is talking."

"In his sleep," says Beth.

"Frankly I'm not even quite registering anything he's saying yet, beyond just the fact that he's *talking*."

"Yeah, finally," says Doomer, loudly, directed at Akaz. "Ya damn mutt."

Givers stir, significantly, at this casual blasphemy.

"Doomer," I say.

"Dogs don't talk," says Beth.

"You're pissing off the Givers," I say.

Doomer rolls his eyes. "Look, is this a prank? Chester gonna pop out with his hidden camera?" He sings, awfully: *"'With a hocus-pocus / you're in focus / it's your lucky day / SMILE!'"*

"Doomer," I say, "are you telling us it's not weird to you that the inside of my dog's head is on fire, and he speaks English, and these folks worship him?"

"Hell," says Doomer, "I'd worship him myself if I didn't know he's a sonofabitch."

"Dogs," repeats Beth, "don't talk."

"Not on Earth." Doomer laughs. "Not this poor guy, at least." He calls over to Akaz. "Glad to be offa that rock again, huh Akaz?"

Akaz shudders. Opens his eyes to fiery slits. "Ugh." Shuts them.

"How many years was it this time?" asks Doomer.

"Fuck you," says Akaz.

Doomer chuckles.

I look around at the Givers. All eyes on Doomer, or me, or Beth.

"Doomer," I say, "I've never heard a dog talk before."

"Or seen one with a headful of fire," says Beth.

"Whaddaya talkin' about?" asks Doomer. "He's like this just about everywhere. Aside from the more mundane end of the human-survivable spectrum."

"Spectrum," says Beth.

"Of parallel Earths," says Doomer.

"Okay what the fuck are you talking about," I ask him.

"What the fuck are you talking about what the fuck am I talking about?"

"Traveling through portals to other worlds," I say.

"A thing," says Beth, "we've never done it before, because it's not real."

"And you're acting as if," I begin, intending to offer an *argumentum ad absurdum* but I realize, as the words pass my lips, that it isn't, and that all of this is really happening. The realization cascades over and through me like the shimmering euphoria of a big balloonful of nitrous from a whip-it. I feel Beth squeeze my hand; maybe I swayed a little? *Friends don't let friends do whip-its standing*, as the saying goes, and I'm glad to be sitting.

"We do it all the time!" says Doomer, insistent, badgering us to recall. "With Jump and Joey and Fuckface and alllll those fuckers! You guys have been doing it for years, ever since..."

He watches me and Beth shaking our heads at him.

"...your City of the Watcher thing," he trails off.

Beth and I stare at him. He looks back and forth between us. Blood Eagle and the Givers observe us with great interest.

"I thought *you* were from *my* fucking future," says Doomer. "*I'm* from *your* fucking future. Fuck."

We just stare at him.

"Wait," he says, testily, "this whole time, all those times I mentioned things that happened when we were on other worlds...."

"We just thought that was your shtick," I say. "You say plenty of other weird stuff."

"We were humoring you," says Beth.

"We just thought you were high," I say.

"And weird," says Beth.

"And nuts," I say.

Doomer turns to Blood Eagle. "We're on the world of the City of the Watcher *now?*"

Blood Eagle points. "The city lies two days run from here."

"And *none* of you have conquered it."

"Nope," say Beth and I.

"We have waited," says Blood Eagle, "over four hundred years."

"Well I'll be damned," says Doomer.

"There's a way back to Earth," says Akaz, "in the city."

"So there's that," I say to Beth.

"Couple of 'em," mumbles Akaz, and resumes snoring.

Wolf of Kaios II

The desert night has turned cold. Fortunately Akaz has finished with his damn nap and burns brightly again. Beth and I hunker under an unzipped sleeping bag, hands outstretched toward his head as though it's a campfire. Doomer, heftier and tougher than either of us, just has a thin wool army blanket draped loosely over his shoulders. Blood Eagle sits nearby, not the slightest sign of noticing the cold despite being essentially naked.

"Whaddaya wanna know," says Akaz, grumbling.

"So the whole time you've been my dog," I begin—

"I've never been *your* dog," says Akaz.

"—that whole time, you've had this self inside of you: talking, thinking, fire-breathing...."

"Yeah, yeah," says Akaz.

"Dang," says Beth.

"Why didn't you say something!?" I ask.

Akaz glowers at me.

"You know what I mean," I say. "Why didn't you write something in spilled cheerios with your paw, piss in the snow, whatever?"

"Give us some kinda sign," says Beth.

"It doesn't work that way," says Akaz. "It's not like my vocal chords don't work. I'm existentially different. More mundane. Like Beth said, dogs don't talk. They don't spell out S.O.S. in cheerios, either."

"Drag," Beth and I say together.

"Tell me about it," says Akaz.

"Well," I say, "welcome back, I guess."

"Thanks," says Akaz.

"Guess you're not coming to California, then," says Beth.

"Ha." Akaz coughs. "Fuck no."

"What?" My voice cracks.

"What what?" asks Akaz. "Surely you jest."

Oh. "Fuck." Akaz has been my dog for most of my adult life. I guess this explains why he never seemed to age in over ten years, never got sick or injured. I had thought he just had good mutt genes. I can't imagine going back to Earth without him. I've struggled to keep an even keel in the face of the losses of recent months—family, friends, my home city, my reputation, my naive hope for the people of North America.... And in recent days, I've been able to maintain despite being kidnapped, suffering the agony of that high-tech nerve torture gizmo, the loss of my eye.... But now, facing the loss of my dog opens a yawning gulf of despair in my heart. Only losing Beth could hurt more. I start formulating arguments to convince him, but he is already gone from us. His whole time with me, with us, was a time of exile and debilitation. He is home and himself for the first time since I have known him.

"First," says Blood Eagle, "we march on the City of the Watcher."

"Uh, no," says Beth.

"Au contraire," says Akaz, "uh yes."

"C'mon," says Doomer. "We don't even know how to get back to Earth yet. May as well kill some fascists while we're here."

"Fuck, fuck, fuck, fuck," I say in tandem with Beth.

"It'll be fun," says Doomer.

Cannibal-Queen

Beth and I lie on the platform in back of the van, crammed near the roof above all our gear, cozy atop eggcrate foam and under not one but two sleeping bags, spooning under the skylight full of stars and crescent moon. I press my face against her long red hair and inhale her scent.

"No fucking way," says Beth. "As if it's our place to play white savior. As if we have any idea how to lead an army in battle. As if they weren't fucking *cannibals*—who the fuck could their enemy *be* that we'd consider *them* the bad guy and not these guys?"

"Fair enough," I whisper in her ear, holding her tight. I recollect the City of the Watcher from my D&D game, though, ruled by its pair of evil demigods and their legions of black-armored cannibal stormtroopers.

"Fuck that American Empire style police-the-world bullshit," she says.

"Okay, baby," I say. "Thanks for havin' the Power to Clear My Mind." And soon enough we collapse into sleep.

In the dim early morning we awaken to cold noses and misty breath under a frost-framed skylight. We warm up by making love spooning, keeping as silent as we can. Then, adrift in contentment, any urge we might have had to get the drop on the day instead evaporates into a snooze. The frost follows suit, thawing fast under the rising sun. We re-awake stifling in our little crawlspace, collars of our long-johns clammy with sweat, sunshine angling in through the skylight to roast our feet. We kick off our sleeping bags and shove open the skylight. Startlingly cold dawn-wind knifes its way in.

"Fucking desert weather." Beth lowers the skylight to all but a crack and pulls the covers half over herself.

"Fucking van life," I say. "I look forward to getting to Ohlone City so we can unload this thing."

"Sleep in a building," she agrees, shoving covers aside and wrenching off her long johns, top and bottom.

She notices me watching her. We find ourselves making out, then start making love again, as quiet as we can. We do hear someone walk up to the van, so we get a notch even quieter, but to no avail, Doomer's muffled voice from outside says, "If this van's a-rockin'," to which Akaz replies, "Christ."

This is not to suggest that we're some sorta idealized nympho dream couple, fucking twice every morning regardless of gunfights with Feds or interdimensional mindfuckery no big deal; au contraire, this is our response to stress: a little nurturing, a little reaffirmation of solidarity, a little letting off of steam, a little shared retreat into oblivion.

Before long we're out back, bundled up and heating water for coffee on a little butane stove set up on the bumper, hiding from the morning east wind on the shadowy lee-ward backside of the van. Literally hot in the sun and cold in the shade. Fucking desert weather. Givers sit motionless in a perimeter around us fifty yards across, out there all night naked and hairless and heedless of the cold. Soon Doomer and Akaz drop by again.

"Blood Eagle says he wants you to meet someone," says Doomer.

"Great Shamash," says Akaz, "wants your blessing."

"Back at the volcano?" I ask.

"Can we get outta this world the way we came in?" asks Beth.

"In," says Akaz.

"Yeah," says Beth. "The way we came in. Through a gate at the base of the volcano, no?"

"What?" asks Akaz.

"What what?" asks Beth.

"I was answering *his* question." Akaz nods his snout in my direction.

"What question?" I ask.

"I'm lost," says Doomer.

"You said, 'at the volcano,'" says Akaz. "I'm saying no, 'in.'"

"In the volcano?" I ask.

"Yeah," says Akaz, "Shamash is in the volcano."

"He wants my 'blessing'?"

"Yeah," says Akaz. "It's been his standing request for centuries: whenever the prophecy finally comes true and the Cannibal-King appears, before you march on the city as foretold, he wants you to drop by and give him your blessing."

"We're not marching on the city," I say.

"What?" asks Akaz.

"We," says Beth, "are not marching on the city. We're going to California. By way of a Nevada full of Feds if need be, but hopefully not, if you supposedly veteran interdimensional travelers have any bright ideas how to get us straight to Ohlone Island."

"Dammit," says Akaz.

"I got nothin' in the way of bright ideas," says Doomer. "But hell, I'm stayin' with Akaz. See this thing through."

"Have fun." Beth spoons coffee grounds into the pan of water.

"I'm not keen on going into any volcano," I say. "Also."

"Seriously," says Beth.

"No worries about that though while Akaz is around," says Doomer. "He protects us from fire. I've stood in fuckin' lava with him around and not even needed a shoeshine after. It's awesome."

"Yeah, thanks but no," I say.

"When have you ever gotten a shoeshine?" asks Beth. Doomer sticks his tongue out at her.

"Can Shamash come out of the volcano?" I ask.

"Would we *want* him to?" asks Beth. "Volcano god coming out of the volcano sounds... not so hot."

"So to speak."

She squints at me.

"No," says Akaz, "he can't come out."

"Why," I ask.

A jagged harpoon, line and all, flies straight down out of the sky and hits our coffee, splashing hottish water and wet grounds everywhere including on me and Beth. "Fuck!" we shout together. The camp stove flips and falls to the ground, fuel line severed so that a little foot-long flamethrower shoots up from it at an angle. "Back up!" I say, but Beth just reaches in, grabs out the butane canister and chucks it. It doesn't explode. The harpoon is reeled back up, along with our impaled saucepan.

Twenty yards above us, emerging from a ripple of invisibility, hovers something not unlike a viking ship, its prow bearing sharply down at us. Hanging agilely from railings and rigging, a dozen men with generic bone-white faces and enameled black armor—glossy like the carapaces of carpenter ants—heft harpoons and javelins and fling them down at us.

I don't see what happens next, since I dive on top of Beth. Nothing stabs either of us. I hear a clank and a crash from the roof of the van, and Doomer shouts, and Akaz barks once in a mighty *kiai*. Then come grunts from above. When we look, we see Akaz snarling upward. Doomer stands frozen, shuddering with tension, hands over his head, three spears sticking up out of the ground so closely to him that he can't move from the spot without rubbing against at least two of them. Not a drop of blood, though, looks like. A few more spears stick out of the ground here and there like flagpoles, and two pierce the roof of our van—one of them, I can tell, stuck straight through the skylight and into our bed.

"Dammit," says Beth.

"Hope it doesn't rain," I say.

Up above, four or five of the spearmen hang from rigging, impaled on their own weapons, presumably bounced back at them by my Sovereign Shield. Assuming no one else has one? What if Beth gets one here, as 'Cannibal-Queen'? What a fucking relief *that* would be. Akaz? Blood Eagle? Looks like Doomer doesn't, but all them spears missing him looks like Weird Luck if I've ever seen it.

Harpooneers jerk their lines, pluck their spears up from the hard-packed dust and rapidly reel them in. Others ready new javelins, staying their throw for obvious reasons. Holding onto rigging by one hand and one foot, a blue-skinned fishy-looking guy in a dark blue robe makes some sorta weird gesture with his free hand.

The ship goes invisible again.

I stare at the spot where it vanished.

A second or ten later I hear Akaz barking at me, "Jack! Oi!" 'Oi' being what I snap at him when I want his attention. I turn to him, but he's running off to do something. I look around. Doomer is throwing spears back up. Everywhere Givers jump to their feet, rattling their little one-handed finger-drums... spitting fireballs at the ground. *What?* Why?

The ship reappears, wheeling around our perimeter. Spears rain down through thighs and torsos. Wounded Givers snarl. Impaled or not, they grab up handfuls of molten glass from the spots where they'd spat their fiery breath. The ship vanishes again from view as balls of burning glass rain against its deck. A couple of harpooned Givers get hauled on board and disappear into the shroud of invisibility, their all-too-audible screams harmonizing with sounds of snarls and rending.

Next thing I know, Beth rapidly levers my rifle Victoria, and starts unloading round after round in the direction the ship seemed to be going in. The ship reappears for a moment, a quarter of the way around our circle, and a few more Givers get impaled by its black-armored crew. More glowing glass balls shatter-splash against the hull, charring wood but sadly far from making it drop out of the sky. A couple of shipboard soldiers are hit with hot glass—one falls tumbling and burning to the ground, where Givers set upon him. Beth fires at the ship, hitting someone I think, before it vanishes once more.

"Beth," says Akaz, "oi."

"Huh?" She looks at him.

He jumps into her mouth. There's not really any other way to say it. Yes, our giant black wolf-dog just leaps into the air, aimed at Beth's face, and disappears into her mouth.

Her eyes blaze bright with flame.

As she turns and aims at empty air, flames lick down the length of Victoria's barrel. Beth squeezes the trigger and out comes a thunderclap, a glittering ray of fire, a .30-30 bullet infused with the power of the God-Dog of Fiery Destruction. The ship reappears, flames dancing across the deck, mast blasted in half. The boat begins to sink toward the ground. The blue guy in the blue robes leaps nimbly away into the air. He grabs a corner of the sail and pulls it loose with a flick of his wrist, and flies away flapping it on the wind.

Givers cheer as the ship skids hard against the desert floor. A broad swath of dust pours up diagonally behind it. The hull cracks open and the vessel falls onto its side, scattering black-armored spearmen and burning timbers. The Givers swarm upon it, burning and devouring.

Akaz leaps out of Beth's mouth. She starts to drop Victoria and bends over, coughing—I put one arm around her and catch Victoria with the other. I hear Doomer and Akaz exchange a slew of "Yeah!" and "Wicked!" and the like.

"I'm fine." Beth coughs. "I'm fine. Just... fuck, that was weird."

"Akaz!" I shout.

"Huh?"

"Don't do that again without warning me first," says Beth.

"*Warning you*'?" I ask, incredulous. "How about '*not ever*'?"

She looks earnestly into my eye. "Jack," she says, "you've gotta try that, man."

I stare at her.

"Definitely wanna march on the city," she says.

God of the Volcano

Beth slowly drives back toward the volcano across the hard-packed salt flat. We're surrounded by Givers on foot. Doomer zooms here and there ahead of us. Akaz sits on the hood, motionless, facing forward.

"Sounds to me like he brainwashed ya," I say to Beth. "Hopped inside your head and tweaked you telepathically."

"Telepathy yeah, but he didn't compel me," she says. "He just showed me a bunch of real reasons why the Herax with their flying boats are a goddamn fascist police state that needs to be crushed."

"And we're the guys to do it for some reason," I say.

"'Cause we *can*," says Beth. "Ugh, the things he showed me. You'd agree with me."

"Assuming these things were even real."

"I guess," she says. "But what if they were? Weren't the Herax evil in your D&D game?"

"Dictionary definition of Lawful Evil," I say. "Fashy as fuck. I recall them clear as day, but I gotta say I'm having a hard time using my teenage adventure game as a basis for real-life war ethics. And, bottom line, back home we gave our word to each other never to kill at someone else's behest."

"Fair enough," says Beth. "Just seemed so real."

"For all we know, it was," I say. "Is. But still, we don't even know the barest basics of this situation. Blood Eagle says he's got hundreds? How many Herax are there? A dozen of those ships? A thousand? Just one of them took out over a tenth of our platoon. Plus that blue guy turning the thing invisible?"

"I know, right?" says Beth.

"Who knows how many other sorcerers they have and what other shit they can do." The thought gives me shivers. "And most of all, these Givers don't exactly seem like the Saints of Ultimate Righteousness. Say they do conquer the Herax, then what? Instant ultimate utopia?"

"Surely not," says Beth. "But if there's fascists and we can kill 'em, we kinda gotta."

"If we can pull it off and still get home, *maybe* we have to. You know I'm down." I try to rein it in, but my voice gets that pontificating edge in it: "But I'm not psyched about us taking it upon ourselves to create a power vacuum in what looks like a horrifyingly violent and bafflingly complex context that we barely comprehend. These Givers could be every bit as bad, or worse."

"Yeah." She's deflated.

I persist, failing to rein in the edge. "I can wrap my head around fighting for the liberation of the California Archipelago. I know the players, the risks, what 'victory' might look like. But we can't risk missing *that* fight because we *died*, in someone else's battle, in a world that shouldn't even be possible."

"Fair enough." She stares into the middle distance, takes a deep breath, and sighs, releasing her momentum to go to war.

"Let's find out what's what," I say, softer, not wanting to disrupt her meditation. "Maybe this guy in the volcano can shed some light on the situation."

"Figuratively."

"Right." I laugh.

"Fair enough," she says. "We'll grill 'em."

"Figuratively," I say.

She scowls.

"We are less evil than the Herax," says Blood Eagle, appearing at Beth's window. Both of us jump and put our hands on our guns. "Because we do not eat souls. Whereas they do."

"Eat souls," I say.

"Herax do," says Blood Eagle. "Givers do not. The Good Givers, that is."

"Just the body," says Beth.

"Yes," says Blood Eagle. "Though flesh give only a fraction of the vitality provided by soulstuff, we forego it, preferring to liberate the soul. Thus it can rejoin the Sun Dragon and Earth Dragon, and thence re-incarnate. Thus have we done no wrong."

"You sure about that," I say.

"As certain as fire is hot," says Blood Eagle. "For I have seen a soul released; and I have seen a soul devoured; and I have seen freed souls reemerge from above and below to manifest upon the surface of the earth once more."

"Seen how, with your special Soul-o-Vision?"

"Seen in visions," says Blood Eagle, "in rattle trance."

"Great," I say. I turn to Beth. "More of that great basis for real-life war ethics."

"And the Gods have taught me," says Blood Eagle, "all the peregrinations of incarnation and dissolution."

"Which gods? Akaz?"

"Most of all, Great Akaz has shown me the Way. But the Dragons have spoken to me as well."

"Great. As sure as fire is hot, then."

"C'mon," says Beth. "Why would your dog lie?"

"That is the saddest question I have ever heard," I say.

Before long we arrive at the rubble around the base of the volcano. It angles up through the packed surface of the salt flat, jagged red walls sloping sharply toward the rim. The whole thing can't be more than fifty yards across and half that high, far more symmetrical than a volcano ought to be. Thick black smoke pours upward out of it, forming a perpetual cloud overhead that drifts and dissipates with the winds above.

Beth and I get out. Heat radiates from the sloping red stone, feeling strangely pleasant despite its intensity. Doomer rides up and dismounts. "Whoa, hot," he says. "Good thing *Akaz protects the faithful*, as they say."

Beth and I look at each other, our dog's divinity not yet getting any less odd.

Doomer cracks his knuckles and surveys the slope up and down. "Blows my mind you guys don't know this stuff. We count on him for fire protection all the time."

"The future us," I say, "the ones you know, presumably originally found out 'cause you told 'em. Us."

"Like," says Beth, "just now."

"Yeah," says Doomer. "Maybe. Though if it's an infinite multiverse, they might not be you. Maybe the future you-guys I know are somebody completely else."

"Well," says Beth, "if any other superpowers come to mind we oughta know about, just, y'know."

"I'll let ya know," says Doomer. He turns to Blood Eagle: "Hey, we going up this thing? Or is there some secret door in."

"Up," says Blood Eagle, and the Givers start streaming up the angled face of the little volcano. Doomer clambers after them. Then Akaz.

Beth and I look at each other. Then at the volcano.

"No big deal," says Beth. "At least it's no steeper than for-ty-five."

"I'm fuckin' sore," I say. She hugs my arm and kisses my cheek and starts up.

We hike up stone so rough it serves as an irregular stair-way, using our hands much less than expected. The rocks feel deliciously, burningly, painlessly hot to the touch.

At the rim the lot of us stand side by side in an arc around the edge, staring into a vertical black cloud. Akaz takes a deep breath, and blows. The smoke coils like a tornado and whooshes away, whipping across us as it twists out from the bowl of the volcano and away into the desert.

"That's not how volcanoes work in the real world," says Beth.

"Nope," I concur.

Below us a pool of lava, its surface mostly solidified like puddle ice, crusts around the body of a guy, or thing, curled fetal in it, apparently asleep. He looks to be about a hun-dred feet tall, red as a fire truck, with roaring flames for hair and beard. Huge golden chains run from manacles on his wrists to opposite sides of the volcano, where they are fastened to the inner walls by huge golden staples.

"Hey, Shamash." Akaz's voice echoes in the volcano like thunder.

The fire giant stirs a little, cracking the frozen stone around him, fissures exposing more of the glowing lava beneath. But he does not awaken.

"Duuude," says Akaz in a louder, longer rumbling thunderclap, "wake the fuck up." His voice rings in the volcano, then seconds later echoes back at us from the distant hills.

The giant stretches, flinging its limbs out to send huge sheets of jagged stone flying in every direction, thankfully far below us. Then he sits up, gold chains jangling. He looks around at us, his immense eyes coruscating like forest fires. Hard to judge his nonhuman expression, but he kinda looks out of it. Beth whispers to me, "He looks kinda out of it." I nod.

Then Shamash notices Akaz. "Great Akaz!" His voice thunders even louder than Akaz's roar, the blast startling me and Beth so much we almost lose our footing: not a good thing whether one were to fall forward or back. She sits down. I follow suit. Shamash meanwhile flings himself onto his knees, sending more stone shards and gobbets of magma flying, some of them as high as the rim. Beth and I dodge. A Giver grabs a softball-sized drop of lava out of the air, then watches it drip through his unharmed fingers. Shamash bows his head to the ground, face-down in lava, his outstretched hands splayed on the inner slope. Then he sits up, face dripping, and shakes his head fiercely. Droplets of lava spatter us, doing no harm even to our clothes and quickly cooling to smooth, flat pebbles, easily brushed off.

"Great Akaz," booms his titanic voice, "your wish is my command. Would only that I were unchained."

"Fuck that servitude shit," says Akaz. "And fuck your sob story, you'll be free soon enough. Four hundred years, hell, I've been stuck somewhere worse than this for five hundred, so quit yer bellyachin'."

"As always you speak truth, Great Akaz," rumbles the enormous voice of Shamash.

"Plus could you whisper?" asks Akaz. "Your voice is fuckin' deafening."

"Indeed," says Shamash, his whisper like the sound of a mere rockslide.

"Our dog," I say, "is bossing around a giant volcano-god."

"Yeah," says Beth.

"You should see him in battle," says Doomer. "He's got this one move I fuckin' love, grabs some poor motherfucker by the head and flings them around like a rag doll till the body flies off. Awesome."

"*Body flies off?*" asks Beth.

"Neck spurtin' in air," says Doomer. "Gnarly."

"Our dog does that," Beth says to me.

"They call it the 'Mhabahhpo Maneuver,'" says Doomer.

"The what?" I ask.

"Stands for *Momma Had a Baby and Her Head Popped Off*. Y'know, like poppin' heads off whaddayacallit. Daisies? Dandelions?"

"Dandelions." I know the line from childhood.

"Puffball dandelions?" asks Beth, deflecting us deliberately down a tangent, away from that image of spurting necks. "Blowing their seeds you mean?"

"Naw the raw version," says Doomer, "not raw, ripe, shit, you know what I mean, the yellow kind. Dandelions? You pop 'em with your thumb, or you can wrap it in its own stem like a noose."

I'm also familiar with this technique.

"Ghastly," says Beth.

"Cannibal-King's here," Akaz says to Shamash, nodding toward me.

Shamash jerks to look at me, eyes wide. He stares for a long moment. Then breaks his gaze away, lurches forward in a bow that has his forehead strike the stone at the base of the wall hard enough for us to feel it reverberate up at the rim. His arms stretch halfway up the sloping inner wall.

"Cannibal-King!" he says, deafeningly loud. The Givers join in with him: "Cannibal-King! Cannibal-King!" Shamash raises his head and looks up, again wide-eyed; and in his version of a whisper, says, "We have waited so many years."

Beth elbows me.

"Uh, hi," I say.

"Cannibal-King," he asks, "would you give me your blessing?"

"Look," I say, "I'm not sure I'm your guy."

Shamash looks at Akaz, eyes even wider. "It is exactly as prophesied," he whispers, quieter than ever, barely even loud this time. "He cites the very spirit of scripture."

"Yep," says Akaz. "Interdimensional telepathy across timestreams will do that."

Doomer laughs, elbowing me from the other side. "I love this cargo cult shit when it's done well."

"Holy fucking fuck," says Beth.

"Zackly," says Doomer.

"Just finish up your part," Akaz tells Shamash.

"Cannibal-King," Shamash says to me, still trying to whisper, "please bless me with your promise of freedom." He closes his eyes. Clasps his gigantic clawed hands. His fiery hair and beard crackle and blaze as he continues, clearly reciting from memory rather than speaking spontaneously. *"Bless me with the knowledge of my impending salvation; for you will stop at nothing to liberate the wild folk of the Isle of Kaios: the Deepings, Wilders, and Givers; and with them their respective demigods: Fat Man, and the Bitch-Queen, and Shamash. Bless us with your promise to free us all."* He leans closer and reopens his eyes. The gigantic circular infernos of his irises dominate my field of vision—so terrifying I almost say yes to that crazy bullshit just so he doesn't squish me.

But Beth beats me to it with a succinct, "Aw hell no."

I look at her, surprised, relieved, panicked, and still dazed.

"Kill some fascists, yeah," she says, "we're down with that for now; but 'stop at nothing'? No way, man."

Which snaps me the rest of the way out of it. "Right. Uh, sorry, man, no fuckin' way am I making that promise." Shamash shuts his eyes and it's like someone turning off their high-beams, making it easier for me to blather on: "If you guys turn out to be good guys, and if I can figure out how to break those chains o' yours, sure. And for now, yeah, it looks like we're going along with your revolution thing. But

I'm not gonna risk my life or my wife unreasonably on your behalf, especially if y'all turn out to be assholes, no offense."

Shamash's face is eerily placid, his huge fingers interlaced and still. So I feel emboldened to add, "So we're going to California, soon as we can figure out how. If it turns out we're supposed to do something here then sure, okay. But truth be told, I'm skeptical."

Beth and I hold hands tightly and whisper to each other, "Ready?" meaning ready to somersault backward over the rim and run. But Shamash stays placid. Again as though reciting something he knows by heart and loves with all his heart, in his most peaceful voice yet, he says, "*Cannibal-King, so be it. Your just nature and fearless autonomy are both shown by your refusal to give your word to a false future. By so refusing, you have given an even greater blessing than the asked-for promise: for as our cause against the Herax is just, I rest in my certainty you will find it so, and so choose to align your mighty guns with us. And so I rest assured that you are indeed the one with the power and wisdom to break these chains.*" His chains rattle. He opens his eyes. I feel chills.

"Wow," says Beth.

Beth and I hold each other's hands tightly.

Dungeon Master

The Givers walk each alone, arrayed for a distance around us, Akaz alongside Blood Eagle. The ground lies so flat that once we get the van rolling—in neutral, engine off—it takes almost no effort to keep it moving. I take position alongside Beth as she lounges in the driver's seat, my hands braced at the base of the side mirror, Doomer opposite me on the passenger side mirror, he and I moseying along barely pushing. The motorcycle's hitched to the back. Beth and I had briefly entertained the idea of riding around on our crappy old bicycles. But just trying to take them down off the back of the van made us realize how exhausted we already were, and we thought better of it. It really caught up with me. Hanging onto the mirror makes it easier to remain upright.

With the windows rolled all the way down, Beth, Doomer and I can converse pretty well. The heat of the day is intense, sort of, but also somehow feels mild and comfortable. Doesn't seem to bother any of us. Presumably another manifestation of the protection from Akaz, but I haven't quizzed Doomer for confirmation—I have other questions for him. "Doomer, I have questions for you."

"Like what?"

"Well, what the heck do you know about this City of the Watcher business?"

"Not much. Just that it was y'all's first trip offworld, and got you on your start as interdimensional space pirate revolutionary types."

Beth and I look at each other.

"It's one of those classic Fuckface scenarios where, you know, he's there like twice," continues Doomer, "trying to finagle shit but totally hapless. This time I think there's *three* of him here, ell oh ell." He cocks an eyebrow at Beth. "*'That fuckin' guy.'* Am I right?"

"What do you mean, *'that fuckin' guy'*?" she asks.

"That's what you always say when his name comes up."

"Who's name," I ask.

"Fuckface! Shit. You haven't met him yet, spoiler, sorry."

"Great," I say.

"Bodes well," says Beth.

"Can't wait."

We proceed in silence for a minute.

"Here's one thing I'm wondering," says Beth. "What's that riddle, from that weird sci-fi book?"

"Bilbo and Gollum?" I ask.

"No no no," she says, "it's kinda psychedelic, and there's ancient Egyptian gods, and this one guy teleports to different worlds...."

"Oh," I say, "oh, you mean the Riddle of Thoth, from *Creatures of Light and Darkness*."

"Yeah," she says, "like if you can travel to infinite worlds, how do you know if you *found* the world you travel to, or *created* it?"

"Kinda solipsistic, no?" I ask.

"Well, here's the thing," she says. "You already said you created this world."

"Wait wait," I say, "I didn't say *that*."

"Sure you did," she says. "You invented the Givers, and Akaz with his flaming head, and presumably Shamash and that volcano. When you were twelve."

"Seems kinda likelier I somehow *saw* the world when I was twelve," I counter, "with interdimensional telepathy dreams or some shit, and *based* my D&D game *on* it."

"Touché," says Doomer.

Beth looks at him, says nothing, turns her back on him. "Sure," she says to me. "Obviously. But there's something funny here, correct me if I'm wrong—if there are infinite worlds I guess you'll find anything and everything somewhere or other."

"If," I reply.

"If," she says. "But take these Givers for a sec. Doesn't it seem odd to you that this desert is inhabited by a tribe of weird-acting religious fanatics with inhuman bloodthirstiness?"

"What?"

"Is that a word? *'Bloodthirstiness'*?"

"What do you mean it's odd?" I ask.

"Religious fanatics?" says Beth. "Bloodthirstiness? Doesn't it seem like some white twelve year old American boy's racist caricature of 'Ayrabs'?"

"Givers aren't even human," I say. "They're, like, elementals."

"That's so much worse," she says, laughing.

"But they're like white as fuck," I say. "Color-wise, at least."

"Which is exactly the sort of fig leaf a twelve year old white boy would come up with to conceal a racist stereotype. No? The Givers are so white they're like thou-dost-protest-too-much white."

"Touché," I say, looking at Doomer. He raises an eyebrow.

"While we're at it, how about the title 'Cannibal-King'? If someone came up with that where we came from, I mean c'mon."

I nod and shake my head. "Makes me think of those mid-20th century racist caricatures of African or Pacific Islander folks. Isn't it from a lyric or something?"

"Truth be told," she says, "I wonder if we'd even feel entitled to meddle in this little someone-else's-revolution if we didn't grow up in the imperial core."

"Though if I did create this place, maybe I am entitled to meddle in it."

"That's such a fucked up concept," says Beth, laughing.

"White savior complex taken to its logical extreme, I reckon." I shrug and laugh.

"Taken," Beth can barely speak for laughing, "taken, taken to its *apotheosis*, if you will." She snorts.

"Yeah but fact is you *do* have godlike superpowers here," says Doomer. "Blows my mind that you fiddlefuckers are indulging in this second-guessing shit. Just use 'em."

"Hardly 'godlike,'" I say. "But honestly, who cares. It makes no difference what the metaphysical truth is. There's a police state we may be able to at least impede, and it seems to be en route back home anyway, so let's do what we can. On our terms, on our timetable, with a use of force we deem ethical."

"But we can't dictate their strategy for liberation," says Beth. "If it's fucked we can bail, we can boycott. Remove ourselves from the endeavor."

"They might not dig that too much," says Doomer.

"If they turn out to be evil enough," I say to him, "I'll sooner fight them than fight beside them. But I'm not playing cargo cult and making them do what I want, however much I may think I already know about this world."

"It's also fucked to bail if we help start shit and good folks are counting on us," says Beth. "I hate being stuck in this lesser-of-two end-justifies-the-means no-good-option shit."

"Fuck," I say.

"Yeah," says Beth.

"You guys are getting bent outta shape just like Fuckface," says Doomer, "tryna outguess the moral implications of a billiard break while yer just chalkin' yer cue. You just said it makes no difference what the metaphysical blahblah. Let's go."

Beth and I look at each other, shrug, sigh. Trying to change the world in coalition with people we disagree with and can't trust? Par for the goddamn course.

Cannibal Ethics

The salt flat seems to go on endlessly, the black craggy hills getting no closer. Still the pounding heat of the day brings us little discomfort, not even sweat. We spend an unknown stretch of hours ambling alongside the van, taking turns pushing and "steering." Occasionally we let some Givers push, though honestly it gives me and Beth the creeps to be served by people whose devotion derives from oddly coincidental fairy tales, and we have a hard time putting up with it for more than a short while at a stretch. Beth, Doomer, and I each ration ourselves to one can of warm beer; but upon Blood Eagle's reassurance that we'd find clean water ("Safe enough for Digglies") in the hills, we give ourselves free rein and down about a gallon of water between the three of us. The Givers drink nothing, eat nothing, don't piss, don't miss a stride—even those who'd been speared by Herax lope along, wounds cauterized by fire Akaz spat upon them, crusted blood dry-brushed with dust and flaking away over the course of the day. Beth, Doomer, and I piss like race-horses, often, leaving behind short-lived mud puddles. Still don't sweat, though. At some point, in the high-sunned afternoon, we stop and eat cold beans from a can, Beth and I both with no appetite and unable to finish a can between us, Doomer sweeping ours and having two cans to himself, emboldened by Blood Eagle's assurance that we'd find "food suitable for Digglies before too long, breads and vegetables and the like, possibly even as soon as we reach the Bad Givers," and we having a whole case of baked beans in the back.

Beth laments the harpooning of our camp stove: "Dammit." The three of us sit on the back bumper, van facing west so we're in its sun-past-zenith shadow. In the distance stands the column of smoke rising from the Seat of Shamash. Upon our insistence, or Beth's anyways, Akaz comes and sits by us. Heat makes ripples in the air over his head.

"So," I say to him, "as you may know, Blood Eagle is not always entirely clear."

"Cryptic," says Beth.

"Vaguey Vaguerson," says Doomer.

"Look who's talkin'," says Akaz. "Spit it out."

"What the hell are 'Bad Givers'?" I ask.

"He fuckin' told you," says Akaz. "In detail. Straight outta scripture."

"What the fuck scripture?" asks Beth.

"*The Books of Kaios*," says Akaz, "the only scripture to speak of on this island."

"We're on an island?" asks Doomer.

"We're on an island," says Akaz.

"It didn't sound particularly like scripture," I say. "I mean, it sounded just like he always talks." Though now that I'm reminded of them, I think for the first time in years about *The Books of Kaios* I wrote in high school, a series of poems serving as prophecy in my D&D game. Didn't I dream them, and then just transcribe them while stoned, something like that? Another checkmark in the 'interdimensional telepathy' column.

"Maybe he just quotes a lotta scripture," says Beth.

"You have no idea." Akaz sighs.

"So what the hell are you saying he told us," I ask. "'Cause I caught nothin'."

It looks like Akaz's fiery eyes do the littlest roll. "Recite it line by line and I'll explain it."

"What?"

"Whaddayamean 'what'?" says Akaz.

"Whaddayamean 'recite it,'" says Beth. "We only heard it once."

"You don't remember it," says Akaz.

"We don't remember it," Beth and I say.

"I didn't even hear it," says Doomer. "I was on the other side of the van."

"Christ," says Akaz. "Got any whiskey?"

"Beer," says Doomer.

"Bowl?" asks Akaz.

"Here," says Beth, digging in our gear for five seconds and coming up with his heavy ceramic bowl, enameled black, with 'Akaz' on the side in red. She drops it in front of him.

"Beer?" repeats Doomer.

"Fuck yeah beer," says Akaz.

Doomer upends another warm can into the hot ceramic bowl. Akaz slurps up the foam before it overflows, his fiery tongue splattering boiling beer. Delicious-smelling beer-steam wafts toward us. We watch him, captivated. Before long the bowl sits dry, and he looks up at us. "What," he says, seeing us all staring at him. He belches fire.

"Nothing," say the three of us at once.

"What was yer question again," asks Akaz.

"Oh," I say. "Right. What was it...?"

"What the hell are 'Bad Givers,'" says Beth.

"Yeah. What the hell are Bad Givers?"

"Bah," says Akaz. "That's his annoying moralization talking. They're just another Giver tribe. Well, it's most of the other tribes. Pretty much all the Givers, come to think of it. But you'll change all that."

"So what was the scripture?" asks Beth.

"Fuck. Okay, just the highlights. Repeat after me."

"No," we say.

"Okay, fuck, just listen then," he says, and recites:

> *Though the flesh give us only*
> *A fraction of the vitality*
> *Provided by soulstuff,*
> *We forego it;*
> *Preferring to liberate the soul:*
> *Thus it can rejoin*
> *The Sun Dragon and Earth Dragon*
> *And thence re-incarnate.*
> *Thus have we done no wrong.*

"...or some shit like that," says Akaz.

"What the fuck's that got to do with 'Bad Givers'?" asks Beth.

"Are you serious?" asks Akaz. "Have you guys followed anything that's happened so far?"

Beth gives him a Look.

"Okay, okay," says Akaz. "I'll just pretend this is the first you've heard of this shit. So you remember the Herax? The guys in the flying boat? Speared your coffee?"

"Don't remind me," says Beth.

"So, remember when they hauled some Givers on deck and ate their souls?"

"Wait, what?" I ask.

"Ate their *bodies*," says Beth.

"And the souls along with 'em," says Akaz. "They may be elementals, but Givers still have souls. They're embodied spirits. Normally when a body dies, the soul zips back into the astral plane and reincarnates into something else later. But you can eat the soul, totally destroying it in the process but gaining a huge amount of, you know, 'blood magic energy' or whatever. Some folks can just rip yer soul out and eat it without even touching ya. Some need to drink your blood like Count Dracula. But those are rare refinements. Easiest way is to just eat the organs, heart and brain, especially. Or, for the least skilled, eat the whole damn body."

"Gross," says Beth.

"So when you eat the soul," I say, "it's destroyed."

"Right," says Akaz. "You just, like, ate it."

"Forever," says Beth.

"Right. Now, though, if you know *how* to eat the soul, you *can* eat just the body, and still skim a little of the life-force without destroying the soul itself. The soul doesn't really miss it. Minimal lasting harm. Like Blood Eagle said, you get maybe a tenth of the juice you get from eating the soul and a tenth of the high."

"*'High'*?" I ask. Beth and I exchange creeped-out glances.

"So resisting the urge to eat it is pretty hard for most of us," says Akaz.

"*'Us'*?" asks Beth.

"Not you," says Akaz.

"But... *you*," I say.

"Yeah, of course," says Akaz. "What the fuck sorta death-and-chaos god do ya think I am?"

"I dunno," I say.

"The kind that doesn't eat souls 'cause it's mean?" Beth has a glimmer of hope amid the resignation in her voice.

Akaz shakes his head, eye-fires flickering upward in a slow, condescending roll.

"It could happen," I say.

"Dude," says Akaz, "at the end of time I'm gonna consume the entire *astral plane*. Not just some souls. Not just hella souls. Not just *all* the souls, their entire *plane of soulstuff*. And then, who the fuck knows what happens to me. Prolly explode." Akaz sits up on his haunches and gestures oratorily with his forepaws, "So yeah I may be charming and personable, but do not misjudge just how few fucks I give. 'Since we're all going to die,' as the saying goes, 'it's obvious that when and how don't matter.'"

Beth elbows me in the elbow. "Any of this ringing a bell with you, O Dungeon Master?"

"Some of it I remember clear as day," I say. "Like, I remember deciding the world would have reincarnation. I remember coming up with the ideas for the Givers and the Herax. I remember tying together psychic vampirism, blood vampirism, and the sorta cannibalism that gives you extra life, like in Lovecraft's 'The Picture in the House'—"

"Lost me," says Beth.

"Me too," says Doomer.

"I was like, what if all those different forms of feeding on life force—what if they're the same thing, just different techniques."

"Exactly," says Akaz.

"But you're saying," I continue, "on a world with reincarnation, so long as you don't destroy the soul, killing people *doesn't* matter."

"That's Blood Eagle's trip," says Akaz. "In a nutshell."

"Yeah, uh, no," says Beth.

"Yeah," I say. "Suffering still matters."

Akaz shrugs.

Giver Names

So we dawdle there for quite a while before continuing on our way to the Bad Givers.

"I dunno why the soul-eating creeps me out so much more," says Beth.

"It's so much worse!" I say. "Body dies, you just reincarnate. Blood Eagle is right, on a certain level."

"Gross," says Beth.

"Stockholm Syndrome," says Doomer.

"What?" says Beth.

"Stockholm Syndrome," he repeats. "Feelings of loyalty to yer captors 'cause they're all you've got and they're oh-so-nice for not killing you."

"We know what it means, Doomer," says Beth. "The origin of that term is misogynist copaganda bullshit, by the way."

"Like your guy in the Nevada desert," says Doomer.

"What?" My voice cracks. "I was the fuckin' captive. Unless you're positing Reverse Stockholm Syndrome."

"And Blood Eagle's the same," Doomer continues, heedless. "That's why you guys buy into his ethical cannibal shtick, 'cause you're fuckin' lost out here without him. I'm not saying shame shame shame," wagging his finger, "it's natural to let your ethics bend when you're in this kind of shit. Hell, I'm always in this kind of shit. Anyway my ethic is *I.D.G.A.F.*, kill fascists on sight, I'm just glad you're on board and I wish you'd put a sock in any more debate about it."

"Duly noted," I grunt.

Blood Eagle shows up. "Cannibal-King," he says.

"Do you have to keep calling me that?"

"Yes."

"Milk, it, dude," says Doomer.

"Okay, whatever," I say. "What's up, O my loyal follower?"

"We wish for you to drill us," says Blood Eagle, "before we reach the Bad Givers."

"Whaddayamean 'drill you'?" I ask, moderately concerned that this is going to be a chore, or worse.

"In the ways of hand to hand combat," says Blood Eagle. "Your ways. Whatever it is you wish to teach us."

So I find myself introduced to each of the three dozen or so of Blood Eagle's Givers, minus the few that got fished up by Herax harpoons and eaten alive. Both Beth and I thought the name 'Blood Eagle' might be some sort of North American Native stereotype from my twelve year old brain, twisted to fit this horror-fantasy genre we find ourselves in. Or are we just imagining such tropes now, where all we're really encountering is the inevitable shitload of variation in an infinite multiverse?

Turns out it's nothing of the sort anyway. It's not entirely clear what Blood "Eagle" means, but the other Givers are named Head Turner, Throat Chopper, Eye Socket, Thigh Fountain, Rib Liver, Rib Lung, Rib Heart, Spine

Folder, Flat Head, Knee Cutter, Bell Ringer, Glass Ball, Fire Ball, Sky Fist, Jaw Taker, Gut Reacher, Glass Floor, Blacken, Throat Eater, Cinder Face, Glass Spear, Fire Feast, Gut Hauler, Collapse, Glass Eye, Glass Mask, Glass Feast, Fist Feast, Collarbones, Knee Folder, Face Eater, Fire Curtain, and Fire Mask.

Beth and I sit on the van's back bumper. Akaz and Doomer banter in a whisper nearby. The Givers stand in a circle. Under Blood Eagle's direction, one by one the Givers step forward, name themselves to me and Beth, and demonstrate a different little bit of choreography—spitting fire from their mouths or flinging it from their hands, striking or clawing or biting the air, while tapping a rapid beat with one hand on their tiny drum. These movements match their names in disturbing pantomime; sometimes concrete and literal, sometimes stylized yet disturbingly evocative. "What was that?" Beth whispers to me after an especially abstract move. "What the fuck does *Glass Feast* mean?"

"Maybe that's just a literal movement for something that we just don't know what it is yet," I say, inarticulately.

"Yeah, but *what?*" she says. "Ew."

Each of the Givers is burly yet lithe; white as marble except for the pale pink scars crisscrossing the skin all over their bodies and inhumanly angular faces. Their features vary as much as those of humans, despite universal dispassionate expressions and irisless eyeballs the color of blood.

"They're not, like, albinos." Beth directs the question at Akaz, who had wandered up to sit by our feet.

"They're not, like, biological," says Akaz. "Their eye color is a side effect of their blood magic."

"How ya gonna train these guys?" Doomer squeezes in beside me on the bumper, making both me and Beth shift over a little.

"So how do you want me to drill them," I ask Blood Eagle without enthusiasm.

"You are our King," says Blood Eagle. "Whatever you choose to do will prove to be correct. Perfect. Divinely pre-ordained."

"Great," I say. I look at Beth.

"Go for it, sensei," she says.

"Okay." I do my best to summon up my martial arts instructor self, and my resonant leaderly riot-inciter outdoor voice, and announce, "Okay, gather 'round." The Givers do so swiftly. "First: explain to me that move you each have—so you're named after it?"

"Yes," respond a few of the Givers, then some more, then the rest.

"Our 'killing move,'" says Blood Eagle.

"You don't really call it that," says Beth.

Blood Eagle nods to her.

"So it's your trademark," I say. "Okay but—" I interrupt myself. Look at Blood Eagle. "What the hell is a 'blood eagle'?"

"You are not familiar with the blood eagle?" asks Blood Eagle, eerily dispassionate.

"Two guesses." Beth scowls at him.

"No," I say, "I'm not."

"I am hopeful that you will have opportunity to see it before long," says Blood Eagle earnestly.

Beth and I look at each other, wincing a little.

"Cannibal-King," asks Blood Eagle, "what is your drill for us?"

"Oh, uh, right," I say. "Well—do you all know each other's super-move?"

"Indeed, do we?" Blood Eagle asks the Givers. Much murmuring among them. "It is as prophesied," he says, then turns to me. "Cannibal-King, it is forbidden to us to study one another's 'killing move.' Forbidden by the spells of Minister Apraxos, the Watcher of Melkhaios."

That name sends a chill down my spine in a wide, cold wave like an icy river. I remember making it up—or so I thought—when I was twelve. The evil sorcerer who rules the city:

...who devours souls daily and feeds on literal factories of suffering; who sees through the eyes of every soldier and spy of his General's army; who has sorcerously enhanced his False Sovereign Shield to repel not only sling-stones and arrows on the material plane, but even bad intent on the luck plane: to oppose him one must approach at a tangent, through intermediaries, subtly skating along the edges of the web of fate.

Shit. That's right. He's about the vilest villain I ever made up. My loathing of him eclipses any care I might have for any repercussions of killing him. Isn't it white savior hubris to assume we can control repercussions anyway? No, that's gibberish, we need to consider every angle imaginable and do our best accordingly. But sometimes you just have to pull the emergency brake. Apraxos must die.

Maybe I can just assassinate him, sneak into town possessed by Akaz and wielding Victoria?

Blood Eagle busts me out of my reverie. "We have been forced to limit our martial repertoire, physically incapable of imitating certain special moves. Our curse can only be lifted by the word of the true Cannibal-King; He and He alone has power to lift the Lesser Binding."

"Oh," I say weakly. "He does this how?"

"Command us," says Blood Eagle.

"What," I say, "like, tell you all to teach each other your super-moves?"

"Yes," says Blood Eagle.

"Uh," I say to the assembled Givers, "all of you guys, teach each other your super-moves."

"*'Killing moves,'*" corrects Beth.

"Killing moves," I say. "Don't hurt each other though. No injuries."

After a pause, the Givers roar: "Cannibal-King! Cannibal-King! Cannibal-King!"

"Fucking weird," said Beth.

"Seriously," I say.

"Cannibal-King! Cannibal-King!" continue the Givers, ecstatic.

Tactical Dispositions

I find them uncannily easy to teach and train, as if they have photographic memory and reflexes to match. Their attention doesn't waver. They have no resistance to corrections, no defensiveness blocking their ability to simply listen. No having to think for a sec when I say something like, "Put more weight on your left foot," wondering which foot I mean or how to accordingly adjust their spine, pelvis, head, and limbs; they just do it. Their responsiveness is unnerving. I can't help but find them "inhuman," their manner and features falling into that uncanny valley of perception where their almost-humanness makes them feel all the more alien. My own response to them makes me sick. Despite being elementals, more magical than organic, they still have individual minds, wills, souls, as Akaz said. They are people. Also, I really do not like being called "King."

In any event, I ask each of them to again demonstrate each of their moves to the rest of the group. Then Beth and I circulate among them as everyone practices, same as we did at our dojo before the shit hit the fan on Earth. Mostly we watch, learning what these guys are capable of. We offer whatever refinements we notice, sometimes encouraging them to work in pairs. "No injuries," we keep repeating. "Slow." At times the practice-ground becomes spectacular, blossoming with dozens of fireballs or flame jets. Within an hour or two, every one of them knows the full repertoire of killing moves.

Observing and participating in the process entails a sustained period of mostly-wordless mindfulness. Beth and I keep glancing to one another wide-eyed, simultaneously observing a maneuver that is exceptionally athletic or terrifying. Especially in contrast with the nonstop anxiety and trauma of the past weeks, this extended shared trance drops us into a psychedelic combination of dreaminess and focus, intensity and flow. Our surroundings only enhance the surrealness: vast empty plain around us, smoke from the volcano on the horizon. I watch the Givers working in pairs and try to imagine what sort of maneuvers and tactics we could develop together over time, given the chance.

I'm about to suggest we start drilling in threes when, as if on cue, a half dozen Herax longboats creep over the horizon, flying low above the craggy black hills.

"Whoa," says Beth. "Fuck."

"Bad timing for them," I snarl, my wrath sparked. Doing my best to unleash some sorta 'kingly' voice, I say to the assembly: "Behold, the Herax!"

"Corny." Beth laughs.

The Givers cheer once and then fall silent.

"Creepy," says Beth.

"Don't hate," I say.

"So you wanna be a king now, hmm."

"Oh hell no," I say.

"Cannibal-King?" prompts Blood Eagle.

Everyone is looking at me.

"Uh," I say to Blood Eagle, then turn to the assembly. What the hell do I want to say to these people? "Uh, right, Herax. Well, we can hope that they know not yet that I have come; perhaps all they know is that strange fire sorceries were used against them near the volcano of Great Shamash." What's with the hackneyed antiquated speech? It just comes out like that.

Akaz chimes in. "They saw me, that's for sure. They prolly just think I helped one of the Givers draw some extra power from the volcano god."

"The Herax would not send a mere six boats against the Cannibal-King," says Blood Eagle, gesturing at the distant enemy.

"Right," I say. Beth and I look at each other, not entirely comforted by the implication that if and when they figure out I'm here, things could get worse than this. I address the assembly: "The Herax know not yet that the Cannibal-King is come; for if they knew, they would send a vast armada against us. Still, those six ships on the horizon are five more than we faced before; and we lost lives last round."

"Death is nothing," proclaims a Giver, I think Glass Feast. "It will be the highest honor to expend this life in destruction of the Herax, and to dissolve into cosmos until my soul reemerges into the form of another being of earth and fire."

"Unless they eat you," says Beth.

"Which they will!" I say, as kingly as I can manage. "And even should your soul escape, your body gone reduces our small army by one, and we need everyone we can get. We must meet up with the Bad Givers and add them to our army. And that means we must get to them before the Herax get wise to who I am. So we must kill those"—I make a sweeping gesture at the approaching longboats—"quickly."

"Stop talking then," Beth says to me, "and let's shoot them."

"Yeah but no. We wanna keep as D.L. as possible, you and me. Let the Givers kill them off with their brand new skills. We don't wanna tip off that we've got guns and stuff." I ask Akaz: "Right? The guns are in the prophecy, and Apraxos knows it?"

"Kinda," says Akaz.

"Minister Apraxos has the *Books of Kaios*," says Blood Eagle, "in which the coming of the Cannibal-King is foretold."

"So the guns are a giveaway."

"Stop talking," says Beth. "You're not thinking. We're vulnerable to harpoons. The Givers are mostly hand to hand."

"They can all throw fireballs now!" I say, loud.

The Givers all cheer once, then resume silence.

Beth looks askance at them. Then, to me, "Let Akaz jump into your mouth, hop on the MG, and you'll be throwing fireballs that carry a shitload more kick."

"We call that 'Wargus-Fire.'" Akaz grins.

"Great Akaz!" cheer the Givers. "Cannibal-King!"

"No way!" I say.

"The rifle is more magical than the machine gun, actually," says Akaz. "It's not about rate of fire. One good shot to the mast will snap it. As we saw."

"The MG has more range," says Beth.

"Don't matter now." Akaz points to the approaching ships, which are now near enough that they must be able to count us. "Where's Victoria." Beth hops into the van. She hops right back out, bearing my lever-action .30-30 carbine with the spiral-branded stock. She hands it toward me.

"Your aim as good as hers?" Akaz asks me.

"Ain't no dog gonna jump in my mouth," I say.

Beth takes the rifle back, "Okay, I'll do it then," grabs shells one by one from my bullet belt and loads them into Victoria's side.

"Wait wait wait," I say, inching back from her with each bullet-grab; but she keeps pace with my retreat. She turns to Akaz, who says to me—

"Open wide."

"No!" I say. "Okay, I'll do it." Beth shoves in the final shell and hands the gun back to me. I look at Akaz. He looks at me. I look at him. He cocks his head. "What," I say.

"Open wide!"

"Oh. Uh....." I open my mouth as wide as I can and close my eye.

It feels as though the contents of a blacksmith's furnace are shoved down my throat and into my belly. Roaring heat bursts out through my torso, down all four limbs into my extremities. I open my eye. The world seems covered in a curtain of fire; through it, I can perceive every facet of every surface, at any distance, with the unearthly detail of *samadhi*. My mind spins, buzzing, burning, too chaotically active for a straight line of abstract thought. The Herax air-vessels approach, winking in and out of visibility—but either way I can still see them clear as day in the Fire Plane or whatever this radiant world is that I behold through Akaz's eyes. Around me in all directions, the thundering clamor of little Giver drums. I heft Victoria, lever her action, take aim on the mast of a longboat a few hundred yards away, and fire. Flames burst forth from Victoria's muzzle as from my mind, as from the center of the earth; the recoil against my shoulder merely grounds me deeper into my inferno-filled body, feet inseparable from the earth, this strange earth, my sovereign dominion. The mast splits. Its sail afire, the ship slowly sinks toward the ground. Givers rush out to meet it, rattling their drums as they run.

The remaining five longboats part to either side—to encircle us and approach from all directions, I assume. I fire upon another and sever its mast. It falls, burning, to be swarmed by Givers. Four boats left. They aim their noses up. Hoping to get up out of range, perhaps, while keeping their masts mostly concealed from my angle of fire by the hulls themselves, till they can drop on us from straight overhead in a hail of plummeting harpoons. So I hand Victoria to Beth, jump up on the hood, and drop down through the ring mount. I ready the M240, crouching low on the passenger seat so I can aim up, and blast a little meteor shower up through the keel of a longboat from stem to stern. It begins to fall in flames. By the time it crashes fifty yards from us, the last three longboats have turned and are taking off in three different directions, cranking for maximum elevation.

I don't want any survivors to come back at us later. And I want to amplify our fearsome reputation; that's one of my few real weapons back on Earth, and it comforts me to cultivate it. Might that bring more of them down on us? That's always the risk. We'll be at the Bad Givers before long anyway. And dammit I just want these fuckers dead. Dead on the ground. I want my Givers strong, well fed upon flesh and souls. Wait, no—just souls. Just flesh I mean. Flesh, and unscathed souls flee freely into the beyondo. Christ, way too easy to get carried away on this rush of power.

A fiery rage engulfs my interior. I unleash a volley of bullets at one distant ship, blasting enough of a hole in its side to cause it to list, exposing its mast, which I blast away. The next one has angled so I can see only the very top of its mast; but that's enough for me to loosen its sail and cause the boat to drop. The last boat takes the longest: too far for even the MG to hit with any precision, pilot keeping its mast well concealed, I simply pelt its hull with endless fiery bullets, punching charred holes through planks and sail and unlucky soldiers, every detail visible to me from a mile away through Akaz's incredible eyes. I gradually gnaw away at its enchantment till it too falls, becoming another broken bonfire releasing its column of smoke skyward.

I look around, emerging from my gunner's trance. Everyone's gone but Beth. I hear them in the distance, reveling at multiple slaughters, drums clattering, trying out their new killing-moves. Akaz barfs his way up out of me and runs off to the nearest feast, and I collapse over the side of the ring mount.

"Jack!" Beth comes running.

I right myself, slump back down into the van and drunkenly let myself out the passenger side door. Beth catches me and keeps me on my feet. In the middle distance, a pack of Givers mops up the crew of one wreck, molten glass and fireballs flying. Then they run off to join the next wreck.

Doomer, astride Beth's motorcycle, skids to a stop near us. He pulls down a dusty bandana and pries up dusty goggles. "The fuck did I miss?!" he asks.

Beth and I sit on the front bumper of the van, passing a warm beer back and forth. The Givers, having first made sure every Herax was dead, proceed to spend an uncannily short hour or two eating each and every one of them, leaving (as we soon learn) nothing but gnawed bones and untouched organs, each Giver impossibly (you'd think) eating what must be at least twice their own body weight in Herax flesh. After Beth and I finish our beer we retreat to our bed, clear it of debris, and lie there under the broken skylight, staring up at the darkening afternoon sky, trying not to hear the faint distant sounds of ravening. After a while or so I roll onto my side, and Beth spoons me while I weep.

The Bad Givers

Close to nightfall we roll up on the Bad Giver fortress set into the wall around the edge of the desert. An obsidian crag looms jaggedly a hundred feet high from the flat sands, encircling the salt flat in a curtain as far as the eye can see to right and left. The fortress front gate stands as nothing but a pair of tall narrow metal doors, twelve feet high, together only six feet wide. Big as heck for a house, say, but eerily small as the only way into a fortress. "Not wide enough to get the van in," Beth observes. The fortress doors sit more or less flush with the sheer wall of obsidian towering above them. Can't tell if they're solid metal or sheet metal over wood. Can't tell if they're brass or gold. Can't focus so well on them, not with those javelin slits staring down at us from the cliff face.

"Apraxos built this," says Akaz. "Taking it was one of the Givers' greatest victories."

"The fact that the crag disappears," I say to Beth, gesturing in both directions at once, "that proves the curvature of this planet, right?"

"There's fucking Givers in there," she says, sensibly ignoring my digression. I follow her gaze. Ten, twenty, thirty javelin slits, tall apertures and very skinny, built originally for Herax harpoons but now inhabited like nightmare peepshow booths by slim glimpses of Givers. Little flickers of flame strobe broad shadows from their fingers across their scarified limbs and faces.

Till they see that we are Givers, immune to fire. Then they let their flames flicker out, and from within their shadowed cubicles we hear clinking echoes as they take up sharp missiles of glass. Only an occasional curve of thew or glint of glass makes it into the last light of the sun.

"Great," Beth and I say to each other.

Then the Givers see Akaz. The doors open wide in welcome. A chanting cheer emanates from the many openings in the wall: "Akaz! Akaz! Akaz!"

Blood Eagle says, "Behold, your Cannibal-King! He who has come to liberate the whole of the Isle of Kaios! From the Seat of Great Shamash, through the Temple of Fat Man in the twice-damned Herax city, to the Witch-Queen's Throne in Gomothrax-Beyond-the-Bay—behold!"

The Givers stare out at me in silence.

"Akaz," I ask him, "you sure you know what you're doing?"

"I don't want to go in there," says Beth.

"C'mon." Akaz leads the way.

Our Giver platoon walks in after him. From outside we watch Giver guards in the foyer bow down before Akaz. "Bring us to Larynx," he says. "He's still boss-man here, right?"

"We will lead you to General Larynx, Great Akaz," says one of the Givers.

"Great," says Akaz.

Doomer dismounts, gets Beth's motorcycle settled, and follows. Beth and I reluctantly leave the van behind, half-heartedly locking it, unconfident that'd make a damn bit of difference, even with the M240 dismounted on the passenger seat and the trapdoor shut. I carry my carbine, Victoria, slung over my shoulder, pistol and kukri and hatchet at my waist. Beth has a pistol holstered on one hip, the bayonet on the other, and her own hatchet in her hand. I squeeze her free hand as we pass through the gate, trying to act like I'm not nervous. She gives me a glance that tells me she's not convinced. Which eases my worries, and I stop trying. The relief is short lived: I kind of feel like I might need to shit. Timely. Fuck. Our Givers gather closely around as we squeeze into the foyer, turn down a hallway alongside the inside of the wall with javelin slit emplacements stocked with barrels of glass. We turn again and enter a room that had once been a barracks. Once I wrap my head around what's going on, I see this has become a weapons factory.

The bunks are shoved against the walls for use as shelving, laden with barrels and footlockers. A half dozen irregular-sized circles cover most of the floor, maybe six to ten feet across, faintly worn into the stone. In the center of each sits a barrel of sand, beside it a footlocker full of glass: soft-ball-sized balls, leaf-shaped blades. Givers occupy two of these circles even now, walking around and around, one clockwise, one otherwise, each holding a glowing piece of red-hot glass, haloed in fire. After a few orbits they suck away the fire and even the glow from the glass ball or knife. Then they drop it, cooling, into a footlocker. Sometimes something breaks. No one seems to care when that happens.

I wonder if Herax have to shit, whether there's a bathroom, whether it's been repurposed beyond usefulness.

"General Larynx," says Blood Eagle.

One of the pacing Givers stops in his tracks, turns his red-hot glass blade point-downward so it won't bend, holds it hanging before his face and blows on it. He turns his eyes to Blood Eagle. Rights the sword. The blade bends only slightly.

"Blood Eagle," says General Larynx. "You're telling us you've finally found the Cannibal-King."

"He has come," says Blood Eagle.

Larynx sees Akaz. His hairless brow rises. "Akaz," he says.

"Yeah, this is the real deal," says Akaz. "I don't need you sonsabitches to pay the reverence that some say is due me, I don't need you to stop imitating the fucking Herax with your factory thaumaturgy bullshit here, but please just do what this guy says." He points his snout at Blood Eagle.

Beth's eyes meet Akaz's. Akaz looks back at Larynx. Beth elbows me. "Huh?" I say.

"You mean do whatever *he* says," says Beth, indicating me. "He's the Cannibal-King, right?"

"I am but his prophet," agrees Blood Eagle.

"If you are Cannibal-King," says Larynx to me, "how can you prove it? Aside from a fire-demon and a desert charlatan vouching for you."

"Well," I say. As uncomfortable as it was, I preferred the reception we got from Shamash.

"We can make Herax ships fall from the sky," says Beth.

General Larynx's forehead furrows.

"On fire," Beth adds.

He looks back and forth between me and Beth.

I nod affably. "From hundreds of paces away."

"And as foretold," says Blood Eagle, "he has lifted from us the Lesser Binding."

General Larynx's brow lifts again.

"Even should your Givers of Fort Goodbye have no reverence for Akaz," says Blood Eagle, "or his prophet, or his Cannibal-King, please at least recognize the might of these new visitors to our world, and allow them to lead us to victory over the Herax."

"If all this were true," says General Larynx, "I might even accept him as Cannibal-King."

"Then," says Blood Eagle, "as you and I wagered many years ago, if I brought to you our King, you would abstain from eating souls."

General Larynx dejectedly drops his glass sword into a chest. It breaks. "I must argue," he says. "If we march upon the Herax, we will need to feed on blood energy more than ever before."

"We gain more from the Cannibal-King," says Blood Eagle, "than we lose from letting our victims' souls fly free. Free to return as more men for us to feed upon henceforth."

"If we feed truly," says General Larynx, "if we devour enough spirit, we may transcend into immortal demigods."

"You will not," says Blood Eagle, "for the Cannibal-King and the Cannibal-King's Wife will not lead us unless we all swear to abstain."

"How then," asks General Larynx, "can we still call our-selves 'cannibals'?"

"You worship a word," says Blood Eagle, "yet you call *us* superstitious? Ha. This is the Law: neither you nor any of these Givers shall eat the soul of anyone or anything: not now, nor till our Cannibal-King leads us to victory or death. Not soul, nor heart, nor brain."

General Larynx pauses for a moment. "Agreed. As you and I bargained so many years ago, we will abstain from soulstuff. But I decline any permanent vow. With victory we feast."

"Uh," I say.

"No," says Beth. "We're not killing fascists to make room for more fascists."

"Look," begins Akaz, but alarums interrupt him.

Voices echo down the hall, approaching in little waves, chanting: "Herax! Herax! Herax!"

Fort Goodbye

Beth and I look at each other. "Fuck," she mutters.

Akaz growls at us. "We can debate systems of social organization later. For now we kill Herax."

"Are these guys feasting on the dead or no?" I ask.

"If you prove you are Cannibal-King," says General Larynx, "we will refrain from eating the souls of the dead."

Blood Eagle butts in. "Then your warriors may only feed upon the muscles of the fallen if they vow not to eat the soul as well. If you recognize the Cannibal-King, you must recognize his doctrine of sparing the soul, and you must fulfill it with rigor."

"Exactly," I say.

"After," says General Larynx, with a touch of something I feel sure is asperity, "you prove you are Cannibal-King."

"No fucking victory feast till that gets sorted out," says Beth.

"You're in a fortress," says Akaz, "that's under attack right fucking now. C'mon!"

"Okay," I say, "but as soon as we secure this place we're gonna talk—"

—but Akaz leaps into my mouth.

Fire flashes across my field of vision. I bound out of the room and lope down the hallway, dodging agilely between Givers, sometimes running halfway up a wall to pass them. Victoria on her bandolier, and kukri, hatchet, and pistol on my belt, all swing wildly yet I somehow manage to not drop or bump any of them.

"Jack!" says Beth, racing after me.

All down the hallway Givers speed back and forth to their battle stations, already growing white-hot fires between their palms. Warriors position boxes and barrels of glass weapons alongside each javelin-slot. At top speed I thread my way among them, trailing smoke from my mouth and nose. Upon arriving at the double front doorway I find it barred with a log. I grab it and fling it backwards over my head. Kick the doors open.

Shimmering above the horizon, soaring low in their approach over the salt flat, at least a dozen Herax ships.

I jump onto the hood of the van, shrug out of Victoria's bandolier and unhitch my belt, setting my weapons on the roof. I fling open the hatch and dive feet-first in through the ring mount, demigod agility finally giving out for a sec as I whack both elbows painfully on metal. Cussing, I haul the M240 up, notch it into the ring mount, and unload a fan of piercing fire at the distant ships.

Although Akaz seems to have taken control of my voluntary muscles, inside my mind I have been able to maintain a lively dialogue with him. While running through the fortress it consisted chiefly of a long sequence of me repeating the question, "What the fuck? *What* the *fuck?*" Now, though, in the relative stillness of standing here shooting down Herax boats, my thoughts are able to catch up, and I articulate my inquiries more precisely.

"I'll agree to fight in self-defense for now. But explain to me how these guys are any better than Herax. This place is fucking awful."

"Well, these *are* the 'Bad Givers.'" Akaz laughs in my mind.

"How did we even agree to come along with you guys in the first place?" I ask. "You even got Beth to do it. What the fuck?"

"That desert does strange things to a mind," says Akaz.

"You're telling me. Well, don't be surprised if I ask you to help us Earthlings get the hell outta here with our lives. Those guys will not be psyched for me to cut the King routine. Blood Eagle seems dead set on me playing that part for him."

"The scale of evil isn't even comparable," says Akaz. "Think of it this way. If the Givers are Jonestown, the Herax are Auschwitz."

"So tell me why I want to put Jim Jones in charge of Auschwitz?" I ask.

"No, jackass," says Akaz, "the Givers don't want to run the little Herax 'empire.' They wanna break it so it don't work anymore."

"So you claim," I say. "I'm not killing people just 'cause you say so."

"You are doing exactly that right now." Akaz laughs. "And yet they'll all come back, into a better world, without any Herax in it."

"Like I'm gonna bank on reincarnation being real," I say.

"You know it is," says Akaz quietly. "Whether you created this world or just discovered its lore in your dreams, you know reincarnation is part of it."

"Fuck that," I say, remembering a summer day age twelve, out on the patio killing ants, pondering the ethics of the arena combat in *Melee/Wizard*, and the idea coming to me: what would it mean if people truly knew that reincarnation was a fact, same as gravity? How would that affect the culture around killing, in a swords and sorcery world? And so I baked that idea into my D&D world when I created it—a context where running around and slaughtering "monsters" for their treasure isn't quite so horrifying.

I stop shooting for a moment. But Akaz reasserts control of my trigger finger and resumes the rain of fireballs.

"That's part of why I'm so heedless," says Akaz. "Not bloodthirsty, heedless. I'm a god of chaos and death, sure; but everybody just comes back, so no big deal."

"I reject the hypothesis that I 'created' this world," I say.

"As long as the cannibals eat only flesh, and not souls," says Akaz, "you can truly liberate this world, even by your own standards—heck, even if innocent folks die in the process."

The last of the Herax boats falls in flames out of the sky. A dozen giant bonfires blaze at different distances upon the hard-packed desert floor. No one got close enough, I think, to identify this mysterious new Giver super-weapon, even with a spyglass. If Herax have spyglasses.

A loud cheer of many deep voices comes from within Fort Goodbye, and out of the main gate pour dozens upon dozens of Giver warriors clutching fistfuls of hot or molten glass. Some carry buckets of glass weapons. A riot descends upon several of the closest burning ships at once, completing the slaughter of any survivors, then quickly spreads to the remaining boats. Beth and I sit on the hood of the van, watching the distant silhouettes dance around the fires.

Dead Fatman Dreams

Then somehow I've fallen into a doze on the back bumper of the van, nodding off into dreams of dark cold water. Deep in the sea I swim-stride up a broken cobblestone street toward a temple of strange spires, slick with green ooze and emanating sinister vibes. And a voice. Not a voice. But words:

Dead Fatman lies dreaming

and

Don't crawl
Seek his burn of war
When the fallout comes
He is fire

I awaken cold, t-shirt sweated through, crick in my neck from slouching sideways over a couple of stacked toolboxes. But most of all frazzled from that voice of latent horror.

I hop up, jolting both Beth and Doomer awake. How did we all fall asleep at a time like this? They both say, "Huh?" absently. I wrench off my clammy, clinging t-shirt with no small difficulty and hang it casually on the latch inside the cargo door as I grab another shirt from the pile. My soaked shirt slides down and falls into the dust.

"Shit."

Beth rolls her head in slow circles to work the kinks out of her neck. "Okay baby?" she mumbles.

"Stress dream." I realize our iJuke is quietly playing the penultimate movement from the epic song "Through Silver in Blood," with the lyrical refrain

> Don't crawl
> Seek his burn of war
> When the fallout comes
> He is fire

over and over and over.

"Me too." Beth yawns and groans at the same time. "Fucked up underwater city."

"Yeah, and that song was in it," says a barely-awake Doomer, fumbling to turn off the iJuke and failing. "C'mon." No luck with the gizmo. "Fuckin' lyric gonna drive me nuts."

"You dreamt the same thing?" My daze does not lift but deepens.

"It was like fuckin' with me, too," says Doomer. "'Dead fat man's dreaming, dead fat man's dreaming,'" in a nasal brat singsong. "I like to eat, fuckin' problem with that?"

Beth reaches over and pulls the jack out of the iJuke, bringing the music to a sudden stop.

"Fucking finally," says Doomer to the iJuke, to the dream, to the endless desert.

King Jack

The Givers return in scattered waves, leaving behind an array of smoldering wrecks populated only by charred gnawed bones, unless they ate the bones too. Akaz scrambles up to the van, trailing a plume of dust. "Check it out check it out check it out," he says, unusually animated. Flames whoosh around his eyes and muzzle. "Put that song back on. The 'don't crawl' part."

"Huh?" Doomer looks down at the wee iJuke in his big hand.

"Here." Beth takes it from him. She's as mystified as I am by our dog's insistence, but likewise infected by his enthusiasm. "The whole song, or just that part?" she asks Akaz, peering down at the screen and tapping at it.

"No no no not the whole fucking song," says Akaz, "just the 'don't crawl' section. Could just be part of it, doesn't matter, just hit it, they're here already." Little jets of flame shoot from his nose. He dances in place a little with excitement.

I lean over Beth's shoulder and start to say something, but she cuts me off with, "I know, I know, Mr. DJ Argus—" But the song begins playing from the beginning with its eerie, echoey factory sounds, at my guess a full eight minutes before the 'don't crawl' section. "—oh shit."

"Great," says Akaz, watching the first few Givers shuffle past the van and into the front gate of Fort Goodbye, trailing aromas of charred meat, their glossy white bellies hugely distended. Wisps of fire dance around their lips, nostrils, eyelids.... Occasional sheets of fire erupt from their pores and wash across a swath of skin.

"Chill, dude," I say to Akaz, "take it from a DJ, if that section's so special they'll turn back for it, and that amps up the vibe for anyone who sees them do so, everybody wants to know what the big deal is."

"Yeah," says Beth, scanning forward on the iJuke. She drops the digital needle right into a screaming chant over thunderous bass and drums, with guitars and keyboards like collapsing buildings:

> *Don't crawl*
> *Seek his burn of war*
> *When the fallout comes*
> *He is fire*

again and again through the tinny little built-in speaker.

"Yeah, take it from a DJ," says Doomer.

"What the fuck are you talking about," says Akaz.

"You may be god of death and whatnot," I say, "but I know how to run a party. But what I'm trying to ask you is, *why* the fuck do you wanna play the 'don't crawl' part of 'Through Silver in Blood' for the Bad Givers."

"Not just the bad ones," says Akaz.

"'Cause the thing is," I continue, "all three of us just dreamt this fuckin' lyric at the same time. No big deal, the song was playing while we slept, it just crept into our dreams. Except we also all three dreamt of the same fucked up underwater temple, with an eerie voice chanting those lyrics. Bit of a co-incidence. And we just woke up from this dream like five seconds ago, and I for one am still spaced out and spooked as hell from it, so excuse me for rambling but I'm feeling pretty fucked up right now that you picked that verse of that song to play for these dudes. So maybe you could, like, explain."

"Sure," says Akaz. "Those lyrics are from their ancient prophecy about you. So, if they hear it now, it might help cement the deal."

"Cement the deal."

"Yeah. Of you. As Cannibal-King. Shooting down all those Herax was pretty monumental, and it fits in with prophecy. So right now they're all yummy in the tummy, and potential-ly predisposed to accept this idea that you're their guy from scripture. But c'mon, please, this is the perfect mic drop."

I rub my forehead. Doomer plugs the iJuke into the van's P.A., inspiring furrowed hairless brows from passing Giv-ers, they never having heard this type of music. Akaz en-gages with passing Givers like a peepshow barker, draw-ing their attention to the lyrics. One by one they fall to their knees in awe, raising a small ruckus in sync with the music on their loud, uncannily small drums. All Givers in earshot gather at the sound, adding their drums to the growing cacophony, the sound drawing others from farther. They start spilling from the fort. They chant along with the lyrics, sometimes alternating into shouts of "Cannibal-King! Can-nibal-King! Cannibal-King!"

That night Blood Eagle calls Bone Council, and my king-ship is debated briefly by a hundred fat-bellied, fire-flicker-ing humanoids. Each point of discussion gets raised once—prophecies from scripture that might or might not refer to my companions, my hand weapons, my guns (including one eerily named in prophecy as "Victory"), my van, my bandolier (*"lo, His girdle of fireballs"*!?), my shirt (a sleeve-less old Army Ranger shirt with a patch reading "Follow Me": Givers don't read but Akaz points out these further words from their prophecy), and various things I'd said since I arrived—and after a succinct description of the ar-guments for or against, the council unanimously acknowl-edges the legitimate fulfillment of prophecy, point by point. Then Blood Eagle offers his theological-ethical ultimatum: stop eating souls. "Your King commands it, and will only lead us to victory and liberation if we assent to his decree."

This raises a loud and sustained ruckus, a sudden and severe alteration in the tone of the council from eerily uni-form harmony to what feels like the brink of riot and mas-sacre: Blood Eagle's two dozen followers sit motionless and silent in grimaces of broiling rage, while the remainder of the assembly roars and threatens them. Some even leap to their feet, fire streaming from mouth, nose, eyes, ears, and hands, poised to attack.

"SHADDUP!" says Akaz.

Everyone freezes.

"Your gluttony," Blood Eagle intones into the quiet, "con-ceals from you the deeper truths of cannibalism. Why fore-go the surge of power from fully devouring pure spirit? Why settle for the paltry wages of mere flesh? Because, you avaricious voracious pits of unthinking hunger, when we release the loosened soul back into the wilds of the astral plane, it returns to us as flesh again. If we do not, it does not. This might not have been a concern to the crude-minded magicians Augermath and Apraxos in ancient days of godtime and Empire, when the world teemed with life and soulstuff seemed endless. But, my kindred, our world lies drowned except for this tiny Isle of Kaios, and the astral plane lies withered and bereft of soulstuff. Most spirits were either devoured or disintegrated in the time of the Great Breach; and most of the rest have been eaten since. All that remains is our few thousand scattered in the ruined lands of Kaios. If we release, if we sustain the herd, the astral plane will slowly grow to flourish again, and we, who live and hunt forever, will feast in ever greater portions, in time even surpassing the tenfold rush of energy we derive from destroying a soul forever."

"Apocalyptic balderdash!" cries out a Bad Giver.

"Twisting myths like liar Apraxos himself," adds another.

"Heretic!" say several more.

"*Shut! The fuck! Up!*" Akaz's roar hits like a thunderclap.

Silence.

"If your belief in the future is insufficient," says Blood Eagle, "perhaps your desire for tactical advantage against the Herax will prevail."

Blood Eagle reaches *into the back of his own neck* and draws forth the Spine of Kaios from his back. A sweeping gesture at his followers with it, ending in a clattering metallic rattle. They stand. "For our Cannibal-King," he continues, "has lifted the Lesser Binding." He rattles the Spine. His followers fling jets of fire from their hands to the sand at their feet, melting it to glass, and then scoop up dripping handfuls. They blow on them, leap into the air, and hurl the molten glass into the spot whence they'd grabbed it, the half-solidified substance half-splashing, half-shattering. Scores of Bad Givers gasp, stunned to witness their fellows able to emulate each other's choreography.

Blood Eagle shakes his rattle again, and his Givers stand tall, each of them thrusting one hand straight up, and from it, a jet of fire a dozen yards high. "Not only that," says Blood Eagle. "Not only has our Cannibal-King lifted the Lesser Binding placed upon us by Apraxos, robbing us of our power to embody each other's mastery. Not only that, he has also lifted the Greater Binding. Restoring to us our full power of unity."

The jets of fire spiral around each other, braiding themselves into a writhing column of flame a hundred feet high. The Bad Givers all leap to their feet, shouting in ecstasy, none of them, I take it, having seen this for centuries.

"Swear!" says Blood Eagle.

"We swear!" The Bad Givers hurl up jets of fire to join the intricate helical tower of flame, broadening it, lengthening it, another hundred feet, another hundred still.

And then, together, they sweep their hundred-yard cyclone of fire back and forth through the air like a titanic sword, its surface shimmering with shifting facets like fluttering autumn leaves.

Giver-Tots

I dream again of the sinister spired temple, green with underwater slime, the voice that isn't a voice emanating eerily from it:

In his house at Wiggly Bay
Dead Fatman lies dreaming

murmuring over and over. I awake soaked in cold sweat and delirious with nameless terror.

Beth wakes, shaken, having dreamt of a clown with a knife. "That's all?" I ask, which is not the right thing to say. But we manage not to start the day with a fight. Later Doomer tells us his dreams had orbited around a raucous Louisiana backyard barbecue with a whole pig. Despite having shared it with no one, the voice from my dream lingers persistently in the back of my mind.

The Givers of Fort Goodbye seem hale and fit, bellies flat after the mysterious fashion of Giver digestion. Beth and Doomer and I spend the morning smoking joints outside in the shade of a tarp hung off the van's roof. We pass around a few cans of warm Red Bull from our backup supplies stash, which mostly manages to keep away the caffeine withdrawal headache but the synthetic substance still makes us feel gross. Akaz visits often to debate the ethics of the coming assault upon the city. Beth remains unshakably skeptical of the reincarnation thing simply as a matter of ethical rigor, with scathing critique for my almost willingness to use it as a loophole. Doomer remains unreservedly in favor of killing 'bad guys,' entirely regardless of any afterlife. At one point we get the news that scouts caught a handful of escaped Herax survivors limping away across the desert and ate them—their flesh only, of course, not soul nor heart nor brain—on the spot.

Most Givers busy themselves within Fort Goodbye, gathering any necessities for the march. I wonder what those might be, marveling a little at the strategic implications of an army that has no need for shelter, sleep, equipment, or food—logistical limitations that have always fundamentally defined military activity on Earth. Conflicting impressions roil in my brain, breast, and gut about the relative humanity and inhumanity of these Givers. They are not biological beings of animal origin, but spirits of earth and fire bound into humanoid shape. They betray no empathy, no love, no gentleness; their thinking seems more mechanical than that of the most heartless man; and even their movements seem reptilian or insectoid. Yet they have souls. Whatever a soul is on this odd world, these folk have them, and Herax eat them same as Givers do. Clearly this must be simply a metaphysical (or physical?) fact: even if Akaz was lying, Blood Eagle's cannibal ethic must have a real referent (i.e., actual souls you can eat, or not), or it wouldn't have been such a point of contention. These folks would know. They use that power to throw fuckin' fireballs. You'd be able to tell the difference between enough juice to throw a dozen fireballs vs. enough to throw a hundred. Right?

So whatever a "soul" is here, these guys have 'em. They're not just automatons masquerading as men, fooling me with a convincing android facemask. All these differences I see are cultural, or psychological. The brutal Spartans were human beings, no? As is any psychopath...? My mind wanders through thoughts for a while of what to do, ethically, with a psychopath. Do you simply kill them preemptively, even if they have done no harm? Surely not. Surely the absence of empathy is not, in itself, evil. Empathy is a neurological trait in humans, not an ethical one.

All this runs through my head while Beth and I prepare the van for transport over the wall, putting things away or tying them down. "The sand walkers will be able to keep it mostly level as they lift it over the cragwall," Blood Eagle had said.

"'Sand walkers,'" Beth and I repeated.

"But I suggest securing any objects within, to be safe," Blood Eagle continued.

Doomer revvs Beth's motorcycle and rides it into Fort Goodbye, the sound of the engine at first bellowing out at us through the mouth of the main gate, its echo amplified. As he turns a corner it mutes dramatically, then fades to a distant purr. Out of the gates march twenty Givers, each of them dragging what looks like a fat Giver child, ivory-white except for scattered pink scars. "What the—?" Beth and I ask each other.

The sound of the motorcycle engine comes faintly from over the far side of the cragwall.

The twenty Givers brandish twenty glass knives and begin chanting. The child-things sit in the dust, staring at nothing.

I yell at no one in particular, "No!"

"What the fuck!" says Beth.

"By your command," says Blood Eagle, "a summoning that one might have cost but one soul, now must cost ten bodies. But their eternal souls persist, and shall return."

"No!" Beth and I both say.

Twenty throats spray blood onto the sand. Flittering at the periphery of my horror, I idly wonder why Givers have blood if they're not biological entities.

The chanting continues. Up from the bloody sand rise two shapeless lumps five feet high, ten feet, twenty, which sprout pseudopods of sand, ultimately resolving into two shifting, vaguely bipedal forms.

They take hold of the van, front and back, and carry it up the steep crag, half climbing, half flowing, keeping the van impressively level despite their bizarre quality of movement. The sand walkers lift it over the crest out of sight.

Beth and I look on in silence. The Givers drag the dead inside.

Beth and I sit alone together on the hard-packed dust where our van had stood. Eventually I say, "'Giver-Tots.'"

"'Giver-Tots,'" says Beth. "Is that like kids, or tater tots?"

"Yeah, kinda both. I forgot all about them. They're like a stunted sub-race of the Givers, bred as cattle."

"You were a sick fuck as a kid," she says.

"I'm kinda preferring the saw-this-place-via-interdimensional-telepathy hypothesis."

"Yeah, me too."

"It's so 'me,' though, you know? Horror fantasy satire of the world during the Reagan era?"

"Although," she says, "if you were immersed in dark influences from this world throughout your formative years…. It's chicken or egg, who killed Bambi, one hand clapping type unknowable. So who gives a shit."

"True. Formative influences."

"Speak of the devil," she says, as Akaz saunters alone out of the Fort's front gate. "No pun intended."

As soon as he gets within earshot he begins speaking: "C'mon c'mon c'mon c'mon c'mon. Everybody's out and ready to march. We've got more Givers to convert, and then the Wilders. Though with them the hard part is just gonna be getting them to team up with Givers." His words race, his voice carrying a breathiness like a blacksmith's furnace. Fire dances at his eyes and mouth. He comes to a stop face to face with us. "You're not standing. C'mon. Showtime."

"What," says Beth, "the fuck."

"What," says Akaz.

"Fucking Giver-Tots," she says.

Bursts of flame roll in Akaz's eye sockets like quick little hurricanes of fire. "Oh god, c'mon. Seriously? Who gives a fuck?"

Beth and I look at him, stone-faced.

"I got them to stop eating souls for you!" he says. "What the fuck more do you want?"

"You—" Beth begins, but Akaz cuts her off at once.

"I'm not fucking omnipotent, sorry! Fucking Christ on a pogo stick, if you want to conquer fucking Mr. Rogers' Land of Make Believe, you shoulda got your boyfriend here to invent *that*, rather than this fucked up texas chainsaw road warrior wonderland!"

"I'm betting you had more of a hand in making this world than he did."

"Well here you are," says Akaz. "And you can be king and queen of it, or you can walk back across the desert without any food or water and try to pry open a gate to Earth in the side of the Seat of Shamash." He turns and trots away.

I call after him. "Nice job getting our van out of reach."

He freezes in his tracks for a second, then spins around. "That was under your orders." He lopes away. "Jackass."

Souleaters Anonymous

Beyond the cragwall stretches a desert of low rolling hills pierced by formations of jagged rock. Sparse, dry scrub plants dot the arroyos. A flat stone road, uncannily intact, aims straight for a pale mountain on the horizon.

Giver coalition on the move. I sit in the van's driver's seat, Beth beside me. Holding hands. The motorcycle purrs in the distance, Doomer scouting far ahead with Akaz running alongside him. The van rolls along under Giver power. Letting them push us down the road doesn't irk me much now; a deeper injustice occupies my mind, and Beth's: in addition to the hundred Bad Givers who've just joined us, a hundred flabby, stunted Giver-Tots trudge along, ropes knotted to their iron neck-rings, leashing them to small carts loaded with barrels full of glass balls and knives.

As they march, the Bad Givers and Blood Eagle's disciples rehearse each other's signature moves, practicing salvos of fireballs, sweeping curtains of flame, or that spiraling fountain of fire blasting into the sky. I wonder if any of the other Givers we seek, or any Herax spies or scouts, can see our lights from the distance. Dimly I wonder whether after dark I should order them to still their fires, or if it might better serve us to light up the sky, heralding us, brewing our fearsome reputation.

I also wonder whether I have any hope of ordering them to do anything. Occasionally, Beth and I touch upon the subject of the Giver-Tots, and how to gain their release, so soon after levying the outrageous demand to cease eating souls.

"It could be said that you have nothing to lose by trying," says Blood Eagle, appearing at my window.

"Thanks for eavesdropping," says Beth.

"We have shitloads to lose," I say.

"In one sense," says Blood Eagle. "In another, you have nothing, therefore no risk of loss."

"Yeah, we know that song," says Beth.

Blood Eagle cocks his head.

"What song?" I ask.

Beth rolls her eyes.

"I recommend you decree a taboo on eating Giver-Tot," says Blood Eagle, "upon our meeting with the Rockeater Givers."

"They have Giver-Tots too?" Beth asks. I stare at Blood Eagle, dreading the answer.

"All Giver tribes keep Tots as livestock. Or other manlike creatures."

"All but your disciples," I say.

"Soon, all your followers may cease," says Blood Eagle, "and all new groups of followers. If you give the command in the right way." He strides off.

"Great," I say to Beth.

"No pressure," she says.

We travel indistinguishable miles down the road, getting seemingly no nearer the distant mountain. At dusk the Rockeaters start emerging from their hiding-places and gathering around our caravan. Many of them. By full dark there are hundreds surrounding us, bidding us to stop, and only our guns and our Givers' liberation from the Greater Binding give us any chance of safety if things go badly.

Things seem poised to go badly. Akaz calls a small Bone Council of we three Earthlings, Blood Eagle, General Larynx, and chief-priests of two different Rockeater tribes. The conversation, punctuated by Blood Eagle rattling the Spine of Kaios, seems unnervingly tense and indirect. The claim that I am Cannibal-King seems pretty well demonstrated by the absence of Lesser and Greater Bindings. But deep-seated theological differences, not entirely comprehensible to me or Beth, stand in the way of unity.

"Aren't the Herax more of a threat than how you interpret scripture?" I ask.

"If we differ in our axioms and principles," says one of the Rockeater chief-priests, "then all that extends from them may differ."

"Great," says Beth.

"You guys are dumb as fuck," says Doomer. "You're gonna let each other die because you disagree about a fairy tale?"

The Givers in the council stir, and some start to get to their feet. The hundreds of onlookers see and stir as well.

"He's right," says Akaz. "Agree to fucking disagree and let's get to work! If you wanna break up after the Herax and the Watcher are dead, great, whatever."

"Without principle," says the other Rockeater chief-priest, "we are nothing."

"Principle is not the same as dogma," I say. "Some ideas underlie Right Action; others are just theories."

"Or opinions," says Beth.

"Or fucking fairy tales," says Doomer.

"Doomer," Akaz says to him, "you realize we're talking shit that happened in my living memory. It's a little more tangible than some reinterpretation of a one-to-three-thousand-year-old translation of a translation. We're not on Earth."

"But even here the theology is interpretation, not the facts themselves," says Beth.

"I.e., fairy tales," says Doomer.

I hold out my hand for the Spine of Kaios and Blood Eagle hands it to me. I shake it, wince, stop—at such close range, the clanging golden vertebrae make a deafening racket.

"Tell me your theological differences," I say. "Peacefully, no arguing. We can do that later if we must. First, we'll see if any of these differences matter to this war."

The council stirs, muttering among themselves. They tell the history of Shamash.

> Before the beginning of time, there was the void. And in the void floated the Sovereign Before Time.
>
> Nay; before the beginning of time, there were the Sun Dragon and Earth Dragon, the polarity inherent to any cosmos.
>
> Nay; hanging in the void were the twin Rock and Fire, which were discovered by the Sovereign Before Time and imbued with sentience. Only then did they become Sun Dragon and Earth Dragon.
>
> Nay; they were first concepts in the mind of the Sovereign.

"None of this," I say, "makes a difference to whether you can fight the Herax together."

"Yeah, so table it," says Akaz.

Murmuring, then assent.

During the earliest days of Godtime, the twin dragons spawned AKAZ, the Fire Wolf, and SHUM, the God of Metal.

Akaz the Chaotic: the wild shadow of fire.

Shum the Immutable: the material epitome of earth, its densest core. For the earth was not yet hollow. Shum, embraced by the sphere of the Earth Dragon, Shub-Niggurath; stretching veins of metal out through her, all the way to the surface, where frolick her Ten Thousand Things.

On this we are agreed.

Then Godtime gave way to the Empire of the Sun, and the archimages Augermath and Hoggoth counseled the Sun Dragon to take up his Throne of Day, and ride across the sky and around the world in an endless perfect circle. And the wild gods gave way to Order and Unity.

And to forge an avenue of escape, the wild gods begat Kaios; the Spirit Friend, the Rebel, the Anarch.

The Son of Akaz and Oshta.

Nay, the Manifestation of the Sun Dragon, eternal and unborn.

Nay, he is both.

Both, indeed; and the son of rape, righteous rape.

Akaz leaps to his feet, breathing a gout of roaring white fire upon the chief-priest who had proudly called him a proud rapist. Screaming, although Givers supposedly can feel no pain, he blisters, boils, and chars under the blast, although supposedly Givers are immune to heat and fire. Akaz steps up and chomps out the middle of the black-broiled corpse, gulping it down in a mighty swallow. Then the legs in another bite; then, in a third and final bite, the head, arms, and shoulders.

Akaz says to the murmuring multitude: "I never raped Oshta! You hear? Get that shit out of your myths already!" Then he flops back down on the ground beside Blood Eagle.

The assembly chants, "Akaz! Akaz! Akaz! Akaz! Akaz!" Five times, and five times only.

"What the fuck?" asks Beth.

"I keep killing them," says Akaz, fuming, "whenever I hear folks pitch that slander. But there's this twisted idea that death by my jaws sends you straight to Giver-heaven or whatever, so it's useless as a deterrent. It's so fucked."

"Did you?" asks Beth. "Whoever Oshta is."

"NO!" says Akaz. Little streamers of smoke rise from the sizzling corners of his eyes. Not smoke, steam: tears boiling away as quickly as they form.

"Continue," I say. The crowd still murmurs. Blood Eagle begins, and the talking dies down.

Then the archimages Augermath and Hoggoth, aided by their apprentice Apraxos, used magicks they stole from Kaios to further entrap the Sun Dragon and Earth Dragon.

Nay; the Rites of Augermath come from Great Akaz, just as we have inherited them from Him ourselves. And the Rites of Hoggoth come from Akaz as well, though we eschew them.

Nay, how could even Oggo and Hoggo master the mysteries of Akaz? How could they have drawn power and wisdom from Him against his will, He calling them enemy?

He calls them enemy; but He sent them, just as He sent Kaios, and just as He has now brought Kaios reborn, our Cannibal-King. He calls them enemy to complexify the game. For this whole world has been made for us as but a test.

I feel the Givers in the council and surrounding crowd solidifying into their positions and oppositions, so I butt in before things heat up. "Again," I tell them, "None of this stops you from fighting the Herax together."

Some stirring, some quiet reflection. I see occasional telltale facial expressions that I've come to associate with my Power to Clear Men's Minds taking effect. There's a palpable release of tension from the gathering.

"So," I say to the council, "keep going. I challenge you to find a point of dogma that prohibits you from gathering against Apraxos and the Herax."

Blood Eagle again speaks.

Thus Augermath and Hoggoth and Apraxos slew Kaios, channeling the power of the manifestation's soul into two mighty rites.

On this we are agreed.

And so did they cage the Sun Dragon in Akaz's jaws; and by permutation of their Sovereign Shields, Akaz became frozen motionless in the sky, Sun in his gullet, together forming the unmoving Eclipse itself.

On this we are agreed.

And so did they cage the Earth Dragon within the body of Shum: She drew Her spirit into a small point at the center of Shum's mass, and Shum was tricked into forming into a hollow sphere around her. But he was frozen in place; and Oggo & Hoggo ruled the Ten Thousand Things.

On this we are agreed.

And so did Augermath and Hoggoth draw power from the enslavement of the Sun and Earth Dragons, and reign unchallenged.

Nay; they were challenged.

Not before Shum's veins of metal, broken off from the rest of his body, were mined mercilessly by the Empire. Even here, [gesturing to the mountain on the horizon] Mount Kaios was mined by the Empire until no metal remained in it, leaving behind only the Well of Apraxos.

Whereby we shall raid the House of the Watcher and erase all dominion over the Hollow World and Surface World both!

End forever any trace of Empire!

On this we are agreed.

And when Akaz freed himself, devouring Augermath and Hoggoth, he hurled himself down that mine to Shum. Whom he freed by "enlightening" him.

By melting him.

And Shum became Shamash.

On this we are agreed.

And Shamash, mad with rage, devoured the entire interior of the Hollow World in his efforts to liberate Shub-Nig-

gurath the Earth Dragon; to no avail. Her soul-binding held, just as the Sun Dragon held powerlessly, mindlessly to his orbit.

Then a memory hits me from age thirteen or so, daydreaming about Shamash zoomin' around and hollowing out the world—after I'd spent an afternoon with a pocketful of quarters playing way too much DigDug and drinking way too much caffeinated soda at the Pizza Store.

Causing the sinking of continents, and the collapse of the Empire of the Eclipse.
THIS WAS THE GREAT BREACH.
On this we are agreed.
But Apraxos used his mighty spirit-taming magic to trap Shamash in place; and trapped in the Seat of Shamash he now remains.
On this we are agreed.

Silence for a bit.

"So, just agree not to fight each other, at least not until Apraxos is dead."

"To this we agree," says Blood Eagle.

"To this we agree," says General Larynx.

"To this we agree," says the remaining chief-priest of the Rockeaters.

I stand. "The rest of you?" I ask the assembled Givers. "Swear not to fight each other until Apraxos is dead."

"To this we agree," came quite a lot of voices.

"Do any *not* agree?"

Some murmuring.

"If you do not agree," I say, "speak up, so the rest of us know not to trust you."

More murmuring.

"Speak up," I say, "speak freely with no fear of retribution, or we take your silence as assent. Speak up now, or leave, or consider yourself sworn."

Silence.

"Blood Eagle," I say to him, "General Larynx," I say to him, "command your warriors to hurl a Fireball Swarm into the sky."

Blood Eagle and General Larynx stand, command their warriors to stand, and dozens upon dozens of fireballs fly straight up overhead, rendering the Givers on the ground shadowless for a few moments.

The Rockeaters stare, speechless.

"Fire Fountain," I shout.

A hundred jets of fire flare upward, coil around each other, spiraling into a roaring cyclone.

"Enough," I shout.

The fire stops. I address the multitude:

"Stop eating souls, and I'll lift the Greater Binding."

Animated murmuring among the Rockeaters.

"Stop eating livestock," I say, "and I'll lift the Lesser Binding."

Murmuring among the Bad Givers as well.

"You realize," Beth says to me, "these people want to free Shamash?"

"Yeah."

"And last time Shamash was free, he almost ate the whole world?"

I grind my teeth for a moment. "Shit." I take a deep breath. Then over the horizon creep a hundred Herax longboats.

Harvest Their Return, Those Who Drive Away the Sun

Panic jolts through my body, but I stand up smoothly, and announce in a loud, steady voice, "Okay, it's time."

But dozens of Givers on the fringes are running off, rattling their strange small drums. "Yo!" I holler, to no avail, as scores and scores of warriors scatter in the general direction of the distant ships. "Shit." Two paces to Blood Eagle and I hold out my hand and he places the Spine of Kaios in it. I shake it, grabbing the attention of those nearby. To the Rockeater priest-chief I say, "Gather your warriors. It's time for tactics."

"The Herax approach." He gestures westward.

"Yes, and they won't get here for minutes."

"Nay." He laughs and lopes off.

"Without plans, we're all dead!" I shout after him.

"Without hidey-holes we're dead," he says over his shoulder as he vanishes into a trench. Most of the hundreds of Rockeaters scatter and drop into trenches, tunnels, and pits.

I rattle the spine.

"We form one titan Fire Fountain," says General Larynx.

"Nay," says Blood Eagle. "We wait direction from our King."

"We gotta get in the van," says Beth.

"Can I use yer bike?" Doomer asks her.

"Akaz, come." Beth stands up. "We gotta get on the MG."

Akaz looks at her.

I shake the spine-rattle fiercely. "Yo!"

"Council is broken," says Blood Eagle. "The Bone is only honored in the confines of Council. One does not invoke Council simply by shaking a Bone."

I toss the spine back to Blood Eagle and stride over to the van. Beth starts to join me, saying, "C'mon, Akaz, now," but she is held up by his blank refusal. A moment's rummaging and I come up with a bullhorn. I flick on its siren and hold it high, turning it in a semicircle. Surreal echo of intimidating urban cop-sound in this barren barbarian wasteland, drowning out any drums it touches. Most Givers freeze and look my way, baffled by the eerie, tremendous yowl. I wonder if the still-distant Herax hear it at all, and if so, what the hell they think it is. I thumb off the siren and hold down the mic button. "Rockeaters!" my voice booms out at them. "Who among you has vowed to devour neither soulstuff nor Giver-Tot? You come here."

A few dozen saunter back toward us.

"The rest of you to your hidey-holes," my voice's authority inflated through the bullhorn. "Fight the Herax however you know best. But watch us; and know that you will never fight as we do as long as you devour souls, or feed upon bipedal livestock." Lowering the bullhorn, I address Blood Eagle and General Larynx. "Gather your forces."

"Givers of Fort Goodbye!" shouts General Larynx. "Attend!"

Blood Eagle glances around, seeing all his followers are already nearby.

Speaking through the bullhorn, I command them: "Form into five groups. Blood Eagle, take your followers due west, toward the center of the oncoming Herax. General Larynx, split your warriors into four groups, and send them out alongside," pointing to suggest equidistant approaches to the Herax line. "Each squad, cast your jets of flame in unison, extending them into a Fire Fountain; and burn the sails of the boats. Rockeaters stay near, but stay out of the way. You have not trained since your release from the Bindings. Join if you can, but stay out of the way."

"My King," says General Larynx, "if we all form one mighty Fire Fountain, we can build a burning cyclone to sweep away all these Herax."

"And we will have demonstrated the maximum extent of our power, giving them the information they need to formulate a suitable response."

"There is no conceivable counter to annihilation," says Blood Eagle.

"And once we demonstrate that power," says General Larynx, "we have all the Rockeaters, who will surely join us, thereby extending our powers far beyond what they are now."

I hadn't thought of that. Should I admit it? Fuck yes, I don't want to be in a pissing contest with this dude, I need him focused on fighting Herax, not me. "I had not thought of that. Nonetheless, the more the Herax underestimate us, the better. We *start* with five fountains, joining them only if we must." Then to Blood Eagle: "And we dare not underestimate the ingenuity of Apraxos and Goromath. Is this the entire Herax fleet, bearing down upon us now?" I gesture at the approaching boats, now close enough that we really need to get a move on, like now.

"Surely not," says Blood Eagle.

Damn. "So even if we smite them all from the sky, we only invite a far stronger response," I say. "Perhaps from the entire fleet."

"Then we will smite their entire fleet!" says General Larynx. "Cannibal-King!"

"Cannibal-King!" shout the nearby Givers, clattering their finger-drums. The chant spreads outward in a couple of waves, accompanied by the cacophony of little drums, until it encompasses all my converts: "Cannibal-King! Cannibal-King! Cannibal-King!" The racket threatens to shred my nerves.

Criminy. I hit the siren on the bullhorn to cut them short. Then, my amplified voice: "Five squads, five fire fountains! Go!"

"Should we not bring Giver-Tots," asks a freshly-converted Rockeater, "for more power, in case of emergency?"

"No!" My amplified voice shreds the air. "No Giver-Tots." Then a phrase leaps to mind and out my mouth, a quote from something, no idea what. But it resonates here in a way that it presumably did not in its original context: "*Forage on the enemy.*"

I hit the siren again for a sec. "Run! Spread out, a few hundred paces. Cover their approach. Hit them all at once, when I sound this siren." I blast it again. "Burn their sails. Then feed on the fallen bodies of your foes. Go! Run!" Then, as they run off, "Bring glass!"

"C'mon," I say to Beth. I swat Doomer on the shoulder. "We stay at the van. We still don't want a single Herax near enough to spot us. We gotta stay outta sight and shoot 'em outta the sky if they get close. You too, Akaz." He looks up at me. I point into my wide open mouth, "unh unh."

"What if I don't wanna?" he asks.

"You got other plans?"

"Nah," he says.

"Doomer," I say to Doomer, "maybe you let Akaz hop in your mouth, and you man the MG if you want."

"Fuck yeah I wanna make fascists explode and fall and burn," says Doomer, "with a death god in my gullet." He bends over Akaz: "Git in mah belleh!" he brogues.

"Okeydoke," says Akaz, and leaps into Doomer's mouth. Fires flash in Doomer's eyes, and he bellows, "Fuck yeah," flames billowing from his mouth. With a couple of inhumanly long strides and a hop he is on top of the van, then slips down through the ring mount with previously unseen nimbleness.

"Don't waste ammo!" I turn to Beth. "Let's go get Victoria."

"And binoculars," she says.

"Good point." As we walk back to the van, I realize I don't really know the range of our five Fire Fountains—yet I told them all to fire on my order, with the siren. Shit, I can't judge that. Even with binoculars, even from atop the van, I won't be able to gauge the distance between the five sections, much less how far into the sky they can reach. Undershoot and we scare them off unscathed, but before they're in harpoon-range from the boats. My kingdom for a rangefinder. The siren should reach them simultaneously enough, but they're out of earshot for intelligible changes of plan via bullhorn. We can't risk getting closer and being seen.

We get to the van. "I'll get binocularses," says Beth.

"Akaz!" Doomer hunches lustily over the M240, aiming down its sights, pointing it this way and that, firing single shots that land with devastating effect far away. "Akaz!" I repeat.

Akaz's snout bursts out of Doomer's mouth. Stunned, Doomer stiffens vertically, flings his arms out, throws his head back so Akaz speaks straight upward: "What!?"

"How do I judge the right range. I don't know the reach of those Fountains, and I can't tell how far apart they are anyway."

Akaz's whole head sticks out so he can glare at me. The flames of his eyes turn upward in their sockets. "How the fuck do I know? Just fucking guess, you goddamn baby. Jesus Christ." Then his head slips back into Doomer's mouth.

"Jesus Christ," grunts Doomer, and shakes his head as if shaking off a punch to the face. Then he wraps himself around the MG again, aiming at one ship, BLAM, and another and another. "This is a rush." Wisps of flame dance out of his eyes, ears, nose, and mouth; helical flurries of fire occasionally flit down around the barrel.

"Don't waste ammo," Beth repeats up at him. She hands me my binoculars. Looking through them tells me more than I expected. I clamber up on the van. Yep, Herax look like they might be close enough to burn, maybe. Fuck it. I sound the siren across the face of the desert.

In five locations, tendrils of fire spiral upward, coil around each other, and form into towering arms of writhing flames. They sweep slowly across the Herax line, burning sails away to cinders, causing longboats to plummet and break on the ridges and gullies and boulders. Givers rush out from everywhere to forage on the enemy.

The Herax catch on instantly, and nine out of ten of the considerable number of boats still in flight turn tail and make all effort to get out of range. Most of them manage to. So be it. I toot the siren a couple times and the titanic whips and tentacles of fire flicker out. They get it: save your strength, fuckers. Indeed, increase your strength: *forage on the enemy*.

Beth and I watch through our respective binoculars as about a dozen of those boats and ships stay in range but simply don't burn. They close in on any clusters of Givers within reach, and rain javelins down upon them, spearing many limbs and bodies. But the Givers let fly volleys upon volleys of boiling glass, which harm at least the Herax spearmen on board, if not the sails, decks, and hulls. Robed fishmen aboard also remain unscathed by high temperature, and so become targets of glass knives and spears—and when they fall, their ships go up like torches.

I feel a surge of sickly, evil pride as I watch even the fire-proof Herax airships one by one turn away, successfully repelled by the Givers' armed resistance. (Are we resistance, or a conquering army? Or both? Theocratic, no less. Fuck.)

"Doomer?" I find myself asking, feeling a bit sick even as I do so.

"Hanh?" he says over his shoulder, transfixed down the gun-sights. Flames flicker out from the edges of his eyes as he unloads magic 7.62mm slugs at the retreating Herax ships. Slugs enchanted in this moment simply by Akaz's presence in his body as a possessing divine spirit. Controlled bursts of a half dozen deck-piercing explosive fireballs full of Wargus-Fire, blasting into one retreating longboat, then the next, then the next, down the line, back and forth, taking down every last retreating Herax in view.

From the whole distance ahead of us comes the sounds of a riot of cannibal mayhem.

Akaz jumps out of Doomer's mouth. Doomer slumps over the gun, snorts, then starts snoring.

The road ahead aims at Mount Kaios. I remember naming it that and wondering if it was cheesy. From the rocky terrain flanking either side of the road comes the sound of chanting. Hundreds of voices, hundreds upon hundreds, Rockeaters, Bad Givers, and all: "Cannibal-King! Cannibal-King! Cannibal-King!"

"I hope we don't regret this."

"Seriously," says Beth.

"Cannibal-King! Cannibal-King!"

"Fuck."

"Fuck."

Interlude in Aleck's Smoking Room III

A stone room cluttered with bookshelves, display cases, and desks. Knickknacks, oddities, and piles of books cover every horizontal surface above floor level, and some of the floor as well.

XAX and WARLOCK peruse the collection. CLARK enters, dressed in Shakespearean garb. He stops in his tracks.

CLARK: H-how...

Xax bursts out laughing at the sight of Clark's outfit. Max looks quizzically from one to the other.

CLARK: Impossible.... How did you get in here...?
XAX: Cool threads, Clark. *(claps him on the shoulder)* That gate I gave you had a trace on it, my good man.
CLARK: But—it's *inside* the Archive. You can't see anything within the confines of the Archive....

XAX: Not till you opened it. But once you did, I could spot it from the Melkhaios side.

Clark looks utterly crestfallen.

XAX: *(cont'd.)* Where you headed? Costume ball? Ren Faire?

CLARK: Wait a moment—on the Melkhaios side, the portal opened into the Melkhaios *Archive.* You still shouldn't be able to—

XAX: 'Cept we were *inside* the Melkhaios Archive, waiting for the signal, Clark.

Clark looks crestfallen again.

WARLOCK: Woad's *Guidebook* is quite clear as to the Archive's geographical location in the City of Melkhaios.

XAX: That reminds me, Clark. I couldn't help but notice you stealing that manuscript of the *Guidebook*.

Clark freezes, aghast.

CLARK: I—

WARLOCK: It's probably a substantially worse infraction than you think. Multiple adjustments apply, increasing the offense level.

XAX: Now now, we don't wanna scare the guy.

WARLOCK: I'm simply stating facts.

XAX: So, Clark, where you heading in that getup?

CLARK: I... this... none of your business.

XAX: *(to Max)* You don't think he's headed to Melkhaios dressed like that?

WARLOCK: The *Guidebook* offers no indication that towns-folk would wear such attire.

CLARK: It's the best I could do!

XAX: So you *are* going to Melkhaios.

CLARK: What? No! I—

WARLOCK: Where is the *Guidebook*?

CLARK: I never—

XAX: Are you going to warn Woad what I'm up to?

CLARK: I don't even *know* what you're up to!

XAX: Perhaps give him the guidebook written by his future self, to help him evade us and other perils?

WARLOCK: Rather a few infractions piling up here.

CLARK: I... you... this is entrapment!

XAX: A-*ha!*

WARLOCK: You are singularly inept at enduring interrogation, Prof. Clark.

Clark glares at him.

XAX: Rest easy, Clark—guess what!?

Clark frowns at him.

XAX: *(cont'd.)* We *want* you to bring the *Guidebook* to Woad. But the wrinkle: he mustn't see you.

CLARK: How... how is that even possible?

XAX: C'mon. *(heads toward door)* I assume you have the *Guidebook* on you? In subspace?

Clark hangs his head and trudges after Xax.

XAX: *(cont'd.)* We'll get you to him. And as long as you do your part to stay unseen by Woad...

WARLOCK: No easy feat in that particular getup.

XAX: ...we'll protect you.

Clark follows Xax to the new portal to Melkhaios. It's in the same spot as the portal Aleck and Beth Woad went through.

Max steps through after them.

Skull of Kaios III

I'm floating above the van and from over the mountain come the eerie voices of the Deepest murmuring up from under the bay:

Fatman dreams
Fatman dreams

I'm floating but I can't fly—I'm pinned in the air by the force of collective will emanating from the Deepest. I can't tell if they're audible or telepathic. Feels like both. I try to ascend or land on the roof; no dice, best I can do is turn in place. The voices definitely come from the bay behind the mountain.

Fatman dreams
Fatman dreams

But rumbling comes from within the mountain as well. Within me. Within the mountain.

Not just Fatman. I'm dreaming, too: my body launches through the air at a zillion miles an hour at the side of the mountain, through it, and out the other side. My face a huge mask of stone slammed out the far side of the mountain, my body the body of an erupting volcano slamming down to engulf the city.

And an even deeper voice emanates from under the bay.

C'mere

"What?" I arrive at the bay's edge, the touch of my talons raising a small wall of steam.

Come to me little boy

I step into the bay to discover an underwater city mirroring the city on the shore. I boil the bay and smash the buildings of the undersea city.

Up from the depths arises a fat lumbering giant, or dragon, a mile high—my height exactly. We face one another in the evaporated basin of the bay, shattered ruins in a vast plain of cracked, baked clay.

The dragon-giant mutters contentedly,

Liberation

And everywhere around us, to the horizon and beyond, the survivors in the ruins shout and kill and revel.

I wake up inside the van, not hovering above it, with a splitting headache, drenched in clammy sweat. It's still dark. I wrestle my way out of my shirt, flip my wet pillow over, fold

down the soaked part of the comforter, and lie there next to
Beth, who's curled up facing away from me and mercifully
unconscious. Soon my bare skin is dry but freezing. Rummaging for a nearby alternate shirt or blanket I come up
with a tattered half of a bath towel. Getting myself situated
under it I elbow Beth in the elbow by accident and wake her.
"Sorry," I say. She grunts and curls back up and falls right
back to sleep.

My head pounds.

From outside the van, seemingly in rhythm with the
pounding in my head, I hear chanting. What the hell? I open
the broken skylight and poke my head out. Starry electric
blue fades to gray twilight behind us. The Givers sit surrounding the van in all directions. After a dazed moment I
can make out their murmuring as

Kaios, we beseech thee
Kaios, we beseech thee

"What the hell?" I whisper.

I look around for clues. Against the pre-dawn sky the
foothills of Mt. Megalon run black alongside the road like
a wall. Some distance ahead, the road turns westward to
wind between Mt. Megalon and Mt. Kaios to the city. A few
Givers spot me and switch their chant to a cheer of, "Cannibal-King! Cannibal-King!" I spot Blood Eagle staring at me.
After a bit longer, he speaks up over the chanting cheer and
they shut up right away.

"Givers of Fire and Flame!" he begins. I look down at Beth.
She's looking up at me, agitated to the full extent that she is

awake, which is only partial. I take her hand. She squeezes mine. My head is killing me.

"What now?" she asks.

"Dunno," I say. "Assembly. Looks like everyone, I mean everyone."

Meanwhile Blood Eagle has been talking about prophecy, about crowns and skulls and shields. "—thereby passing the mantle of his Crown and Shield to his Herald." I shiver and pull the towel around my shoulders.

The back door to the van clanks open. "Hey," barks Beth down past her feet. I duck back down into our cramped little loft and see Doomer ducking his head in our rear cargo door.

"Hey," says Doomer. "Some kinda ritual. The King's presence is requested."

"It's the middle of the fuckin' night," says Beth. "Why now."

"'The stars are right' or whatever," says Doomer.

"Fuck." I groan. "My fucking head is killing me."

Beth and I get dressed, difficulty compounded by close quarters, sleep deprivation, and stiffness from the cold. My headache lingers at a pre-migraine: godawful but still a bit shy of incapacitating. Definitely dehydrated, stiff neck adding tension, who knows what else, brain tumor from USSA cancer ray for all I know, fuck. Our canteen is empty. I get down from the loft with difficulty, dropping the canteen. It clangs on the bumper next to Beth, startling the hell out of her. "Yikes!"

"Sorry," I say. "Sorry. Fuck." I sit on the bumper and grope under it for the canteen. "Need water." I feel dizzy.

"Here." She wipes her mouth and hands me an almost-full canteen. I guzzle. Guzzle more. It hurts my belly and doesn't help my head one bit. They've resumed chanting

Kaios, we beseech thee
Kaios, we beseech thee

and in fact the waves of throbbing pain intensify in time with their chanting. "Fuck."

Beth hands me three ibuprofen. "Here."

I swallow them with another swig. Beth takes the canteen from me with one hand and helps me up with the other. Standing makes me gasp a little.

"You up for this?" she asks. "Doomer can tell him to fuck off till later."

"I know," I say. "I don't know why, I have no idea what he's up to, but it feels like I have to at least put in an appearance." It's more like a compulsion than I dare let on. It's not a good feeling. I take a few deep breaths, just standing there. My stomach hurts. My head pounds in crashing waves as though the voices of the Givers have formed into the dragon-giant from my dream and my head is the bay in which it splashes like a wading pool. Dizzying delirium confuses my own staggering steps with those of the sound-giant stomping through my head: all one cascade of vibration, up through my legs and torso and in through my ears, all resonating like a bell across the world. I faintly hear Beth call my name as I fall to my knees. Blood Eagle catches my head in his hands, helping me kneel upright instead of falling on my face. I think Beth is calling my name again, or something, but all I can hear, all that I *am*, is the clanging of my head, a hollow golden bell the size of the world.

Blood Eagle's material hands cradle my skull on either side. Something cold oozes from his fingers into my head. Not cold: *eerie*. Somehow I know these to be his spirit-fingers, taking hold not of my spirit-skull but something else, something nearly contiguous with it but not quite—something not native to my aetheric body, that has long resided within it, indistinguishable. But Blood Eagle distinguishes it. His hands on the spirit plane seek and obtain a grip on the unwavering surface of this *other skull*. It reverberates like a heavy church bell with every round of chanting by the Givers:

Kaios, we beseech thee

each chant resonating with an underlying echo that is already shuddering back and forth throughout the astral plane. The stars are right? The astral tide is right?

With each sequence of waves, Blood Eagle wrenches this impossible skull-within-my-skull a quarter-inch up out of my head. My astral and physical bodies shudder in response to the grotesque sensation. Deeply unsettled, I do my best to drop myself into a meditative state, which partly works; my breathing slows, my body calms. But this is how I endured the tortures of Agent Xax, all too recently. Feels like moments ago. Feels like I'm trapped and tortured again. Still. Turning my attention to the Givers' chant does not help:

Kaios, we beseech thee
Grant us your Skull
Kaios, we beseech thee
Grant us your Skull
We have want of it
We have need of it
Kaios, we beseech thee

My gaze wanders out toward the horizon of the astral plane. Ley lines crisscross the vast plain of voice, capillaries of spirit-energy webbed between them, and auras everywhere, corresponding perceptibly to the material world and contiguous with it. The echo of the encircling Giver horde causes jangling ripples in the network of light, waves all focused upon me. Not me, this Skull being hauled up out of my head. From the horizon in the west come larger ripples in the astral tide. What is it? What's out there causing those ripples? Some event past present and/or future that harmonizes with this, me incapacitated, Blood Eagle stealing something out of my head that his people think is the Skull of Kaios?

Akaz wanders past, in his mundane solid black wolf form despite the radiant ethereality of the astral plane around us. Blood Eagle slides the Skull out of my astral head. He holds it up and announces, "Behold: the Skull of Kaios!" It gleams gold. He turns it upside down and presents it with both hands to Akaz, who holds a paw ceremoniously over it. Blood pours from Akaz's wrist into the Skull, filling it. Blood Eagle upends the wolfsblood into his own gullet.

I jolt awake in the material plane, Blood Eagle silhouetted in front of me against the dawn, a golden Skull in his hands. No sign of wolfsblood. Silent Givers surround us. My eye meets Beth's and we stay there, gazes locked, both of us dazed and terrified, our only solace each other's presence.

Then the Skull snaps in half, a crack bisecting it vertically. A thunderclap crosses the sky at us from the west. Blood Eagle jumps in surprise, but manages to hold the skull-halves together. They skew only a quarter inch, but the Jawbone drops to the dirt. Akaz pounces up beside us and blasts the Skull with fiery breath, welding the two halves back together. Blood Eagle snaps the Jawbone back on the slightly skewed Skull, then attaches it to the golden Spine of Kaios like the ornament atop a scepter.

Then he hands it to me.

"The Spine of God," says Blood Eagle.

"Cannibal-King!" chant the Givers. "Cannibal-King! Cannibal-King!"

Live Stock

Beth and I spend the morning in a bit of a daze, riding atop the roof of the van as insistent Givers push it along the road. Akaz sits motionless on the hood below and before us like a gigantic sooty ornament. I've left that "Spine of God" on the dashboard. I don't want to touch it. All this "king" bullshit creeps me out enough without wielding an actual scepter. Creepier still: that Skull came *out of my head*. Akaz's clarification of how it got in there in the first place ("The Master Summoner put it there") does exactly nothing to ease my disquiet about the gilded skull of a previous messiah having been contiguous for years with my own head.

Beth and I slowly make our way through a can of pineapple chunks, enjoying the temperate morning as it evolves from mildly brisk to mildly hot over the course of a couple of hours. Pleasanter than the stark and sudden cold/hot of the desert. We don't talk much. The road proceeds alongside the cliffy foothills as we gradually make our way past Mt. Megalon. In the distance looms Mt. Kaios, and sooner or later our road is going to turn into the wooded pass between them. For now we skirt the stony hills.

Late morning Doomer clambers up through the ring mount, sits down with us and lights up a joint. Offers it to us. Beth and I look at each other, shrug *why not?* and each gesture for the other to help themselves. Then we both reach for it at once. I duck my hand back quicker, so Beth ends up with the next hit.

Despite this morning's downtime atop the van with Beth, I'm still frazzled from my sequence of fucked-up dream, broken sleep, migraine, and Skull retrieval ritual. I make room in my lungs with a long exhale, then hit the joint as long and hard as I can manage. More than I can handle, perhaps, and as I pass the joint to Doomer I struggle not to cough or splutter. Doomer doesn't notice the joint at first. My effort to hold in smoke escalates under the additional mental and physical strain of holding the joint out and waiting without the ability to use my voice. But a year and a day later Doomer notices and takes the smoldering joint from my hand. I exhale as slowly as I can, refusing to cough although my lungs tickle and my diaphragm leaps and jumps a little. The high hits me like I've been launched out of a cannon. Maybe this was not the best idea. Though hmm, the euphoria is comforting, there's no denying that. I sit and sway atop the van, enjoying the sunshine within and without. I hope nothing happens to interrupt this bliss. I could use another couple hours of hassle-free nothing time with Beth. No chanting, no combat, just nothing. I open my eye.

Beth is staring at me, laughing at how stoned I am. And at how high she is herself, I can tell. We laugh together for a couple of seconds. Then the stench hits us.

The smell is like an invisible cloud, sparse enough at its fringe to sneak up on us for a few moments without raising conscious alarm. But upon entering the thick of its rich, heady noxiousness, the mind reflects automatically upon that hint of warning and can only interpret the memory with regret: *Had I only been paying better attention, couldn't I have done something to prevent reaching this point? For example, do our gas masks keep out smells? Or could we have just doubled back, found another route around or over the mountains? Or turned tail entirely and fled back to the desert from this infinite awfulness?* For by "reaching this point" I mean the complete saturation of the nose, mouth, sinuses, and brain with a thick, grotesque reek as of miles upon miles of open sewer.

Presumably the fact that we just shared a joint, with the resultant hypersensitivity to stimulus and loosening of control over attention, enables a more precipitous descent into overwhelm than would have happened while sober. Beth and I both retch but resist vomiting (for now), our watery gazes meeting in mutual lamentation.

"Fuck," says Doomer, "gross," and shoves plugs in his nose. He looks at us. "Don't you guys have omnifiltration noseplugs?" We frown at him, forlorn, tragically aware that we come from a timeline where whatever he's talking about has not yet been invented. The Givers notice nothing.

"The fuck is that stink?" manages Beth, finally, summing it up.

A wooden palisade stretches across our path in the distance.

"Behold!" says Blood Eagle. "The Megalon Tot Factory of the Herax! How will our King destroy it? Loosing the Tots into the wilderness? Slaying them in order to liberate them? Devouring them all as a mercy killing, in a wise and subtle exception to his decree?"

"Cannibal-King!" roar the mob of Givers, mercifully only once. They and Blood Eagle look up to me as if for an answer.

"Let's go see?" I manage, reluctantly. We march on toward the palisade, the Givers unfazed by the stench or possibly unable even to perceive it, like their inability to feel pain.

"Fuck," says Beth.

"Seriously," I say. "Sorry."

"No," she says, "I mean, yeah, that smell, but—look at us." She looks around at me, herself, and Doomer sitting atop the van like colonizing royalty, surrounded by natives on foot. The van sways slightly as the Givers push us up the bumpy, rain-rutted road. "C'mon." She slides to the edge of the roof and slips down, landing nimbly.

"Yeah, fuck, when did we start letting them act like dray animals?" I ask Doomer.

"Huh?" he asks.

"She's right." I scoot to the edge. "I'm gettin' the hell down." I lean over to look at Akaz on the hood, sitting perfectly vertical despite the lurching of the van, like a toy with a gyroscope in it. "Akaz, c'mon! We should be walking with the Givers, not being chauffeured."

"Fuck off," he says over his shoulder.

"He *is* their god," says Doomer.

I frown at him. "C'mon, let's all walk."

"No way," says Doomer. "Take your white guilt down in the dust if you want, *kemo sabe*." He shooes at me and stretches out, stoned in the sun, heedless of the olfactory hellscape thanks to his nose plugs.

The reek of whatever's beyond the palisade not only sickens me but stirs in me a growing dread. "You got any more of them nose plugs?" I ask him.

"Nah," he says.

I drop off the side and land somewhat less nimbly than Beth had, stumbling in a rut right beside her. Nothing turned or sprained, though. We trudge along, exhausted.

"Please ride atop," says a nearby Giver.

"Seriously, no thanks," says Beth.

"We should help push," I say to the Giver, grabbing the cargo door handle and leaning into it.

"Nay," says the Giver, as does another behind us in earshot, both of them gesturing for me to let go. It's hard for me to concentrate on anything in this reek, much less debate fanatics.

Then a wind hits us, spitting dust and grit from the road at us, pressing an even denser stench against my and Beth's vulnerable senses. The wall of warm, fetid air feels palpable and overwhelming on a whole other level. Beth and I cling to each other and gag. We rush behind the van and find, to our relief and surprise, some actual respite in the leeward pocket.

"What the fuck," she and I agree.

Overhead, we notice a convulsive gathering of slate-dark clouds. The wind grows cooler and, mercy of mercies, gradually less stinky. A wave of hail rattles against the steel skin of the van, then quickly passes, only to be replaced by distant rumbles of thunder fast approaching. The wind intensifies, its roar blending with the oncoming thunder, rapidly pushing the wave of stink past us. Then wind and thunder stop as one, echoing down the crags, leaving us in crisp, ozoney air with only a lingering residue of stench pervading it. The low ceiling of black cloud looms overhead.

Beth and I peer out past opposite sides of the van. A few hundred yards away, the palisade of sharpened logs stretches across the road and into the flatland beyond. Enclosing a couple of acres? Hard to see inside, though the uneven terrain might get us a glimpse from a certain angle. Looks like a few little things—not Herax ships—are hovering above it. I start toward the passenger side of the van, to grab my binoculars on the passenger side of the dashboard, and I bump into Beth as she grabs for the rear cargo door handle. "Binoculars," she says, hers being inside the back door.

In a few seconds we're back atop the van, both gazing at the stockade with magnification. The few little things hovering above it are men, or manlike things, robed and gesturing. Four of them. We can also catch sight of an angle of high ground within the palisade. That section, at least, is teeming with what looks like people.

"What the fuck," Beth and I ask each other again, still looking through our respective binoculars. Neither of us reply.

"'Sup," asks Doomer, becoming aware of our presence.

"Those look like Giver-Tots," I say to Beth, still looking.

"Yup," she says.

"Who?" asks Doomer.

Beth looks at him and points at the palisade with her binocular-hand. "That stockade is packed with Giver-Tots."

"Well," I butt in, "that one corner we can see is packed with them, anyway."

"With that stench?" she counters. "That's a factory farm, dude. That's like Cowschwitz, you know, alongside the highway."

"What?" I ask, not clicking on this 'Cowschwitz.'

"Route Five," she says, "halfway down the Central Valley."

"Ooooh," I get it now. "Between 'Frisco and L.A."

"Dude," says Doomer, "don't say 'Frisco,' they hate it."

"You got a problem with 'Frisco' but not 'Cowschwitz'?" I ask.

"Who hates 'Frisco'?" asks Beth.

"Herb Caen," Akaz says back over his shoulder from his seat on the hood.

"What?" all three of us ask.

"Step lively," says Akaz, "shit's about to get real."

A massive thunderclap rolls along the drumhead of dark cloud, emanating from the stockade and approaching in a wave that ripples and rumbles out to the horizon in all directions, echoing back at us from the foothills. As the wave of thunder cracks overhead, torrents of rain cascade down upon us. Flickering attracts my eye upward: the low black sky is marbled with faint flowing lights.

"Fuck." Beth also sees them.

The rain stops minutes later. Just enough to soak us.

A flash from above, and a jagged whip of light snaps down onto a distant Giver. Hard to see quite what happens to him. Another strikes, closer, accompanied by deafening thunder. That Giver jumps, flailing, and lands many yards away in a tangle of charred, crumpled limbs.

"Electricity isn't fire," shouts Akaz over the ongoing thunder, "in case you were wondering. I can't protect my worshipers from it."

In the space of a couple of seconds, another dozen bolts of lightning stab down from the roiling carpet of the sky, each killing another Giver. Everyone else dives behind crags and into gullies. Tendrils of fire reach into the air, weave around one another, and form a vast jet of flame pouring toward the sorcerers hovering over the stockade. Winds just push the fire aside.

"Off the van!" says Beth, she ditching down one side and Doomer the other. I, however, possibly incorrectly, opt instead for the ring mounted machine gun, diving across the roof and jumping down into the hatch feet first, whacking my knee and tailbone simultaneously and almost thereby wedging myself into it, femur + butt = diameter of ring mount. But I slip through, scraping my back, and grab ahold of the MG. The gun's roar blends into the endless thunder. Heedless of possible Giver-Tot casualties, I unleash a stream of bullets in the direction of one of the flying wizards as best as I can manage, which isn't impressively well as I can barely make them out in the randomly-strobing dark. Another dozen bolts of lightning render another dozen Givers to cinders.

But then a swath of darkness passes across a quarter of the sky as that section's lightnings stop. The marbling flows of light soon stream from the rest of the sky to fill the gap. But I've hit one!

"Jack!" Beth yells from below.

I make out another speck of flying sorcerer and let fly at it, aiming as best I can in the dimness. Focused though I may be on my target, my peripheral vision picks up the flickering lights in the clouds. The glimmers coalesce into a narrow section of sky, a band like the Milky Way, stretching from the stockade across the sky overhead. I *may* be centered below the ecliptic. I keep firing. I can't hear her but I know Beth is shouting my name and wrenching open the passenger side door beside me. Akaz clambers up the windshield at me. Blood Eagle leaps down from crag to crag like Spider-Man and dives in the driver's-side window. Numberless flash-bangs go off all around us as lightning hits the ground in front of the van, behind it, to either side.

It occurs to me now, as the storm-wizards offer this spectacle of destructive wonder, that my Sovereign Shield was never innate, but came to me only with the Skull of Kaios. The one that's down on the dashboard right now rather than inside my head. Unfortunate.

Akaz dives into my mouth, though, filling me with super-human vitality, and somehow, I know, transferring to me his own Sovereign Shield.

Blood Eagle leaps onto the hood of the van, brandishing the Skull and Spine of Kaios. A flash of lightning touches the Skull and arcs down the road to end at a speck hovering over the palisade. Despite the afterimage from the horizontal lightning bolt I can see the speck fall, trailing smoke.

"Two remain!" Blood Eagle says to me. Then he dives off the hood and bounds down the road toward the stockade.

C'mon! roars Akaz within me. He makes me leap up out of the gun mount.

I land beside Beth, who lies unmoving on the ground.

"Beth!"

She starts to stir.

Beside her in the mud lies my rifle Victoria. Unable to do otherwise under Akaz's influence, I reach down and snatch up the gun, then find myself sprinting away.

"Beth!" I shout over my shoulder as I run full-tilt down the road after Blood Eagle, heart rending to be forced apart from her. I struggle to slow my pace but cannot.

C'mon! says Akaz again within me.

"Stop! Stop! Please!" Tears well into my one eye, ducts around the other socket dead from cutting or burning. Terror clenches my heart, not knowing what's wrong with Beth or how badly she's hurt.

As we run, lightning bolts—sparser than before—rain down among the Givers. The mud gives way to dry dirt as we get closer. I find myself cocking and aiming Victoria at one of the two remaining air-mages. I fire, miss, lever the action, fire again. Miss. The lightning stops. Reassuring, but no, that just means they've got something new brewing. I shoot again. Despite possession by Akaz, with the corresponding demigod strength and precision, there's no way I can aim worth a damn while running. I can see the sorcerers more clearly now, though, as Blood Eagle and I race closer and their robes whip sideways in the wind. A small sandstorm seems brewing before the palisade. For a sec I think they're planning on hitting us with another stench-wave in the face, but no: they're brewing a cyclone. Whether around themselves or between us and them, there's little hope of shooting them through it. A dust devil rises from the ground before the gates of the stockade and stretches gradually upward a few dozen yards. *If they hit us with that*, I think at Akaz, hoping to dissuade him so I can get back to Beth, *we're in trouble.*

Nah, he replies.

It spins its way toward us down the road. I head straight for it, a helpless marionette to Akaz's will, Blood Eagle alongside. The spinning column of airborne dirt, dust, and grit grows rapidly larger as we approach. As worried as I am for Beth, my fear for my own soon-to-be-sandblasted flesh grows and finally eclipses it as we get near enough for the cyclone to dominate the view. Blood Eagle does not slacken, but only raises the Spine of God overhead as though already victorious. Akaz still rules my limbs, so my sprint persists: still no fatigue, after hundreds of yards, and my lungs feel like the huge bellows of a forge. The wall of dust looms before us, cascading from right to left in the clockwise cyclone—and we dive in.

Not a grain of sand touches us. Anything that would have is instead flung up in two pairs of jets: the *Sovereign Shield* in the Skull of Kaios sending a stream of grit up at each of the two collaborating sorcerers, anything that would have touched Blood Eagle; likewise Akaz's shield diverts anything aimed at me. The cyclone dissipates quickly enough then, both mages stunned, double-blasted from head to toe. They float there for a moment—long enough for me to aim Victoria at one and squeeze her trigger. Fire blasts forth. I land painfully on my back. A half-second later I hear the *splortch* of the mage's mangled body landing in the dirt. The final mage recovers their senses enough to blast me and Blood Eagle with a mighty gust of wind, but it just reflects off of us and blows the hapless wizard tumbling out of the air. It recovers just before hitting the ground, but Blood Eagle has pounced. Grabbed an ankle. The two of them rise just a few feet in the air before Blood Eagle swings the Skull of Kaios into the mage's chest, crushing ribs and organs. They both fall. Blood Eagle drops to his feet. The magician does not.

"Alive!" I manage to shout, as Blood Eagle raises the Spine of God for a coup de grace. Blood Eagle freezes and looks up at me blankly. I run up. The fallen final sorcerer looks as close to human as any Earthling I've met, fortyish, bald, van dyke beard, brocaded robes of red and gold. Lying there, legs bent askew, clutching his torso clumsily, wheezing, weeping hysterically. I was about to ask something, something tactical, but I'm at a loss for words. I stand there staring. The wizard writhes. Akaz wants him dead for Akaz reasons but I just have no more appetite to watch others suffer, so I'm happy to let Akaz raise my arm and shoot him. Recoil lifts me off the ground. The wizard's body explodes in bloody chunks, with more than enough burnt blood splashing me.

I gag, retch, and forcibly puke out Akaz.

"Hey!" he says.

I stagger and turn.

"Get back here!" says Akaz.

I stumble back down the road toward Beth.

Tot-Slop

I run up to the van, lungs heaving. Beth and Doomer sit side by side on the front bumper, she with a blanket around her shoulders and sipping beer from a can. I drop Victoria, stumble up and fall at her feet, clasping her thighs, head in her lap, heaving with sobs.

I feel her free hand run through my hair. "I'm fine, silly. Got a little shock through the door."

"C-cool," I manage between sobs.

"Any of this your blood?" she remarks on the wizard-gore spattered across my shirt, face, and hair.

"No." I sigh, and stop crying. Expressionless, I look up at her. "We don't have Sovereign Shields."

"Who does these days," mutters Doomer, half asleep.

"I never did," she says. "But didn't you just crisp that dude with his own lightning?"

"That wasn't my Shield. That was Akaz. But the one I've had all along, since I was twelve, it came from the Skull of Kaios that was in my head."

"Was." Beth stands in place, craning to see the dashboard above and behind us, where the Spine of God isn't. "Fuck."

"Blood Eagle took it."

"Right," she says.

I can feel the absence of my shield, like a never-before-experienced climate, the pressure of potential danger whispering at me from all directions.

"How the hell do you let me lead you into such danger?" I ask her. "I can't believe we've lived the way we have."

She shrugs. "That's life in dreadful times, baby." She gestures around to indicate the whole wide world. The whole multiverse, apparently.

"I've never felt so vulnerable. I can't believe how heedless I've been."

"You just had 'Sovereign Shield privilege'," she says with a laugh.

"You gotta let Akaz possess you," I insist.

"Ha. Or you, if you're gonna be besieging forts on foot and whatnot!"

I take a deep breath. "I guess we'll see."

An hour later we're at the gates, Beth and I wearing bandanas soaked in vinegar against the stench. It kinda works, same as it kinda helps with tear gas. Akaz sniffs with shameless enthusiasm.

Blood Eagle ushers us through. Railingless wooden walkways a foot above the ground crisscross the interior of the stockade. Everywhere else are obese Giver-Tots, standing or sitting in several inches of filth. Troughs everywhere brim with a brown slop indistinguishable from the shit-mud of the ground.

"This Tot-factory is the primary livestock supply for the Herax army this side of Mt. Kaios," says Blood Eagle. "This is a major victory."

"So why the hell wasn't it better guarded?" I ask.

"Seriously," says Beth.

"Those were four mighty apprentices," says Blood Eagle. "Without you, they could have easily fended us off."

Beth and I look at each other, unconvinced.

"Can I have the Spine o' God back?" I try, curious as much as anything whether he'll ever relinquish it.

Without any hint of hesitation, though, he hands it to me, rattling the vertebrae a couple of times as he does so. "Cannibal-King!"

All Givers in earshot say, "Cannibal-King!" Then everyone else, out across the plain: "Cannibal-King!"

"I am so fucking sick of that," I say to Beth.

"Tell me about it."

"So how do we free these Giver-Tots?" I ask Blood Eagle. "They don't seem too eager to escape this hellhole."

"They are entirely tame," says Blood Eagle. "They will stand in their paddocks until they die."

"You sure of that?" asks Beth.

"Not even the Cannibal-King's Power to Clear Men's Minds will affect them," says Blood Eagle. "Of this we can be certain. The Herax sorcerers have designed them with care, over centuries."

"Fucking horrifying," says Beth.

"This is far from the worst of Apraxos's factories," says Blood Eagle.

Beth and I look at him, silent, aghast.

"Yes," says Blood Eagle. "We have much work to do."

I crouch down and meet the eyes of a Giver-Tot. I open my mouth beneath the vinegar-soaked bandanna and form the words, "You're free now, you can leave—" But whatever telempathic connection underlies my Power to Clear Men's Minds, it simply finds nothing over there to attach to. I feel nothing but absence, dizzying like an unexpected stair. Surely I'm simply not finding it...? The tot's empty gaze drifts away. I stand, feeling woozy on top of the physical nausea, and stagger my way out of this pit of hell, Beth steadying me. As we walk I half-heartedly tell myself I'll come back for them after we take Melkhaios, find a way to free their minds somehow, knowing it's almost surely not true and feeling all the sicker.

Interlude in the House of the Watcher

A stone chamber, lit by numerous candles but still dark. APRAXOS THE WATCHER, robed and masked, paces the room angrily. He takes frequent, anxious glances into a small golden sphere. GENERAL GOROMATH reclines on a divan.

APRAXOS: How can the Givers be casting such fire, at such range, while my Lesser and Greater Bindings still hold?

GOROMATH: Presumably they have innovated some sort of long-range fire weapon.

APRAXOS: But what is it? In the name of accursed Wargus-Fire!

GOROMATH: Bite your tongue, heh.

Apraxos spins to face Goromath.

APRAXOS: I detest your cavalier attitude in the face of this loss! How could you have left the factory guarded only by four air-wizards?

GOROMATH: As you'll recall, it was your direct order to move our ships out to scan the entire frontier for Giver and Wilder activity.

APRAXOS: Under your advisement!

Apraxos paces angrily, then turns again to Goromath.

APRAXOS: You must render the sails of our fleet impervious to flame. And armor the hulls.

GOROMATH: Would that it were possible. Can you ensnare and ensorcel fire elementals to weave fireproof sails for us?

Apraxos slumps into a chair. Puts his masked face in his hands.

GOROMATH: Stop worrying, you fool. Even all the Givers and Wilders united could never stand against us. So the Givers have crafted a fireball catapult? Let them fling at us what they will. They will never reach the city.

APRAXOS: *(looking up)* I know you are correct. But I detest being made a fool of.

GOROMATH: Apraxos, please. You embarrass yourself by being so thin-skinned.

APRAXOS: How dare they! *(slams a fist on his thigh)* Savages!

GOROMATH: You could be made far worse a fool than this.

Apraxos absently shakes his head. Goromath grins, unnoticed.

Elders of the Wild

The van purrs its way up the Great Winding. The pass between Mt. Kaios and Mt. Megalon slopes only slightly upward, at least so far, but it's enough that we can't stand to let the Givers push any longer. It's only a few miles, looks like. We can spare the gas. Good to run the engine a little anyway.

Beth masterfully maintains an even seven or so miles per hour, slow enough on this rutted road to minimize our bouncing-around inside the cab (her behind the wheel, me in the middle, Doomer standing beside me up through the ring mount), slow enough that a few hundred trotting Givers can keep pace with us (do elementals get tired? still haven't seen sign of it), quick enough compared to our walking trudge alongside the Megalon foothills as to seem speedy. The kinetics of the bouncy road probably enhance the sensation of velocity.

The road is made of packed beige sand, randomly carved with ribbon-gutters by rivulets long gone from rains of a distant season. Huge boulders loom in all directions. Dry desert shrubs and small gnarled trees start right at the road's edge to either side, growing increasingly dense as we ascend. In surprisingly short order we find ourselves in actual forest, the road now a rich brown of packed soil, still rutted but less jaggedly so, our traction tangibly better now that we're off the crumbly dust. Deciduous and pine stretch in all directions as far as we can see—which, before long, is as little as a dozen yards.

We stop for a breather. Beth, Doomer, and I share a can of warm beer at the back bumper. Doomer lights up a joint, which Beth and I, still shaken up from encountering the Tot Factory while stoned, emphatically decline. Akaz moseys up, followed by Blood Eagle, General Larynx, and Lord Jawsplitter of the Rockeaters.

"Woods are creepin' 'em out," says Akaz.

"Anything we can do about that?" I ask.

"Gimme that." Akaz bites the joint out of Doomer's hand and chews it up.

"Hey!" says Doomer.

"Thanks," says Akaz. "Mmmmm."

"What are *they* afraid of?" asks Beth with genuine concern.

"We are not accustomed to such constrained horizons," says Blood Eagle.

"The Wilders of the Woods," says General Larynx, "are all around us."

"Wait, 'Wilders'?" I look around. Givers line the road on both sides, not quite in fighting stances, but certainly at the ready. Warily they watch the trees.

The trees, I realize, are full of quiet crows. Shapes in the shadows resolve into wolves, deer, bears. "Wilders," I say to Beth. "I remember. Shapeshifters. Wood spirits. Werewolves...."

"Uhh," says Beth, pointing at a pair of crows as they drop to the ground and transform into wolves.

"We are in Old Bear's territory," says Lord Jawsplitter. "Those are his heralds," indicating the crow-wolves.

The two wolf forms approach.

"Akaz," says one.

"Yo," says Akaz.

"The Elders of the Woods wish to speak with you," says the other.

"Is Old Bear around?" asks Akaz.

The two wolves nod. They part.

From the distance, directly between them, comes a rustling. As it approaches it resolves into the sound of something *large*. A flock of sparrows scatters out of its path. Are they Wilders too, or just sparrows? In the shadows stir the long limbs of something far larger than a man. It approaches close enough to see, more or less, though still largely covered by foliage; but not close enough to reach. It bends its huge, gaunt legs to sit on the forest floor.

It is a gigantic bear, skeletally thin, its ratty old fur hanging loosely on its frame.

"Akaz," it rumbles, in a voice older than the boulders around us in the woods.

"Long time no see, Old Bear," says Akaz.

"I am old."

"Hence the name," says Doomer.

"Shut up, Doomer," says Akaz.

"Is the Cannibal-King among you?" asks Old Bear.

"Yeah." Akaz indicates me with a nod.

Old Bear looks at me and bows. "The Elders of the Woods recognize no king. But our Wilders revere Akaz, whom they call 'Great'; and through him, they revere you, and long to walk alongside you as foretold. I am too old to fight, too old for a journey to the accursed city; but other Elders may join you. For my part, I give you my Wilders." Old Bear leans forward menacingly. *"I want them all back."*

Then Old Bear turns and disappears among the trees. We can hear him long after we lose sight of him.

In the next leg of our trek the road begins switching back more frequently. I sit alone on the van roof as we leave the forest and ascend into a landscape of light brown crags and boulders, slopes of gravelly sand broken therefrom, with scrub bushes and trees scattered everywhere. Here and there stand groups of tall, straight trees in half dozens or dozens. Around the column of Givers, walking and flying alongside us on either side, dozens of animals of all sorts: the crows, wolves, deer, bears, and yes sparrows of the forest are joined by mountain goats, rams, and golden eagles. And the occasional lizard of unclear destination but possibly pacing us. Or are there just lots of lizards around the mountainside who spook as we approach and happen to vanish more or less into the direction we're headed?

What is clear, out here in the daylight, without the dense foliage of the forest providing concealment and camouflage, is that these "Wilders" change shape often from animal to animal. Without warning, without breaking stride, a deer becomes a bear. A hopping robin shifts into a wolf. A soaring eagle spirals down and lands on all four hooves as a goat. No sign of the Wilders' humanoid form from any of them, though. Not one of them speaks to me. Some make eye contact; some of those stare without apparent feeling; some seem to smile.

After a while of enjoying the scenery and fauna, I rejoin Beth and Doomer in the van. As I get re-situated between them, I do my best to come up with a pun on the phrase "in the van," jargon for the leading position of an army, we being the foremost unit in the column aside from advance scouts. But all I manage is, "Heh, we're 'in the van.'" I look at Beth, trying to elicit comprehension with an ingratiating shiteater grin, no dice, same with Doomer, just stares from both of them. Doomer pops back up through the hatch, muttering, "'Shmannibal-King.'"

After another half hour of winding switchbacks, we arrive at a huge, lumpy boulder blocking the road.

"Well that's inconvenient," says Beth.

We get out to investigate, and the boulder slowly sits up, revealing itself to be a gigantic stony humanoid, naked and hairless, I'd bet twenty feet tall if it stood. Fortunately it stays seated.

"Uh," I say, "hi."

A thick-boled dead-looking treetrunk looming nearby bends down in a crouch and sits beside the giant stone man, not a tree at all but a gnarled, burly wooden humanoid figure.

"Hello," say the stone man and the tree man in deep, resonant voices, "Cannibal-King."

"Elders of the Mountain," says Blood Eagle, mercifully at hand all of a sudden, "we come for council."

"Hi," I repeat.

Wild Council

Compared to past Councils, this is downright unruly—the Wilders being aptly named, for one thing. Overhead the sky dims toward twilight, and the sky behind the peak roils with magenta and storm-gray. The valley below lies in shadow. I sit holding the Spine of God, Beth beside me. Doomer, Akaz, Blood Eagle, General Larynx, and Lord Jawsplitter complete the inner circle, seated facing outward. All around us, on the gently sloping floors of packed sand, sandstone, and exposed boulders, sit Givers and Givers and more Givers by the hundreds. Among, above, and beyond them are the Wilders, dozens and hundreds of them as well, in all the animal forms we'd seen and more, sitting and roaming and scampering and climbing and flying. And now many Wilders are shifting into their humanoid forms, taller and leaner than Givers, colored in the innumerable brown and gray shades of animals. Many of them retain fringes of fur or feather, or horns, or hooves, or animal ears. Some humanoid Wilders have leaves, branches, or vines to adorn them—no, not adorn; these are body parts, and around us many of the shrubs and trees, I realize, are Wilders. And some of the Mountain Wilders have stone skin, even in man-shape, so surely some of the stones around us are Wilders as well. The plant and stone Wilders sit as silent as the Givers, but the animal Wilders chatter and move.

With low hopes I rattle the Spine of God. To my surprise, the Wilders settle—not to complete stillness, but such a swift and significant shift that it completely changes the tone of the gathering. With me smack in the center of everyone's attention.

What I am supposed to say next I have no idea. Both Akaz and Blood Eagle had briefed me with key points I needed to touch upon, but none of these come to mind just at the moment, just a residue of unease. Well, now if ever is the time for me to speak my own mind, not what those two shady characters want me to say. But what? What do I really know here? What can I honestly assert, and what results can I expect? Scattered thoughts come too fast to track, none of them remotely conclusive.

Yet I open my mouth and speak.

"I am no king," I begin, doing my best to project my voice.

"Use the *King's Voice*." Akaz nods up at the Skull of Kaios.

"Huh?" I ask.

"The Skull," he says. "Just open the jaws."

Skeptical, I press my forefinger to the gold chin and lower the Jawbone. I stare at the Skull for a second, then at Akaz. "And...?"

"Talk!" says Akaz.

Narrowing my eye at him, I repeat: "I am no king." My voice resonates out in all directions, making me jump. I continue: "Kaios called me that in prophesy, to lend me credence. But I will rule over no one."

Many voices say, "Hoy hoy," throughout the assembly. I shake the rattle. The gold teeth clack together and apart. "No scripture is literal," I venture, worried I may have gone too far. No response. Having lived through the end of the Twentieth Century, during and after the fall of the USA, I am naturally inclined to dread the ire of loudmouth fundamentalists. No such wrath here, for whatever reason.

"I am not from your world. So I know next to nothing about any feuds or disagreements among you. I cannot adjudicate them, or anticipate how they might interfere with our battlefield tactics. I must simply ask, then, that you set them *all* aside, *entirely* aside, until we have defeated the Herax. While they hold power, they are our sole opponent."

A rumble of, "Hoy, hoy," around us.

"I demand also that we all abandon any eating of souls," I say, now expecting a real shitstorm to ensue. "The flesh of fallen enemies may be eaten, if needed, but no soulstuff. No hearts, no brains, and never the soul. And never the flesh, not even the carrion, of innocents. Those who defy this decree not only fall back under the Greater and Lesser Bindings...if they apply to you?" I look around at the nearby Wilders. "Do they apply to you?"

Shaking of furry, feathery, leafy heads.

"No bindings on Wilders," says a bear.

"Haha," whistles a sparrow, "bindings on Wilders." Gentle laughter and shuffling among the Wilders. "Bindings on Wilders," repeats the sparrow. "Bindings on Wilders, haha."

"*If they apply,*" I continue, *loud*. Everyone goes still. "Not only the Bindings, but eaters of souls or innocents will also incur *my* wrath and *my* curse."

Lots of muttering. I rattle the Spine.

"I intend for this Council to be short," I state simply, and put down the Spine of God.

There is a stirring among the Wilders, but the assembly is mostly still. I wait. Nothing happens. "Wow," Beth whispers to me, "did you feel that?"

"What?" I ask her.

"Everyone's just... *on board*," she says. "I can't describe it. I feel a little high from it, to be honest. Don't you feel that buzz in the air?"

Maybe? "I guess so."

"Magic from the Spine of God, maybe?"

"Nah, that trick's just amplification," says Akaz. "The Power to Clear Men's Minds is Jack's innate ability."

Beth and I look at Akaz and then at each other. I shrug. "Not from the Skull," I ask.

"Well, yeah, from the Skull," says Akaz, "you had it in your hand there." He gestures with a paw at the Spine of God on the ground. "I mean, you're a charming guy, but the real mind control magic comes from the Skull."

"How the hell is that innate, then?"

Akaz ignores me.

Blood Eagle stands and hefts the Spine of God aloft and slowly turns in a circle as he addresses the company. "Wilders of the Mountain, Wilders of the Woods, renowned for your refusal to obey anyone or anything, know this: we Givers have all pledged to abide by the two dictates of the Cannibal-King: we are a unified force under his leadership, despite our differences; and we abstain absolutely from consumption of astral soulstuff, or so much as the

carrion of innocents, much less Giver-Tot. We may perform the Rites of Augermath upon enemy flesh alone. Do
we take your silence as assent? Do you join with us, to
march upon Melkhaios and rid our world of the scourge
of the Herax?"

A raven lands at Blood Eagle's feet with a flapping of
large wings and shifts into the form of a womanlike creature, seven feet tall and rail-thin, a fringe of black feathers
cresting her head, shoulders, arms; with human thighs,
jack-knees, and scaly black bird-talons for feet. She takes
the Spine of God from Blood Eagle and turns to me. She
shakes the rattling vertebrae.

"What after the Herax fall?" she asks in a croaking voice.

"As prophesied in the Books of Kaios," says Blood Eagle,
"after the fall of the city, our King shall lead us to a new life."

The raven-woman turns to Blood Eagle. "You speak for
him? Should he fall on the battlefield, who 'leads' us; you?"
She taps the Skull of Kaios against Blood Eagle's chest, then
shoves him back a step with it.

"In prophecy," says Blood Eagle, "he lives." Rage seems
to boil beneath his calm exterior. "Do you doubt the Books
of Kaios?"

"Kaios had ideas and words," says the raven-woman. "But
rocks are hard, and water is wet." She shakes the big rattle in his face. Then turns to me and hands me the Spine of
God. "The Raven Sisterhood offers our allegiance for now.
We Wilders have no love for debate; this is perhaps the best
explanation for our silence." She waves an arm to indicate
the entire multitude. "We honor the form of the Bone Coun-

cil, but this is no Bone Council; no consensus or even conversation can occur at this scale." She flaps into the air as a bird and then away somewhere.

"Okay," I say.

"I like her," says Beth.

"Yeah," I say, noticing Blood Eagle frowning down at me.

"Scrawny for my taste," says Doomer.

"Fuck you," says Beth. "Douche."

A tall tree nearby starts shaking as though in an earthquake, its leaves and branches rustling and rattling, its trunk and limbs groaning and creaking. Then it leaps up out of the ground and turns into a sparrow. It flits over to the ground near us, transforms into a gray-skinned man-shaped thing with twigs and leaves growing from its head and back. It bends down and takes the Spine from me.

"Prophecy says you burn our forest," he rumbles down at me. He stared back and forth between me and Beth.

"Prophecy says that *you* burn your forest, Walking Bole," says Blood Eagle.

Walking Bole glances at Blood Eagle, then back at me and Beth. "Heh," he laughs, a short, clipped sound, but deep and resonant. "Heh. Heh." He winks at me, hands me the Spine of God, and snaps his fingers. A poof of flame flashes from his hand and vanishes. Then he flies away as a sparrow once more.

"What," says Beth.

"Yeah."

"Weird," says Doomer.

"Yeah," I repeat.

"Wilder humor," says Akaz. "He's good people. You'll see."

Then a sinister whisper comes from right behind me: "Cannibal-King."

Beth and I twist quickly in place to see the speaker, she clockwise, I counterclockwise, and find ourselves face to face with a smoldering human skull. The rims of its eyes, nose, and mouth glow unevenly like the edges of wood turning to ember. Smoke pours thickly out of it, wreathing it in a shifting veil. Beth and I nearly jump out of our skin. Under the skull, crouching low, the huge, shaggy body of a grizzly bear. The words "I promise nothing" hiss from the skull.

"Uh," I say, "okay."

"Elder of the Mountain," begins Blood Eagle—but Akaz cuts him off.

"We know, Doom Bear." Akaz has a shade of exasperation in his voice. "Seriously, though, join in the fun. You'll be glad you did."

Doom Bear stares at Akaz for a long moment.

"There's a reason I bit your head off," says Akaz. "And there's a reason I gave it back. You should come with us. And if not, you should stay far, far away."

Doom Bear nods, drops the Spine of God to the dirt in front of me—how did it get ahold of it? It stands, towering over us even more immensely than I expected, and strides off, Givers and Wilders alike scurrying aside to clear its path.

"What the," Beth and I whisper to each other.

"That's Doom Bear," Akaz tells us, by way of explanation.

"You don't say," says Beth.

I pick up the Spine of God and hold it tightly.

The sky's pretty dark by now, the remaining sunset a magenta halo around Mt. Kaios, stars coming out over the foothills to the east, the landscape around us nearly lost in shadow. "Got dark quick," I remark to Beth, my amplified voice echoing around us. I shut the Skull's mouth. "Better get flashlights and stuff from the van while we can."

"What about this?" Beth gestures at the crowd around us.

"Is this even a thing?" I ask her. To Blood Eagle I say, "What are we even trying to accomplish here? Consensus with the Wilders?" I gesture at the crowd, imitating Beth's movement, indicating the Wilders' wildness as they wander, banter, play-fight, and shapeshift.

"You have informed them of your presence, your plans, and your wishes," says Blood Eagle. "The Wilders have no love for Givers, but hate the Herax infinitely more. They will fight beside us. Despite their apparent irreverence, they tend toward the devout. They love Kaios and revere his books of prophecy. They believe in you. Some may refuse to march with us—"

"I don't exactly see any of them *marching*," says Beth. "Not literally anyways."

Blood Eagle ignores her and continues. "And some may eat souls. But most will act as you would wish."

I ruminate.

"Best we could hope for, probably," says Beth.

"Hmm," I say. "I guess we could camp here for the night, cross through the pass tomorrow?"

"As you wish," says Blood Eagle.

"What's that," says Akaz, looking ahead downhill. In the distance, where the pass disappears behind the hip of Mt.

Kaios, flashes of firelight flicker and vanish, flicker and vanish.

"What the," I say.

A small falcon lands atop the Skull of Kaios, startling me so badly I almost drop it. The bird leaps aside and turns into a naked man-shaped being with mottled black spots covering his skin like the pattern of a falcon's feathers. "Cannibal-King," he addresses me, and nods his head in greeting or deference or something. I nod back. "The Second Army has arrived." He nods in the direction of the distant little flashes of fire.

"What's the 'Second Army'?" I ask Akaz and Blood Eagle.

"Conscripts," says Akaz. "Digglies and Normals and Deep Ones, forced by the Herax to fight, under pain of death or worse."

"Fuck," I say. To the falcon-Wilder, I ask, "Who's fighting them?"

"The Bad Givers," he says. "The ones from the back of your army. They kept on the march while you held Council. Along with their fat Giver-Tots from the Factory."

"What?"

"They have made good time by eating the souls of the Tots. And now they fight well, each with his jet or ball or whip of flame to roast soldiers of the Second Army."

Beth and I jump to our feet and start making our way through the crowd toward the van. Doomer, Blood Eagle, and Akaz follow us.

"Cannibal-King?" says Blood Eagle.

"Whatcha doing?" asks Akaz.

"Stopping those goddamn soul-eaters," I reply.

Cannibal-King III

The road is treacherous in the dark, but our high-beams compensate. Animals and Givers make way for the van. Before long we reach the rear of the mutinous column of Bad Givers: their hundreds of obese Giver-Tots, leashed together in columns. Ahead, along the line of engagement, the Givers' jets of fire create flashes of light and throw titanic shadows up the slopes to either side of the pass. I honk and honk to get the Giver-Tots out of our way. They catch on, but only one by one as we arrive directly behind them, so it's slow going. Each turns to look at us and squints into the headlights. They all have dried blood crusted around their mouths and dripped onto their big bellies. Hence the stamina and speed to keep up with us on our long march, and to pass us while we talked in the woods: they've been feeding on their own kind.

Ahead we can see the scores of Bad Givers swarming the slopes, running, jumping, shouting, each hurling his own big gout of fire. Big from eating Giver-Tot, eating them body and soul. But also only each Giver to his own fire, the Greater Binding intact.

Trapped in the road between slopes of swarming Givers are hundreds upon hundreds of terrified and ill-equipped spearmen, struggling to impale their teeming attackers but succeeding only rarely, meanwhile themselves being burned dead by the dozens.

I stop the van, insist that Doomer hop out, make my way over Beth and up through the hatch into the ring mount. I shake open the mouth of the Skull of Kaios with one hand, using the other to wield the megaphone as a backup measure. I simply shout, "Stop!" Nothing happens. Akaz and Blood Eagle come around opposite sides of the van and look up at me.

"Good one," says Akaz.

"Eat shit," I say through the squawking megaphone. I see Doomer crack up at that. Something stirs in me, and I feel that Power to Clear Men's Minds feeling. I find myself just talking, a rant spilling unbidden and unfiltered from my mouth and out through both megaphone and Skull: "Givers, hold your fire. As your King I command you. This is your sole and final warning. Against my orders you have eaten the souls of Giver-Tots; and for this you feel the constraint of the Greater Binding, fetters from which your kindred have been released by the force of my divine decree. But you remain weak in your separateness, even as your intoxication seduces you with illusions of personal power. Hold your fire. Withdraw upslope and fall back behind my position. Persist in your attack and die. Yeah, you heard me right. Fall back or die at my hand, traitors."

As these words echo away into the pass, I feel the veil of trance lift from my eye and ears, and I behold the dark battlefield once more.

Most of the Givers have stopped. I can see them, pale and naked, standing on the slopes staring at me, some of them trotting back toward us. Only occasional fireballs and lashes of flame light up the pass as a dozen Bad Givers maintain their slaughter.

In a slightly different flavor of trance than the one that loosed my voice, I find my arms setting down the megaphone and Spine of God on the van roof beside me, then locking-and-loading the MG. I take aim at the nearest flash of fire, and as it vanishes I unleash a small torrent. The pale Giver falls. I kill another. And another. Pausing, I retake megaphone and scepter: "Bad Givers! Do you not wish to avoid a quick and bloody end? Retreat or die!"

"Didn't you already give them a 'final warning'?" says Akaz.

"Shut up," I bark down at him; and for one reason or another, he does.

I take up the gun again and kill more disobedient Givers. Whether because I've killed them all, or they've repented or retreated, the Giver-fires in the pass cease.

From behind us, pale light from the fat crescent moon lands across the Second Army. The trance moves again from my hands into my head, and with megaphone in one hand and Spine of God in the other I address the Second Army, the words again rushing forth without a pause for thought:

"All you enslaved by the Herax, you are now free! Turn your spears aside and let us pass. We march upon the City of the Watcher, and none can stop us. Even if you somehow doubt our might, know that if anyone is to stop us, it will not be you. We will either pass by you or through you. How better for you to join us, to turn your spears against those who dominate you and send you off to brutal death? And even if your death at our hands were not certain, how can you risk your life merely in order to preserve your own enslavement? Step aside, or better yet, join us." I find myself ducking down through the ring mount and letting myself out the passenger door, not quite noticing as Beth tries to speak to me; nor Akaz, Doomer, or Blood Eagle; and striding toward the warriors of the Second Army, scepter aloft, megaphone booming:

"Come and meet your liberator! Come meet your Cannibal-King!"

And as my trance slowly recedes, I become aware of Beth talking urgently to me as she tugs my arm, Akaz dancing around saying something with unguarded enthusiasm, and Doomer interjecting the occasional "Dude!" Blood Eagle takes the Spine of God from me, which feels like a relief—I feel faint, in fact, and stagger a little as I put one foot in front of the other, megaphone dangling from my hand. Givers and Wilders crowd around me as we approach the Second Army, who approach us with spears aimed at the dirt, with stunned silence, with tears of joy. People of sorts I have not seen before outside of my teenage imagination, but which I know to be Digglies, Normals, and Deep Ones, fall to their knees in abject reverence. Of me.

As my faint-headedness starts to resolve into the clarity of full awakeness, and I become gradually aware again of how much I despise this authoritarian messiah-king bullshit, I also notice a disturbing premonition. Something else is happening on the far side of the Second Army. Something is wrong.

"Something's wrong," I say aloud.

Distant squawks echo down the pass toward us. Dozens of large winged creatures descend upon the far ranks of the Second Army, swooping back up with soldiers in their talons and flinging them down from a height upon their comrades. I hear General Larynx shout what sounds like, "Deck-Reavers!"

And behind the Deck-Reavers, dozens of Herax warships coming in low through the pass toward us.

Not just the pass: Herax ships creep over the ridges around us in all directions, flying low and silent.

Then from all around us, an explosion of voices from the decks of a hundred longboats:

"We come as one!"

Wolf of Kaios III

Drums clamor in all directions, Givers rapidly tapping them one-handed as they charge or await charge. I scramble back into the van and man the machine gun. Akaz leaps onto the hood and sits motionless once more. If there was ever a time best spent thinking rather than panicking, I reckon this would be it. I try. Ain't easy. Those Giver drums don't help. Everything happening is so fast and multivalent that at first my nerves are just jangled—but a few deep breaths allow me to get on top of this anxiety and ride it. As long as I don't tense up against it, the anxiety buoys me like a wave. Focus. Now, as quickly as possible, as thoroughly as possible, it's time to assess the situation.

First I cannot help but notice our immediate allies on the battlefield. We and our van are surrounded by Bad Givers behind us and the Second Army in front. That is to say, mutineers from my army so dedicated to rejecting my leadership that they'd rather stay accursed by the Greater and Lesser Bindings than temporarily give up their soul-eating; and cannon fodder who defected from our enemy only a few minutes ago, under some strange telepathic influence

I have no idea how to control and which may not last. Not my most favoritest king's guard for a massive melee. Behind the Bad Givers tremble their Giver-Tots, and further back, the bulk of the Giver army fills the pass, but quite a distance behind us. Wilders are scattered everywhere, but none close at hand. Conclusion: If Herax ground troops break through to anywhere near us, we're in real trouble.

Can we avoid melee yet again somehow? Maybe, but no idea where our enemy is most vulnerable, most concentrated, or most threatening. I'm going to have to scan the dark landscape in all directions before I fire a shot. Fire a shot and announce our location.

Ahead, a couple dozen Herax longboats swarm through the pass, close over the heads of the far fringes of the Second Army. The flock of Deck-Reavers has stopped their dive-and-grab, circling ominously over the heart of the Second Army. They could dive this way any moment. I don't relish the prospect of trying to shoot an oncoming flock of flying velociraptors out of the air before any of them can get at me.

How's the Second Army responding to this threat of death circling overhead? Looks like a scattering of brawls. Maybe those who declare a wish to fight the Herax are confronted by those convinced, understandably enough, of the probable near-future victory of the Herax. Most of the Second Army just cowers under the circling Reavers.

It occurs to me: why aren't there any Herax sorcerers attacking us from up ahead? Were those four we killed a significant part of their war-magery forces? Or are there plenty more, due any minute?

To complete my assessment I start to turn three-sixty (trying to not let my temper flare when the inadequately-greased ring mount catches). Let's assess the specific dispositions of all Herax forces surrounding us.

To our right I see not a single Herax, in boat or on foot, passing over the mountain itself. But there's much movement up the rocky slopes. Who? Wilders? Is that something... big? Several big things, it seems, descending the shadowy slopes. Can't worry about them yet—who knows what else is coming our way from other directions. I force myself to continue clockwise and check six o'clock, back the way we came.

Dozens more Herax boats come low up the pass behind us, toward the bulk of the Giver army. Judging from the formation of dust devils heralding them, they've got wizards. Not good not good not good. Anxiety threatens to stop buoying me and bury me.

A line from Sun Tzu comes to mind: "On hemmed-in ground, resort to stratagem." Yes. Yes. But what stratagem. I stare at the terrain behind us, trying not to be mesmerized by the dust devils, trying to envision a stratagem. Can't think, not with this pressure. If I could just call time out, just for a minute, finish looking around, consider our best moves, figure out what to shout at people through the megaphone.... If only I could see the battlemap from above, and all the wargaming miniatures arrayed upon it....

A handful of ravens croak their death-knell and launch themselves at the Herax behind us: the Raven Sisterhood. A hundred crows follow them, cawing. A few golden eagles soar among them also. I watch long enough to see them dodge around the dust devils, slip under the hulls of the

Herax boats, and hook around behind them; then a hundred birds turn to wolves, mostly; some stags, some bears, and the eagles become huge mountain goats. Herax sailor-spearmen get duly wrenched or butted overboard, each mammal attacker changing back to bird and fleeing to the air before the victims' shipmates can avenge them. Though wounds from these attacks are rarely lethal, and the fall from the low-flying boats often results in nothing worse than a broken limb, none of the fallen Herax are in fighting shape, making the tactic a success. The birds circle around for another pass. Swarms of Herax harpoons hit almost no one, and even then only a wing.

I swing the MG another quarter turn, facing port, out over the driver's side of the van. Boulders define the leftward verge, beyond which is not a mountain limb pressing up against us, as on our starboard; but rather a steep, scrub-grown drop to a small valley. Shit. And forty or fifty Herax boats floating up out of the valley, concealed and covered till now by the cliff edge and boulders.

I kick my way up and out through the ring mount, dive forward over the windshield to grab Akaz by the scruff of the neck. He glowers at me. Opening my mouth wide, I find myself hauling Akaz into the air—

"Whoa whoa *whoa!*" he says.

—and shoving him into my mouth.

What the fuck, man? he asks from inside me as I dive feet-first back into the roof hatch. Ignoring him I take hold of the machine gun and shoot desperately over the driver's side of the van, downhill at these sudden stalking boats. Fireballs blast holes in decks or blow Herax soldiers apart.

Wilders downhill, interspersed with the rocks and trees, erupt from cover as crows and sparrows to fly up to the decks of the longboats, where they turn into wolves or the Wilder man-shape, each wresting a Herax overboard and then flying off in bird form. Herax javelins rarely hit anyone in flight. But the Herax quickly start learning how to use their hive mind to anticipate an incoming Wilder, keeping their eyes peeled in all directions and triangulating their spear-thrusts to fend off or kill anyone who flies close.

A darting sparrow evades notice until it lands on a Herax longboat, then turns abruptly into a hundred-foot tree with roots worming throughout the deck. Its weight quickly overcomes the strength of the air-spirits in the sail, unbalancing the ship enough to tilt, flip, and fall. Herax soldiers tumble to the bouldery slope and die. The tree flits away as a sparrow once more. The ship crashes onto rocks and fallen soldiers, and comes apart as it bounces downhill.

The sparrow lands on the nearest boat and repeats. The Herax move in unison. The trunk of the tree is peppered with spears. The boat falls nonetheless; and when the tree turns back to bird, the piercing spears all simply fall away.

So the Herax air-mages whip winds around the remaining boats downhill from us, making approach by flight impossible. I wish I could spot the wizards and shoot them. I settle for blasting ships with balls of Wargus-fire, knowing the power of Akaz will protect the machine gun's barrel from overheating indefinitely.

Scattered Givers downslope join the attack with narrow blasts of fire. The air-mages easily blow these aside. The Givers throw their fire at the surrounding sands, and fling up handfuls of molten glass. The glass cools just enough on its way through the wind that by the time it hits a hull, deck, or Herax, its shell shatters on impact to release its molten core. The effect on the surface of a boat is unfortunately only a smoldering patch. Herax aren't hit often, but a few get horrible burns and glass shrapnel. Some Givers target sails, but to no avail: the glass doesn't break.

I project as best I can. "Givers!" Where's the megaphone? What the fuck ever happened to our handset for the P.A.? Wait, where is the Spine of God / Skull of Kaios / *King's Voice*? Shit, I just holler as best I can: "Vow not to eat souls!"

Before I can make my case again, there's shouting from behind, and a flare of startling brightness casts the downslope into dark, my shadow atop the van darting ahead the length of the pass. Turning back to look I see a cyclone of fire erupting up from the hands of the Givers on the road, hundreds of them lending their jet of fire to it. The massive, swirling cylinder of flame roars almost horizontally back down the pass toward the Herax, ripping through the middle of their formation, turning a half dozen sails to ash.

"We come as one!" comes the call, not just from behind, but with terrifying, inhuman simultaneity all around us. They're expecting this: the air-mages steer any burning, falling longboats to crash among the Givers. Shit. Smashing timbers crush short swaths through the Giver formation, disrupting the unity of their elemental magics. The cyclone of fire vanishes. For a moment there are just a few hundred narrow jets, each five yards long. Individual Givers form naturally into squads with their neighbors, their flames conjoining to extend ten, twenty yards. These tongues of fire wrap around each other and merge, becoming fewer, fatter, and longer, till we have half a dozen fifty-yard fiery little cyclones whipping through the air with a chorus of massive whooshing sounds.

The Herax longboats ascend at top speed. A couple of stragglers get caught by these smaller helixes of fire. Sails burning, they wreck upon the road. Giver fire-cyclones wink out temporarily as they flee falling boats, but immediately begin to re-form. Torrents of Herax harpoons and javelins fall from far above, too distant to aim but numerous enough to wound and kill by random chance, keeping the Giver-fires from consolidating further and extending their reach.

As I turn back to the Herax coming up from the valley below, I find them already swarming upon us. Hurricane winds buffet me as I shoot any ship I set my eye on. Flat-bottomed longboats land among the Bad Givers, releasing scores of Herax spearmen.

Yeah, this is what I was afraid of.

The Herax move in strange configurations with abrupt changes of direction: dodging blows they could not have seen coming; several abruptly converging on a Giver high and low, front and flank, to spear him simultaneously. This is the Herax telepathic hive mind in action. Their quality of movement is unlike anything I've ever seen from human or animal, disorienting and surreal to behold.

Keeping the M240 on single-fire I try to shoot individual soldiers, but even with Akaz in my brain they're impossible to track. I hit a Bad Giver by mistake, blowing his head and arm into the air. That gives me pause. I look around to re-assess. I want to duck down into the van to check on Beth but dare not take my eye off our situation. I see Doomer just below me, backed up against the passenger side of the van, hunkered behind a big transparent Lexan riot shield (where the hell did *that* come from), propping the muzzle of a forty-four magnum on the top edge and taking the occasional shot at a Herax soldier. I see Blood Eagle, covered in blood, a Herax spear in one hand, the bloody Spine of God in the other. Bad Givers spit gouts of flame onto landed longboats, burning their sails, depriving Herax of an avenue of retreat. (For better or worse; the Herax show no sign of fear and might be indifferent to the opportunity.) But more and more boats land anyway, visibly shifting the Herax proportion of the crowd over the course of a couple of minutes.

Nothing for me to do but keep shooting, then. But from starboard, uphill, the Mountain Wilders descend into the fray: horse-sized goats, huge golden eagles, and stone-skinned humanoids. Ah and those big things I'd seen moving down the mountainside in the darkness? A couple of stone-skinned giants, easily twenty feet tall. One of them grabs a Herax spearman and flings it down onto another, leaving them both motionless.

Witnessing that double-death gives me a twinge of a high, an Augermath blood magic high. Wait, that's not all: I've been slowly picking up flickers of departing life force this whole fight, Akaz sucking it out of the Astral Plane like a baleen whale all along, infusing my soul with its residue as he draws it in through me. Dammit. Euphoric. Physically and morally numb. Standing in the ring mount, Akaz burning joyous within me. Longboats afire all around. Bodies and parts strewn everywhere. Brutal hand-to-hand combat surrounds us, spearmen against goats and wolves and glass-wielding Givers, deck-reavers diving down from above, wind-mages disrupting any large-scale use of fire.

"Jack!" Doomer shouts up at me, snapping me out of trance, with an urgency in his voice that sounds like it must be the second or third time he said my name.

He's pointing at a Herax warship rapidly rising overhead, a black silhouette against the starry black sky.

Then: "Watch out!" A spear clashes heavily against his riot shield and bounces off of it. Another passes close by him to enter the passenger-side window, where it would have hit my leg—but instead it folds back upon itself and flies twenty yards to lodge itself through the quadriceps of the Herax who threw it.

Keeping the machine gun on single-fire, I resume shooting Herax.

And then I see stars. A curtain of shimmering light like television static descends over my field of vision.

First Herald III

For a second I think I must've been speared in the back of the head, but nothing hurts. Hang on, that's not necessarily all that reassuring. I can't feel my body at all. Instead of the screams and clashing weapons of the battlefield, I hear nothing but a far rumble, equidistant in all directions like a sphere of rolling thunder. I see nothing. Sense no one.

"What the fuck?" I find myself saying, hoping I'm not dead.

That thought is swiftly overwhelmed by aching dread for Beth. Never mind my fate, is she okay? The battle has so encompassed my attention that I hadn't so much as looked at her since the arrival of the Herax. What was our most recent interaction? I can't remember. Will that have been our final interaction? Whatever it was, it could never suffice. This can't be it, not even a chance to say goodbye...?

Fuck, says Akaz. *My head, what the fuck....*

"Akaz?"

The distant thunder CRACKS through the entirety of the featureless void, and then unechoing silence. I stand in a featureless plain under a featureless sky. I can see myself both from within and without, as in a dream. I feel nothing. Akaz sits beside me, shaking his head.

AKAZ: Fuck.

He slumps down to the 'ground.'

JACK: Akaz!
AKAZ: *(mumbling)* The Astral Web.

Only now do I realize he's normal-dog Akaz, who I've lived with for years, not the fiery-eyed Akaz of the Isle of Kaios. His eyes are half-open and rolled up in their sockets, shifting like in REM sleep.

JACK: What?
AKAZ: *(muttering)* Finally broke the Astral Web. Here we come, but unstuck.
JACK: Akaz. Wake up.

Kneels and puts a hand on Akaz's flank.
I can feel his hot fur.

AKAZ: Unstuck in time, here we go.

Another thunderclap and the van zooms past, with Beth driving—

—and Jack manning the machine gun.

JACK: *What*

The van vanishes.

AKAZ: I see what you're up to. I see what you're up to.
JACK: What.

Akaz still doesn't seem to notice me.

Jack shakes him a little.

JACK: *(cont'd.)* Who. What who's up to.
AKAZ: Summon us into the past so you have more time. Clever.
JACK: Who are you talking to.

Jack shakes him harder. Akaz remains heedless of him.

AKAZ: But what happens to the kid? Drag back in time too? Oh, of course, he's comin' on his own, you're not summoning him, riiight. Whole thing still seems a little haphazard, chief.

A doorway opens nearby, hanging in the air, and in through it stumbles a boy in his early teens, face and t-shirt covered in blood. He staggers for a few paces and out through another doorway. Both doors slam and vanish.

JACK: What the....

AKAZ: It'll take him a while to get from Earth-Bitchwood to our Bitchwood, though. He'll be stuck in the Vast Plain between them for who-knows-how-long.

I look around the vast plain surrounding us and wonder as to the passage of time here.

AKAZ: *(cont'd.)* But any sec we're all gonna land. The kid in Corpsewater. Us back on Mount Kaios. We'll be done being unstuck, we'll all hit at the present moment, whatever present we happen to hit at. Past, present, future, all are one.

JACK: *(insistent)* Akaz.

AKAZ: Help!

JACK: I've got you!

AKAZ: Help! Help! Ff—ff—ff—father!

JACK: Huh?

AKAZ: Father! Yog-Sothoth!

JACK: Akaz!

Akaz's head perks up and he opens his eyes. Brown dog-eyes.

AKAZ: Where am I.

Jack shrugs.

AKAZ: *(cont'd.)* Fucked up dream.

Interlude in the City of the Watcher

THE ARCHIVE—HALLWAY

XAX, MAX, and CLARK arrive. Xax and Max wear suits, Clark his ridiculous Elizabethan stage costume.

An ornately-robed figure, ARCH-DEAN WERUMEL, stands in the hall, frog-eyes bulging from its blue-green face.

CLARK: Allow me to introduce myself! *(bows)* I am Prof.
    Clark, Provisional Acting Archivist.
XAX: Shut up, Clark.
ARCH-DEAN WERUMEL: Guards!

Max points a pistol at Werumel.

XAX: Leave him.

Xax opens the door to a dark, circular room. Large windows look onto a black bay, twinkling lantern-lights of a small city, a mountain-shaped horizon silhouetted against starry sky.

Behind them, Werumel continues shrieking.

ARCH-DEAN WERUMEL: Guards! Guards!

Max covers their retreat into the round room.

Xax throws open a pair of windows, reaches through and opens a doorway hanging in the air outside. Through this doorway can be seen a cramped room with armchairs in disarray.

CLARK: Where is that a gate to?
XAX: Not a gate. A little ship, hovering outside the tower, invisible. Hop in.

Xax gets in. Clark hesitates. Max, continuing to cover their retreat, drags Clark in with him and slams the hatch.

DEATH MACHINE COCKPIT

Not a cramped sitting room; a roomy cockpit with swiveling seats.

Xax and Max strap themselves in. Clark attempts to do so, has some difficulty.

XAX: Death Machine, take us to the roof of the Tower of the Skull.

DEATH MACHINE: *(robot voice from nowhere)* Aye-aye.

A lurch nearly throws Clark from his seat.

TOWER OF THE SKULL—ROOF

Under dark clouds, a flat-roofed tower overlooks the wide mouth of a black pit. In the center of the roof squats a pedestal. Nearby, a trapdoor lies open.

THRESNER, a steampunk-looking cyborg, lies on the roof, its metal body inert, eyes bulging from a mummified head lying in a puddle surrounded by broken glass. Its lips are sewn shut.

A doorway opens, hanging in the air.

Max exits first, pistol ready.

THRESNER: *(voice emanating from a hole in its chest)* Please....

WARLOCK: *(over his shoulder)* Clear.

Xax follows casually, then Clark, tentative.

Max goes to Thresner.

WARLOCK: Hello.

THRESNER: Please....

XAX: Never mind him. Where's the Jawbone?

Something glitters, poking slightly out from under Thresner. Max taps it free with his foot: a golden jawbone. He picks it up.

WARLOCK: *(to Thresner)* We need this.

THRESNER: Help me....

Xax takes the jawbone from Max.

XAX: *(to Thresner)* For us to get the Jack we want, you see, they need to use the False Jawbone to summon him. Preferably with some kinda extra desecration. That'll skew things just right.

A robed figure emerges from the open trapdoor: APRAXOS THE WATCHER. He looks back and forth between Xax, Max, Clark, and Thresner.

APRAXOS: I heard voices...!

WARLOCK: Those would have been ours.

APRAXOS: *(pointing)* That... doorway!

XAX: Let's say someone wanted to kill a child.

APRAXOS: Who are you? How dare you trespass upon my Tower?

XAX: And let's say this child is somewhere in the vicinity of the village of Corpsewater.

APRAXOS: *(taken aback)* Wh-what? How can it be that you ask these things?

XAX: Wouldn't the perfect guy for the job be that fucked-up child-eating oggerhogg, Zebdod?

Apraxos stares at him, not speaking. Xax smiles, nods, laughs.

XAX: It'd be kinda perfect, right?

Apraxos stares at him for a long moment. Cocks his head a fraction to one side.

APRAXOS: Indeed.

Master Summoner II: Interlude in the Vast Plain

The Vast Plain. Jack and Akaz are there.

AKAZ: Where the fuck's the van?
JACK: You're asking me?

Akaz shakes off in a wave spiraling down from head to tail, ears flapping loudly.

AKAZ: "Van."

The van appears, Beth at the wheel, Doomer in the ring mount firing the deafening machine gun on full automatic into the void.

Doomer screams in surprise. Stops shooting. His scream and the sound of the dozen shots he fired impossibly echo back and forth off the mathematically flat horizon and infinite sky.

Beth skids the van silently to a halt.

AKAZ: Where's Blood Eagle?

DOOMER: They got him!

AKAZ: Dead?

DOOMER: Looked to me like they made sure he wasn't.

JACK: So we're losing.

DOOMER: *(exuberant)* Naw, they're on the run! No thanks to you guys, tho.

AKAZ: Beg pardon?

DOOMER: The Elders of the Mountain, though, man, they're makin' total destroy on them Herax.

Jack and Beth's gazes meet. She nods in agreement with Doomer's account of things, eyebrows raised, clearly quite impressed by the events she'd witnessed.

DOOMER: Did you see the griffin?

JACK: Nope.

AKAZ: Nope.

BETH: *(up to Doomer)* You see that guy with the body of a bird and the head of an eight point buck?

DOOMER: Dude, totally, did you see him flip them boats over by the sail? He fended off a whole formation 'cause they couldn't get past his antlers.

BETH: Best was the Forest Elder sparrow-tree guys though.

DOOMER: And Doom Bear came back, he set some moth-erfuckers on *fire*. *(with a wink and thumbs-up)* Cool name that guy.

BETH: Oh, Jack, here.

Beth throws the Spine of God to Jack. It tumbles slowly through the air. He catches it. It rattles.

From nowhere OLDER ALECK appears. His hair and beard are long. Old, old scars crisscross half his face. Balanced on his head like a mortarboard is a foot-square focaccia.

OLDER ALECK: Hi.

AKAZ & DOOMER: *(together)* 'Sup, Fuckface?

OLDER ALECK: Hi, guys. *(to Doomer)* 'Sup, Billy?

DOOMER: The fuck is on your head?

OLDER ALECK: Haven't you heard? "Bread is hats now." It's anarchy.

Older Aleck takes the focaccia off of his head and throws it to Akaz, who gulps it entire out of the air.

AKAZ: Bleh. Too much rosemary.

OLDER ALECK: *(rolling his eyes)* Everybody's always "waah too much rosemary," what is wrong with you people.

AKAZ: It's cloying. Even worse than dill. Anyways, I figured you were behind all this shit.

DOOMER: You look older than I ever seen ya, buddy.

OLDER ALECK: *(he shrugs to both Akaz and Doomer)* Sorry.

JACK: Where the hell are we?

OLDER ALECK: This is the Vast Plain.

BETH: We kinda pieced together that part.

OLDER ALECK: Naw, I mean that's our actual nickname for it. This little corner of the multiverse is a wee facet of the Astral Plane, that touches just a handful of worlds. *(pointing to Jack)* Your Earth, *(to Beth and Doomer)* your guys's Earth, *(to Akaz)* the world of Kaios, *(gestures to himself)* the Archive of Thoth, etc. First things first though, Jack, I gotta thank you. We wouldn't be here if it weren't for you.

JACK: How do ya figure.

BETH: Who are you?

OLDER ALECK: *(bows to her)* Aleck. *(bows to Jack)* Aleck.

BETH: *(to Jack)* He looks like you.

OLDER ALECK: Correct. We're cognate, as are you and my lovely wife. So the basic backstory is this. I came here as a kid, voila—

Older Aleck draws a square window in space.

Through the window is a pool surrounded with boulders. A crowd of naked people sit around on the rocks. To one side stands the wall of a wooden building in need of paint, with a door in the middle, also in need of paint. Beside the pool sits Akaz, flanked by two people in robes or something.

AKAZ: *(in a loud whisper)* Fuck, dude, don't go opening portals between me and myself!

OLDER ALECK: Not a portal, just a window.

Beyond the window, the weatherbeaten door flies open. A teenager in jeans and a black t-shirt bursts through, blood crusted on his slashed and maimed face. He mumbles something and sprawls into the pool with a splash.

OLDER ALECK: Makes me wince every time I see this.
DOOMER: Gnarly, man. The making of Fuckface. *(to Jack)* You know that's my nickname for him, right? Not just 'cause his face is fucked, but dig, you'd never believe it but chicks went for those scars like crazy. *(to Beth)* No offense.
BETH: What the hell are you talking about?

Beyond the window, one of the robed people pulls the teenager out onto the edge of the pool.

AKAZ: All I'm saying is Other-Me over there had better not fuckin' notice us.
OLDER ALECK: It's only one-way, man, c'mon, I'm no scrub.
AKAZ: Still, fuck, close it, please.

Older Aleck closes the window to the pool.

JACK: Guys.
BETH: Fill us in.
OLDER ALECK: Sure, sure. I can do better than that.

Older Aleck opens another window, this one looking into a dark bedroom. A thirtysomething Aleck, already gray and scruffy, lies asleep beside a sleeping woman who looks like

Beth if she were Black. At the foot of their bed sits a shoul-der-bag.

Older Aleck leans in through the window, holds open the bag, shines a light in: there's a dead crow, a bone wrapped in beads, a few small electronic gadgets, a polished stone, a little plastic brontosaurus. He grabs the crow.

Older Aleck closes the window and hands the crow to Jack, who does not take it.

OLDER ALECK: Here, this is for you. Least I can do.

JACK: What is it.

OLDER ALECK: We can talk through it back in the real world. You'll see.

Jack accepts the Crow Terminal, holding it by the feet and turning it over to examine it. He sniffs it.

OLDER ALECK: So yeah, when I was a kid, I was in the up-coming final battle across the mountain, and I was kinda horrified by how things turned out.

BETH: Spoiler.

JACK: Bodes well.

OLDER ALECK: I spent my life trying to travel back in time and change it all, y'know, driven by guilt.

JACK: Great.

BETH: I'm guessing no dice?

OLDER ALECK: Easier said than done, changing the past, as it turns out. Actually, easy to say, not possible to do at all. If you actually make a difference in the past, you just split off a new parallel universe. Hell, you wanna take it a step further...

BETH: Not really.

OLDER ALECK: ...here's how the multiverse works: everything you imagine is 'real' in a sense, just like love is real or what have you—but under the right circumstances, you can *physically* travel somewhere previously only imaginary. That's how magic works: bending reality to the imagination. Anyway, I knew this "infinite worlds" theory in theory, but it was only from studying your life that I really understood the ethical implications.

JACK: The fuck—?

BETH: —you talking about?

OLDER ALECK: That's how I stopped feeling guilty for being unable to change the past. On the one hand, all possibilities are equally real; and on the other hand, we simply don't get to dictate results anyway. We can only proceed with our best effort. In effect, you taught me humility.

Jack and Beth look at each other.

BETH: *(to Jack)* Who is this fuckin' guy?

JACK: *(to Older Aleck)* Look, man, the messianic shit is bad enough from the Givers. Last thing I need is to get it from a fellow Earthling.

OLDER ALECK: It's not that extreme, man. You just do some cool stuff later in life. Some good choices, some bad, always doing your best to question what's right, though. That's the real thing that makes you a significant figure.

Jack stares at Older Aleck. Looks over at Beth to find her looking back at him.

JACK: That's... encouraging?
BETH: Or a con. *(to Doomer)* You know this guy?
DOOMER: Yeah, Fuckface here knows what he's talking about, he runs the Archive. He wrote books about you guys. He's got your files and everything.
JACK & BETH: "Files"?
OLDER ALECK: Stolen copies of your Reality Patrol files. But that's neither here nor there. Here's a document of immediate relevance, check it out:

Older Aleck opens another window to show Prof. Clark, in Elizabethan garb, at the wooden bar of an old stone-and-timber tavern. The otherwise-empty room is dimly lit by a couple of candles. Clark pulls out a flashlight and leans over the bar, reading an open notebook. He fishes an inch-thick typescript out of an inner jacket pocket, picks up the notebook and slides the typescript under it.

OLDER ALECK: This is Xax using Clark to create you, Jack. When my thirtysomething self wakes up upstairs, he—by which I mean I—am gonna take that *Guidebook* and shove it into your twelve-thirteen year old head. That is where you got your game world from. And thence created the world of Kaios.
BETH: That shit is totally circular and makes no sense.

JACK: Yeah. Where the hell'd the *Guidebook* come from?

Older Aleck closes the window.

OLDER ALECK: During the decades I spent tormenting myself over the Battle of Kaios, I tried writing it, on and off, never with much success. I'm just not at all focused or prolific as a writer. Over time I attained my position at the Archive, not due to any evident archival expertise but based on my facility with interdimensional travel, plus an admittedly enigmatic decision by Great Thoth. This gave me greater access to various records, artifacts, and portals to useful worlds. But never Kaios-X00023 itself. Access to your Earth gave me information about you, leading to my unfinished biography of your youth, and my partially-annotated volume of your Reality Patrol dossier, and numerous other fragments long and short. Finally, though, thanks in no small part to your inspiration, I was eventually able to set aside my guilt and resulting perfectionism, and simply finish a not-great-but-adequate draft of the *Guidebook* so we could have *something* to stick into your head.

JACK: What.

OLDER ALECK: I realized that no version of the *Guidebook*, or any particular action on anyone's part, is actually going to carry the day.

JACK: Then why even bother trying?

DOOMER: We get to kill fascists!

BETH: Yeah why is this even a question.

JACK: Fair enough.

OLDER ALECK: I've seen alternate timelines on alternate Isles of Kaios, where my wife Beth and I had several months to work with, and we made use of all them things in my bag. Dried out those gizmos with rice. The dictaphone was especially handy. But even so, I've ridden multiple timelines myself in person, and I've viewed dozens more through interdimensional windows, or indirectly through stolen Reality Patrol reports. And every one of these timelines has taken a starkly different course—but regardless of the *course*, startlingly similar *outcomes*. *Startlingly* similar.

JACK: Isn't that an ethical cop-out, then, to worry less because we're resigned to fate?

OLDER ALECK: I can't say. I've gone back and forth on that more times than you've drawn breath. But dude, there's only so much one person can do in a lifetime, even a superhero like you. That's reason enough for us not to worry, and just do good stuff as best we can.

BETH: The biggest fuckups always result from the biggest projects.

OLDER ALECK: Sure, on principle. And that's all the more reason not to worry, and just focus on stuff that's actually within your reach. But sometimes, if you find yourself surfing certain tides of history, big stuff comes within reach. And we've got allies in unexpected places.

JACK: That doesn't make it any more under your control.

OLDER ALECK: Exactly true. But I'm telling you, every Isle of Kaios I ever saw turned out the same way. Not identical sequences of events, different body count and whatnot, but not significant in light of the Second Breach, know what I mean.

JACK AND BETH: *(in unison)* Nnnope.

OLDER ALECK: Well, if you win, the Second Breach is pretty much guaranteed; and if you lose, it's pretty much guaranteed. So this whole battle is just rearranging deck chairs. We can't save the Isle of Kaios. On the contrary, the *point*—

He leans in close and pokes Jack gently in the chest.

OLDER ALECK: *(whispering)* —the *point* is to make sure Agent Xax gets left behind.

Jack stares at him while Beth stares at Jack.

JACK: You mean the Agent Xax who cut my eye out in Nevada.

Older Aleck holds his gaze and nods slightly.

AKAZ: In case, y'know, you needed motivation. So. Shall we?

JACK: Shall we what?

AKAZ: *(to Older Aleck)* Stay in touch.

OLDER ALECK: Hang on—

The Vast Plain vanishes.

Interlude in the City of the Watcher II

UNDER THE CIRCUS OF BURNT SKULLS

A windowless torchlit room, walled in crudely carved and fitted stone. BLOOD EAGLE lies chained to a table, covered in bloody gashes. APRAXOS bends over him, meticulously cutting with a wicked-looking scalpel. HERAX SPEARMEN surround them, weapons poised.

APRAXOS: Silly boy. Silly boy. Giving me all these magically-powered markings to deface.

BLOOD EAGLE: *(with effortless calm)* You, of all people, should know that your torture gives me power, Watcher of Filth.

APRAXOS: *(absently, focused on his work)* Be that as it may, this sigil-working gives me all the power I need to reinstate the Greater Binding. Throw all the little fireballs they want, your swarm of savages will no longer be able to join their magics together.

BLOOD EAGLE: We will still win.

APRAXOS: *(standing up straight)* That, little man, remains to be seen.

He punctuates the statement with a deft little stab of the scalpel into Blood Eagle's nose, like a kiss.

Battle of Melkhaios II

"In battle, there are not more than two methods of attack—the direct and the indirect; yet these two in combination give rise to an endless series of maneuvers."

—Sun Tzu V:10

Next thing I know, I'm playing cards underwater with an obese, formless shadow the size of a mountain. Ruins surround us. Although odd, this alone is not enough to constitute a nightmare. Such uneasy vibes emanate from the entity, though, as such things sometimes do in dreams, that I feel terror just being near it. The cards make it worse, because of the stakes we're playing for: a glowing golden marble sitting between us on the ruined flagstone floor, the materialization of my soul.

The mountainous thing puts down a hand of huge cards, fanning an underwater wave at me of sufficient strength to gently push me over backwards and send me skidding a

224 Andrew M. Reichart

few feet. I manage to hold onto my own cards. I right myself, swim-trudge back over, and situate myself at the thing's five face-up cards, now somehow the same size as my own:

Queen of Clubs
King of Clubs
Fool
Magus
Priestess

"Full house major," says Fat Man.

I look at my own cards: four Sevens and the Tower. I place them down over His cards, fanned with the opposite curve to form a fat vesica piscis. There's a momentary lull in my panic from the knowledge that four of a kind beats a full house, but in that lull I recall that a full house *major* beats four of a kind. The Tower indeed. Fat Man picks up my soul and looks at it.

"Yummy," He rumbles.

I wake in a cold sweat, cramped in the passenger seat of the van, clutching what seems to be a taxidermied crow. For a moment I think the light piercing into my eye is that of the aetheric Vast Plain, but no: it is morning in the Great Winding Pass. Beth sleeps beside me, slumped behind the wheel. Akaz sits on the hood facing forward again. I hear snoring, roll down my window and stick my head out to see Doomer asleep on the ground.

Everywhere around us, on the slopes and the road, lie mangled bodies, parts of bodies, and burnt-out hulls of Herax boats.

Akaz looks back at me over his shoulder. "'Morning," he says.

"What the fuck."

"We were in the Vast Plain for a while," he says. "Wake up your friends and let's get a move on. Reality's pretty frayed around the city; we're likely to lose a bunch of hours again before we get to the heart of things."

"What," I repeat.

"Timespace," he says. "Warping. Echoes of the upcoming reality storm. We're all probably gonna skip back or forth in time a little on our way in. Maybe more than once." He cocks his head up the pass. Its highest point seems not far, unless there's a higher rise hidden behind it. Either way, perhaps we'll catch a glimpse of the city below. "So, that-away," he says. "Pronto. The sooner we get going the less we have to lose."

As my daze fades, I notice the Spine of God on the dashboard. I leave it there.

I awaken Beth and Doomer, and we sit in the dust facing the front bumper, keeping our backs to as much of the carnage as possible, passing around a warm and cloying diet Red Bull someone must have bought by mistake. Akaz gives a little speech from his perch above us on the hood:

"Keep your eyes peeled for any of our cognates. That means my other self, Young Aleck, Old Aleck, or OtherBeth. Avoid them at all costs. We may bump into each other sooner or later, but the longer we can delay it, the better."

"How so," I ask.

"Seeing as how we don't trust your intentions one bit," adds Beth.

"Aww," says Doomer. He crumples the Red Bull can in his hand and chucks it downslope.

"Doomer!" says Beth, who has zero tolerance for litter-bugs.

"Who gives a shit," grumbles Doomer.

"How so," I repeat, to Akaz. "Aleck in the Vast Plain just told us it doesn't matter. It just splits off another reality."

"Nah," says Akaz, "That's bullshit. Even he doesn't believe that."

"What?" asks Beth. "Why would he even give us that whole spiel, then?"

"So you'll worry less, probably," says Akaz. "Take the pressure off. He's neurotic enough to assume you're as neurotic as he is, and just as subject to Hamlet Syndrome. Or maybe he just thinks if you're less worried about outcomes, you're more pliable and easier to manipulate. If he's the same old Aleck, it's probably conscious A and unconscious B, and he'd get really defensive if you called him on B, and then he'd get depressed."

"'That fuckin' guy,'" growls Beth.

We hunker down in the van, me in the middle, Akaz poised in his impossible verticality on the lurching hood as Beth drives us out of the battlefield. I offer again to drive and she again declines, to my relief. I wish I could just look down at my hands or whatever till we're through it, but I can't leave poor Beth to have to look at the carnage by her lonesome. So I stare more or less directly ahead down the road, helping her do so as well, we both trying to ignore the corpses and corpse parts—mostly humanoid, some quadruped or winged—splayed all around us in patches of darkened dust. Beth proceeds at a crawl, avoiding bodies, weapons, etc. as best she can, but they are everywhere. I wonder about the gore inevitably collecting on the underside of the van. I imagine it caked in inches of bloodmud, rotting, reeking. Doomer looks out through the windshield and passenger side window, seemingly unperturbed. The Spine of God clanks and rattles atop the dashboard.

Not soon enough, but soon, the corpses start tapering off and then stop. Beth steps on it and we're making decent time up the bumpy road. "Can you check if we're raising much dust?" I ask Doomer. "And keep an eye on the sky? We could be leaving a huge plume for all we know. Fucking homing beacon."

"I've got my eye on the dust." Beth glances in the rear view. "Not too bad, I think. But be a dear and check the sky for foes, wouldja?"

"Alley-oop." Doomer hauls himself up through the ring mount.

We drive on. Nothing assails us. That rise does indeed mark the highest point of the pass. Once we cross over it, the road winds its way down amid crags and scrub to disappear into a forest of autumn leaves, scraggly-looking evergreens, and tangled bare branches. A few miles distant lies a broad dark bay, a small city sprawling at its near edge, straddling the mouth of a narrow river. Between us and the city we see no flying ships anywhere. The river winds its way up to Mount Kaios and disappears into another limb of the forest. Across the bay, the sun hangs a handspan above the horizon.

"That's west," I say.

"Yeah, we've been heading basically westward this whole time," says Beth.

"It was just morning."

She ponders that, brows knit in consternation. "Fucking time warp."

"Creepy," I agree.

She rolls down her window and slows the van. "Hey Akaz, what's up with the time warp?" As if he's likely to offer any more clarity than he already has.

"No biggie," he says back over his shoulder. "It won't bite ya. We just don't wanna miss the party."

Beth rolls her window up and accelerates. We bounce down the winding pass. After jostling and twisting our way around a hip of Mount Kaios we see our army halted a mile or so below, where the scrub thickens into woods. The Giver column spans the pass, with Wilders of all forms gathered on the slopes around.

Looming over us, carved into the side of the mountain, a titanic stone face frowns out over the city and beyond. Beth and I stare at its immensity, speechless.

We arrive at our host to find the Giver-Tots still crowding the rear, hundreds of them sitting glumly in the dust. They lethargically crawl aside to make way for the van. The Givers part likewise, enthusiastically cheering our arrival, and soon General Larynx joins us in the midst of the column. We dismount. Bloody mud indeed crusts the van's undercarriage.

"I had assumed you and your van destroyed," says General Larynx, "as we found no trace."

"We're back. We're here, I mean. No sign of Blood Eagle?"

"Surely not," he says. "I will lead the Givers of Fire and Flame in a direct assault upon the Senate and Circus."

"*Circus?*" asks Beth.

"We definitely want the Circus," says Akaz with deathly seriousness.

"The Wilders, by contrast," continues General Larynx, "will enter the city from myriad directions, as is their way, under no one's leadership. Unless you wish to assert a different plan, for either of your armies, Cannibal-King."

"No need," says Akaz. "Yer plan's fine."

"Um," I tell him. "I'm gonna speak for my kingly self, thanks, and I'm gonna wanna look at some damn maps for starters."

"Let's just go," says Akaz. "These guys can handle themselves. Unless you're some kinda tactical genius that I don't know about."

I scowl at him. "I thought the whole point was for me to bring whatever unique outsider perspective I have to this situation."

"Nah," says Akaz. "The whole point was for you to gather these guys together and get them right here. From now on, we just need your guns and stuff. C'mon." Akaz turns to General Larynx. "You ready with the fire?"

"With great eagerness," says General Larynx.

"And you're in sync with Walking Bole?" asks Akaz.

"The Wilders are ecstatic," says General Larynx.

"What the fuck?" I say.

"You people talking about?" adds Beth.

"Cool," says Akaz, ignoring us. "Let's go." Akaz leaps onto the hood and then up to the roof of the van, stretches his neck skyward and lets loose a massive, echoing howl.

Wilders all around us respond with wolf-howls, and the Givers begin chanting, "Akaz, Great Akaz! Akaz, Great Akaz!" The entire army begins flowing downhill, into the woods.

"Wait," I ask Akaz, "we're attacking *now?!* That's absurd! The Herax will have the setting sun behind them!"

"Wait and see," he says.

A new chant rolls upslope to us, not quite discernable. And in the woods I start seeing many little flickers of yellow light—

—fire. Givers and Wilders shooting and spitting jets and gouts of flame into the dry leaves, needles, and branches of the forest. Starting a forest fire with us in the middle of it. And through it all chanting, over and over and over: "Akaz protects the faithful! Akaz protects the faithful! Akaz protects the faithful!"

Down toward Melkhaios marches our army of fireproof barbarians, increasingly wreathed in flame.

"Fuck," says Beth.

"So you're telling me we'll be safe driving into that," I say to Akaz, "because you grant us immunity to fire."

"All X hundred of us," says Beth.

"That's right," says Akaz. "Fire or heat or smoke or whatever. For the rest of the day at least. Guaranteed. Let's boogie." He hops down to the front of the van and resumes his giant hood ornament routine.

"You gotta be kiddin' me," says Beth.

As we watch, the fire thickens, consuming the twigs and limbs of every tree below us in a widening swath. Its roar intensifies and widens its voice to encompass the world before us.

"Goddamn fuckin' Herax weather-sorcerers," says Akaz, "cursing us with drought for years now—suck on this, suckers." Then, to Beth: "Let's go!"

With some apprehension we squeeze back into the front seat of the van, Beth still insistent on driving, Doomer claiming the middle this time. "You stand in the fire, buddy," he indicates the ring mount. I make a face at him and stand on the passenger seat. Heat radiates at me from the fire spreading across the land below us.

As we drive between our first pair of burning trees, I can't help but worry about how perfectly Akaz's immunity covers, say, gasoline and gunpowder. "Hey Akaz," I say to him, voice raised against the crackling roar of the forest fire.

"This is fuckin' glorious," he beams.

"You *sure* your fire immunity thing protects all our stuff?" I ask. "Like, even the gas tank of this van?"

"Huh?" he asks me absently over his shoulder. "Oh. Yeah, yeah, of course. Shut up, I'm trying to enjoy the fire."

Beth drives slowly down the rutted road. I brace myself in the ring mount against the van's bouncing. Givers march alongside us. Fire, all around us and overhead, blocks the view of anything but the nearby burning trees. A gentle baking heat emanates from all directions, causing us not the slightest sweat or discomfort. It feels exquisite. I crane to see the sky through any gap in the burning trees, worried that the Herax could sneak up on us—but, of course, the fire and smoke also conceal us from above. Before long the continuous roar becomes a hypnotic drone, the writhing walls and ceiling of fire seeming to blot out everything else, as though there is nothing for this world to do but burn.

We catch occasional glimpses of stone ruins scattered among the trees. These crumbling buildings of unremarkable design quickly increase in number, though the trees grow no sparser; soon we find ourselves in what was clearly once upon a time city block after city block, now entirely overgrown. Overgrowth now all transforming into ash.

Then the forest stops, and with it, the fire. Ahead in the distance looms a huge intact building like a small castle, its basic square shape offset by strangely curvilinear windows and crenelations. A broad street stretches forward into the heart of the city. To our left, a cobblestone road in ill repair skims between the edge of the burning forest and a slum of half-ruined buildings. I notice Akaz conferring with General Larynx. Soon the Givers start pouring down the road ahead, heading straight into the city. "Left," Akaz says over his shoulder at Beth, and points with his paw down the ruined road alongside the woods. We turn left and continue down the marginally less bumpy cobblestone road. A wall of forest fire towers on one side, half-ruined city on the other. Wilders of all description bound alongside us, through the slum or between the burning trees.

Stormclouds cover the sky over the bay, opaque to the setting sun, darkening all the land but for the firelight.

After several blocks, a spur of forest, unburning, reaches across the cobblestone road and into the city. We pass through it and upon emerging behold the bay stretched before us. Our road comes to an end, broken off by a cliff. The innumerable and chaotic Wilders swarm to our right, into the city, without hesitation. Dark miles of water stretch before us under the low, dark clouds to end in silhouettes of distant headlands.

"Coming through." Doomer squeezes past my legs to get out the passenger side door. "Mind if I take your bike?" he asks Beth, then without waiting for an answer circles around to the back of the van.

"Um," I hear Beth say, and I hear her door open.

A naked blue woman rises up from the bay, levitates over to us, and hovers in front of Akaz. Her three eyes glow yellow. She looks furious.

I duck down into the van. Beth and I sit there side by side, she frozen with her door open and one foot out, staring out through the windshield at the blue woman bickering with Akaz.

"What the?" Beth asks me.

"Beats me."

"Look at her face."

She looks like Beth, just... blue. "Whoa."

"Creepy," whispers Beth. We continue to stare, even as we hear sounds of Doomer extricating the motorcycle from the back of the van.

"You burn your own forest," says the floating blue woman to Akaz, her voice booming like ocean waves. "How ludicrously indicative."

"A., not my idea," says Akaz, "and B., fire's good for it now and then."

"Our children come to join you in your massacres," she says.

"Kaios?" asks Akaz, startled.

"Our son remains dead," says the woman. "Though you seem to be littering our cosmos with his cognates." She looks pointedly at me, sending a chill through my heart.

"Who then," asks Akaz, "the Nymphs?"

"The Merrows of the river," says the woman.

"Oh, right, them," says Akaz.

"The Nymphs hide in their shrines, praying for peace. The Merrows hide in the shallows of the river, awaiting their chance to spring forth and eat Herax flesh."

"Cool," says Akaz. "Thanks." Over his shoulder, to Beth, he says, "Let's move," indicating with his snout a side street into the slums.

Beth scans for other nearby side streets, gauging them I'm certain on the basis of width, intactness of cobblestones, presence of obstacles such as sinkholes and fallen walls. One second later comes the rattling roar of Doomer starting up Beth's motorcycle. "Shit," she manages to say in response, before a pummeling wall of wind hits us from bayward. The floating blue woman is shoved a few feet inland, and Beth's door slams on her calf. "OUCH!"

"Baby!" I pull her into my arms as she shoves herself in my direction, dragging her leg in through the doorway. The wind slams her door ringingly shut.

"Ow!" she says. "Ow! Ow!" She hauls her leg up, plants her heel on the bench seat and starts wrenching up the cuff of her jeans.

I feel a wash of relief: not what I'd expect from someone with a broken bone. I see an abraded shin. "Broken?" I ask anyway, my voice still edged with alarm despite my efforts to rein it in. The van rocks in the wind.

"Fibula cracked maybe," she says, her voice strained. She presses hard with her knuckles up and down either side of her shin, aborting muscle tension even as it arises in response to the trauma, as we do. This both helps establish clarity as to the precise nature of any actual damage and prevents secondary damage caused by tension. "Ow. Ow. Ow. I think just bruised."

"GUNS, PLEASE!" Akaz roars through the windshield at us.

Out over the bay, not very far at all, three bolts of lightning leap down from the sky, followed immediately by a deafening peal of thunder. A few seconds later they flash again, significantly closer, with another thunderclap; and this time they are close enough that we can see three robed wizards lit by lightning as it flashes down from the clouds directly through their bodies and into the bay. Where the bolts strike, three waterspouts arise from the choppy surface of the bay, quickly cycloning taller and wider until they rise higher than the edge of the cliff and begin reaching toward us.

Doomer zooms past on the motorcycle, shouting something that sounds like "Holy sheepshit!"

Akaz leaps after him. They vanish into a side street.

Beth stomps on the gas without even situating herself behind the wheel, awkwardly organizing her limbs into the space while steering us to a stop behind a solid-looking stone wall nearly as tall as the van. A tendril of waterspout slams against the far side of the wall and whips around at us. The edge of the cliff cuts it off, rendering it just wind thick with seawater. The open ring mount hums ominously in the gale and fat drops of seawater spatter in on my arm and face. I force myself up through the hatch, into seawind buffeting like a thing enraged. I swing around the M240, looking for flying sorcerers.

A massive tower of spinning water slams into the cliff and explodes over the burning forest, dousing a hundred yards inland. An acre of sudden steam hisses into the sky.

Then I see the blue woman, floating in the air a stone's throw from us, light beaming from her three eyes. She says one syllable, and the wind stops dead. She scolds the three sorcerers, clearly enraged: "I did not create our magical pedagogy in order that tyrants could train potent servants for themselves."

The radiance of her eyes lights the sorcerers up. Two of them are fish-faced blue-green men, with bulging eyes and noses like gill-slits. The third looks human. One of the fish-men snarls back at her: "We serve no one, River Witch, not even you. Our mastery is our own, to which we are entitled full freedom of action."

"Wrong," she says. "As you see, I have erased your wind."

The three flying wizards spread their hands, fingers clawing downward, arms shaking with tension. The bay recedes from the cliff, block after block of underwater city exposed to air and light. A couple hundred yards out, the water swells hugely, forming into a massive wave.

Akaz leaps into my mouth, knocking me backward and making me retch. Instantly I recover, though, and find myself aiming and firing the machine gun on full auto. Threads of fire stab through the sky and sweep gradually leftward, occasionally connecting with a levitating sorcerer, causing him to explode into chunks of various sizes and tumble, broiling and afire, into the bay. One, two, three. The tsunami settles.

The blue woman glares down at me, furious.

"Um," I say.

A familiar voice from the other direction hails, "Cannibal-King!"

I turn to see a Giver, hovering half a block away upon a flying raft, with maybe a dozen other rafts floating in formation behind him. It is Blood Eagle. He looks different. The scars spiraling across his body all look... fresh. Ugh.

"Trapdoor Spider has obtained for you the Circomangkus, and its Flying Rafts," says Blood Eagle, of which I understand only a very small portion. "Also the Token of Time Dilation."

"That Token is rightly under my guardianship," says the blue woman. "You are none of you to use it."

Akaz leaps out of my mouth and onto the hood of the van. "Go home, Oshta," he barks at her. "Wait this thing out, and quit trying to control it, you asshole. If this isn't your fight, you don't get to say how it goes."

"Nihilist!" says Oshta.

"Hey!" says Beth. "Nobody can dictate how someone else seeks liberation."

"Yeah," I add.

"Semantics!" says Oshta. She dives over the cliff and disappears into the waters of the bay.

The low stormclouds quickly clear away, revealing a sunset of magenta and slate gray, half a fat red sun shimmering on the horizon.

We catch our breath enough to determine that Beth's calf is fine, just bashed. We wrap it in an ace bandage and she kicks back half of a black market Vicodin with warm beer. We share the rest of the can.

The van fits nicely onto one of those flying rafts. Blood Eagle gives me an odd medallion to wear around my neck, its spherical pendant made of interlocking layers of golden metal. With it I find I can control the rafts simply by thinking—which, despite all the wonders of the past few days, blows my mind nonetheless. I experiment with turning empty rafts upright, rotating them along every axis, etc.; I cannot help but wish I'd had these to use against riot pigs and stormtroopers back home. Handy.

Blood Eagle also hands me a seashell strung on a blue-green thread. "This is the Token of which I and Oshta spoke," he says. "With it you can decelerate the passage of time, allowing you to act in the space of a moment as though full minutes had transpired. Though bear in mind it may kill you."

"Uh, pass," Beth says.

"I will use it, then, upon your command," says Blood Eagle, putting his bald head back through the string. "Or if I behold a tactical necessity. I should be able to use it at least twice without harm. More times than this, however, may stop even my elemental heart. Therefore I will act sparingly."

"Cool," I say, wracking my brains to remember this thing. Is it from the AD&D *Dungeon Master's Guide* (1979)? Did I make it up myself? ('Myself,' under the influence of this world.) Anyway the important point being: what exactly were the rules defining the risks of using it...? I see Beth looking sidelong at me, knowing that I'm debating whether or not I could subject myself to it after all. She shakes her head.

"Don't even," she says.

"Okay okay."

"I go to join my Givers," says Blood Eagle, and runs off.

We pass through several city blocks. I man the M240, skimming the van on its raft a few feet above street level. The other rafts trail behind, sometimes inhabited by Wilders in the mood for a ride. Hundreds of crows, sparrows, and golden eagles flit from rooftop to rooftop of the surrounding blocks; wolves and bears and humanoid Wilders lope along through the streets; deer and goat hooves clack on cobblestones. Echoes of the motorcycle's engine come to us now and then from any direction, Doomer apparently scouting randomly a block or two all around us.

Most buildings look like they've been built out of stacked and mortared rubble, fieldstone-style. No one in sight, though many buildings look inhabited. Empty lots from fallen buildings often lie cleared of rubble and planted with gardens. Occasionally, we pass an intact building that looks as though it was carved from a single piece of stone. I roughly recall some sorcerer-builders in Melkhaios, in my D&D game, using the *Stone Shape* spell—or was it Kaios himself? Allied stone spirits? All of these?

We don't see a soul. Has everyone fled? Or they're hiding? Or is this neighborhood just uninhabited? Doubtful, given the decoration and upkeep of buildings and gardens. Where are they?

We come to a wooded rise, right there in the middle of the city, a dozen or maybe twenty feet of earth plus trees. Akaz calls to me: "Hold up." He hops up from the hood to the roof, sits, and says with inscrutable earnestness: "Okay, so you and I need to cross this ridge together, on foot."

"Uh, why?"

"Complicated," he says. "Simply put, there's a curse on anyone who crosses it, but the magic is partly broken, and if you and I cross it we'll break it the rest of the way, which will let the rest of the Wilders move freely back and forth."

"Okay, what—" I start to say, but he cuts me off by leaping into my mouth. Still reeling, I find myself jumping down the side of the van to the raft, then another yard to the street. Beth honks the van's horn at me, but—dazed by Akaz's presence in my body and mind—I just keep walking. I hear her door open and slam and she runs up to me, limping heavily.

"The fuck you going?" she asks, then sees from the fire in my eye that I'm possessed by Akaz. "Oh."

"We're gonna walk up that ridge." I take hold of her hand.

It's steep, a little slippery with fallen leaves and needles, but exposed roots provide a gnarled stairway of irregularly-spaced steps. When we reach the top, we can see the ridge curving to right and left, and another, similar ridge directly ahead with an intact cobblestone road running parallel between them.

Akaz leaps down out of my mouth. "Well, welcome to the Spiral Mounds. Their magic was interesting while it lasted." He looks up at me. "Tell everyone the magic of the Mounds is broken, and they're all free to walk straight to the God-Dog."

"'Walk straight to the god dog,'" Beth and I repeat.

"Yeah." He runs off down the ridge.

Not knowing what else to do, I levitate the raft with the van over beside me and Beth. We get back in and I float us ahead in the direction the Wilders are flowing. No sign of Akaz. I get up on the roof with the megaphone and announce to the Wilders, "Uh, you can now 'walk straight to the god dog.' The magic of the Spiral Mounds is broken." They cheer wildly and race up the ridge, sprinting, loping, and flying. Was the magic of the Mounds another of the Watcher's binding spells? Did I truly have the power to dispel it?

Looks like there's a big building past the next mound. We float down the slope, across the road, up and then down the other mound. We're in a clearing surrounded by a curving ridge: the center of the Spiral Mounds, or one whorl thereof. In the middle teeters the single weirdest building I've ever seen: an ancient round tower of ivied stone, attached to a three-story balconied and gabled Victorian-ish mansion, shuffled with parts of a Gothic cathedral. The Wilders gather around it in the clearing, cavorting with joy. The sun vanishes behind the Mounds.

Wilders dance, play-fight, howl into the sky; crows flap among the trees, croaking; humanoids drum and smoke. Everyone shifts often from humanoid to wolf to crow, bear, deer. At the edge of the clearing, Wilders haphazardly pile bows and arrows.

Akaz reappears, running across the clearing to leap up to his spot on the hood of the van. His voice fills the air in the clearing. "Though the breaking of the Spiral Mounds means we can travel freely back and forth, it also undermines the magical defenses of the God-Dog and the Shrine of the Nubiles. So we must move now, attack! Yet, the Wild Folk still gather from woods far and wide, and we must defend the God-Dog. So: some of you fuckers stay here, and rotate out as others arrive. The rest of us: let's go light the Wargus-Fire!"

The assembled shapeshifters howl, roar, screech, and cheer into the night, and half of them scramble up the far mound. I float our raft along with their animal tide, wondering what the hell he meant by 'god dog' and 'shrine of the nubiles.' Continuing out of the clearing, we cross over three more wooded ridges, moonlight dappling through the leaves. Finally from the third crest we see some Herax: silhouettes of boats hovering far in the distance. I get on the megaphone: "They could be swarming low and stalking us... They could sneak up on us from any direction."

Then lifting the raft and our van high into the air, I survey the city. Its layout is eerily, entirely familiar. Somehow I feel sure of our path ahead: through a neighborhood of small stone buildings; across a broad plaza full of tents and booths; past a huge rectangular windowless monstrosity with sharp spires; then through a neighborhood of mansions to a weatherbeaten old stone arena. Though I've never before set eye on that far building I know what it is: the setting from the very first RPG I ran, age twelve, the gladiatorial combat of *Melee/Wizard*. Even then I felt the world-building impulse, and had to give the place more of an identity than just a hex-grid battle-map. My players joked mercilessly at the name "Circus of Bright Skills." We enjoyed playing out a few monster duels, but I'd hoped for a little more emotional engagement, a bit less frivolity. So at the opening of our second session I declared the place had been taken over by an evil sorcerer, who ate the souls of losing combatants, and who had renamed it the "Circus of Burnt Skulls," many of which hung from chains over the front gates. That did the trick, leaving my players taken aback by the horror. A couple of residual clown and lion tamer jokes were attempted, but without vigor. I had set the tone.

Anyway, this is that place. Herax ships swarm above it. Somehow I know it plays a key strategic role in controlling this city. What role exactly, though, I have no idea. I just... *want* it. I want my warriors to seize and hold it. Just because it could be a good fortress? Not against flying boats, ha ha. What is this weird intuition?

Speaking of fortresses, a few blocks beyond the Circus: a massive curtain wall with many towers. Behind it, various buildings, including three very large ones. A palace, a keep, and a temple? Each very different from one another and unlike anything I've ever seen, strange towers and domes and spires. I raise us up a little more, squinting through my binoculars past the curtain wall, when an unrelated thought crosses my mind. I duck gingerly down through the ring mount. "Uh, Beth?"

Our gazes meet, and I catch mine flicking back and forth between her two eyes. Her eyes flicker momentarily to my eyepatch, then back to my eye. Huh. "Hmm?" she asks.

"Do you have the emergency brake on?"

Her mouth tightens slightly. As we sit there frozen I hear the slow ratcheting of the handbrake being gently applied.

We look at each other, breathing. We both know the transmission was of course in Park; and I'm not tilting the raft. But. We also both know that the parking brake is nonetheless preferable at two hundred feet.

I lower us back down near the crest of the third wooded ridge, and we float down the far side, the whole train of rafts staying just a couple of feet above the ground. Among the sparse, shifting Wilder army we enter a neighborhood of small buildings rebuilt from rubble. Thick with vines, these stone walls crowd each other along narrow streets of bare dirt. Vegetable gardens fill every front yard.

Wilders in humanoid and quadruped form lope alongside the rafts. Birds fly from rooftop to raft to rooftop, often switching into humanoid or animal form while they alight. We see no townies. Are they hiding indoors, or have they fled?

We flow into a small plaza with two fountains, one filled in with a garden. The other has a bulky stone statue of a square-jawed ogre of a man, dressed in some kind of uptight military uniform, beneficently dripping water out of both hands. Across the plaza stands a ten foot wall of fitted rubble with a wooden catwalk atop it. A pair of square towers frame a wide archway, a courtyard visible through it.

Herax longboats rise up to hover over the wall and unleash a wave of javelins upon us. Several pierce a wolf near us, and it tumbles into the fountain of the fascist ogre statue.

I open fire with the M240 on the Herax longboats, kicking up splinters and killing Herax. Akaz jumps into my mouth, causing me to sway and fire a few rounds wildly into the air; at first simply bullets, then as Akaz's possession takes hold they become streams of fire that explode far overhead. I re-aim and punch big, fiery holes through hulls and decks, or blast Herax bodies apart. The ships quickly duck back behind the wall and I cease fire.

Then a horde of Herax spearmen burst through the wide gate. I open fire on them, filling the archway with explosions of fire and burning meat. But they keep coming, far faster than I can shoot, pouring into the plaza. I've never seen them on foot like this, so many shoulder to shoulder, polished black leather cuirasses and helmets glinting with moonlight, pale affectless faces chanting: "We come as one, we come as one." Why are all the cannibals fucking chanting all the time in this world.

The Wilders aren't: they dodge without a word between bristling spears. Crows and wolves and lithe humanoids dart in to peck an eye, gnash a throat, stab up under a breastplate with a stolen spear. A maelstrom of limbs and wings dashing in and out and around, unpredictable and incomprehensible even to the multi-aware Herax hive mind. Breathtaking to watch, but the fray is too tight for me to shoot without risking killing Wilders. What to do what to do.

I fly a couple of rafts over to the gate and slam them down across it like a portcullis, pinning and crushing a few Herax underneath and shutting the archway against any others.

Or, not quite: there remains a gap of several feet across the top. Herax start to clamber over. I slam another couple of rafts across the remaining space, crushing another couple Herax. I take a breath and assess. Wilders fly and dive and shapeshift with dizzying randomness, rending and goring the hundred Herax who remain in the plaza. The Herax spearmen do better than I could in their shoes: their hive mind enabling everyone to see through each other's eyes, they coordinate their movements like countless limbs of a single invisible body. But they can't accommodate the chaos of the Wilders.

As the massacre slowly proceeds, it's uncanny to see how unresponsive Herax are to wounding. Their identical expressionless faces remain unmoved even when cloven with an axe. For their part the Wilders seem hard to hit in the first place, hard to injure when hit, and it takes a while for me to be sure but their wounds close up even as I watch, leaving behind splashes of drying blood.

Herax longboats, some with smoldering holes, lift above the wall again and unload a single volley of javelins. I hurl hellfire at them again and they withdraw, or fall, behind the wall. Before long all the Herax in the plaza lie unmoving or mostly so, pouring their also-red blood into the dirt.

From the far side of the wall come flashes of firelight. I shove aside the rafts from the gate, ready to start shooting, but the archway beyond is filled with Givers. Out spill the sounds of Giver drums, greeting their King.

I fly us over the wall as the Wilders cross over and through. Beyond sprawls a vast plaza cluttered with booths and tents of all sizes. Here and there burn fallen boats and whatever they fell on. Wilders and Givers skirmish with Herax in shadows and alleys. The far side of the square ends at the foot of that massive, many-spired, window-less monstrosity. To either side, open space—a river! The blank stone behemoth of a building stands across the entire breadth of the river, massive stone pilings holding it up. The water looks to be only a hundred yards wide here, but at a dozen stories high that makes for a titanic building. All of it—pilings to spires, stone walkways bordering the river, even the entire plaza itself—looks to be fashioned out of one seamless piece of stone.

A squad of Herax spearmen holds a position on a walkway halfway across the river, poised, harpoons readied, lines coiled loosely in their free hands. Up from the water leap several somethings, I can't tell quite what; I think I see arms, and fins, and possibly tentacles. Harpooned or not, they each grab two Herax and disappear back into the river, the entire squad swept away in one stroke. I remember the words of the blue woman: *the Merrows hide in the shallows of the river, awaiting their chance to spring forth and eat Herax flesh.*

An explosion catches my eye. I turn to look and see another—an exploding wolf, in the midst of a formation of Herax spearmen. *What?* Two other wolves charge into the phalanx and explode, burning Herax body parts flying everywhere.

Throughout the bazaar I see clusters of Givers, faces and chests covered in dripping blood. At first I can't figure out what they're doing, some standing around, others huddled together crouching on the ground, bobbing up and down. Of course they are feasting on fallen Herax. I spot Blood Eagle, standing surrounded by his loyal company. He raises a long, broad, jagged glass blade, brings it down heavily twice in quick succession. Then he tosses the blade aside. It shatters on the pavement. He bends down, performs a quick series of wrenching movements. The Givers around him cheer. Blood Eagle holds up a still-writhing Herax. It's hard to tell quite what is wrong with his victim, but I could swear its back has been chopped open and its organs are flopping out. Then he flings the Herax aside, scans the nearby sky, and hurls a wave of roiling fire from his hands to engulf a flying long-boat, another, another, all three boats slowly tumbling to earth, trailing blazing sails, dropping burning Herax.

Hmm. I wonder just how deeply Blood Eagle is dining. That blast of fire was huge. He of all people couldn't possibly be eating souls? How many Givers have gone rogue? Dammit, as much as anything I want their vow for the tactical advantage of pooling their magic. But mid-feast is not exactly the best moment to try and sell a principle of abstention.

I do my best to muster that Power to Clear Men's Minds and project it through the megaphone. "Givers! Pledge to eat no souls, and be free of the Bindings!"

A handful shout, "We swear, Cannibal-King!"

But many more scoff. "Just release the bindings, if you are truly King!"

"I wouldn't even if I could, you self-absorbed assholes!" I say through the bullhorn.

"Coward!" some reply. "Idolater of individual life!"

Great.

Wide archways gape in the sides of the bleak spired building, broad streets running into it from three directions. Two of the three gates are flanked or blocked by burning Herax wrecks. I duck down into the cab and ask Beth: "Do you want the machine gun, or do you want the rafts?"

She leans up and kisses me. "I'll take the gun," she says. I kneel beside her and we embrace, kissing some more, the war outside momentarily vanishing in the intensity of our connection. I spit up Akaz into her mouth and she gags him down. "Fucking gross," she says, coughing. "Kissing cool, wolf cool, but both simultaneous, NOPE."

"Sorry," I say. "Duly noted." I kiss her cheek and pop up and out through the hatch. Circomigamagig in hand, I slide down the windshield and sit on the hood in Akaz's spot. I hear Beth ratchet the machine gun. I look up at her. "Don't shoot me," I say.

"You've got a Sovereign Shield," she says.

"No I don't," I say, "it comes with Akaz, and he's in you."

"Oh," she says, "right. Well what if we both had them?"

"Good question." Where's the Spine of God? Where's Blood Eagle? I spot him, shit, he's got it and the skull is covered with blood. He must be wielding it like a mace. Stole it when he handed me the Circomangkus and went off with the Token?

Simply by willing them to move, I fly the rafts down to where Givers and Wilders can climb on them, then speed each raft up beside a longboat, praying that as few of my warriors as possible get harpooned on the approach. The survivors leapingly disembark and unleash mayhem upon the Herax onboard. Mayhem adequate even with the rogue Givers' meager solitary flame jets. I fly rafts over to meet my survivors as they disembark from burning boats.

It dawns on me that the Herax arc of fire doesn't cover directly below. Why the hell are their air-boats shaped just like water-boats? They could be bristling with arrow slits around the bottom. I bring a raft up directly underneath a ship, elevating a pack of my warriors all the way up without one of them hit en route. Then, quick as I can without knocking them off, I whip the raft up alongside the deck. Weapons pierce a few Givers and Wilders as they come into view, but unharmed and wounded alike they board with fire and fang.

Then I try the opposite: flying a raft far overhead, then dropping it straight down toward the deck of a Herax boat. Anything flung from below simply strikes the underside of the raft. It lands with three spears sticking down like spindly legs. Their butts hit the deck first, trapping for a moment a clumsily fleeing slowpoke spearman. I force the raft downward, snapping two spear-hafts sideways, the third stabbing up through the raft and into a Giver. Dammit. I crush the slowpoke Herax under the raft.

A rattling sound from below, and I find myself unable to move, sitting cross-legged on the hood of the van, its raft swiftly lowering all the way down to the street.

Blood Eagle stands directly before me, Herax blood spattering his pale shoulders, swaths of red painting his entire face and chest. He shakes the rattling Spine of God at me, its skull-face face thick with congealing blood. "Circomangkus." He holds out his other hand.

Powerless, baffled, I find myself taking it off and handing it to him. He hangs the glittering chain and amulet over his hairless head. It dangles, clacking against the blood-covered Token of Time Dilation.

"Jack?" Beth can tell something fishy is happening.

Blood Eagle raises the sceptre at Beth, turns and walks away.

"Uh," I manage. I cannot move.

"Shi—" I hear from Beth, cut off presumably as she ducks back down into the van. Our raft starts to lift from the street just as the van's engine roars awake underneath me. Beth skids us off the raft as it is somewhere between one and two feet off the ground, front bumper smashing into the cobblestones and knocking me off. I land hard and Beth manages to brake before hitting me. Ow. I grab ahold of the bumper to pull myself to my feet and it comes off in my hand, clattering to the street as I fall on my ass. I can't help but laugh. Before I can make my way to my feet, Beth is there to help me up, Akaz-fire flashing in her eyes. Over her shoulder I see Blood Eagle soaring away on a raft. She says something.

"What?" I ask.

"Are you fucking okay?" She laughs.

Nothing really hurts, actually. "Yeah, actually," I say.

Akaz's voice rumbles up out of Beth's mouth, she meanwhile looking like she's belching repeatedly: "Weird Luck," he says. "Convenient, sometimes, but keep an eye out. Shit may get increasingly weird."

"Duly noted," I say.

We trade Akaz again, not kissing this time, and I take the machine gun. Smoke rises from the bazaar in a dozen black columns. Beth zigzags us toward the giant bleak building, steering us swiftly between dying bodies and burning wrecks, avoiding sites of active street combat. I open fire on an approaching Herax boat—aiming carefully for mast and spar, the deck swarming with shapeshifting Wilders. Its severed mast leans over slowly as the longboat sinks,

Wilders winging away laughing. The boat crushes its way through a couple of booths before skidding to a stop a hundred yards from us. Givers run up and burn it.

Beth speeds down an empty aisle, van rattling on the uneven surface. A clatter from behind—? I look back to see our crappy bicycles lying fallen in the intersection. Dammit, those pieces of shit have sentimental value. Aah fuck it. No, I should tell Beth. Wait, what the fuck is that in the distance, a Wilder fire-wizard in fire-breathing-wolf form? For a second I think it's Akaz, but Akaz is in me. I duck my head down into the van. "Did you see that?"

Beth looks up at me. "What."

I pop back up and it's gone. "Where are you?" I call after it into the shadows. I feel like I'm fuckin' losin' it. "Where are you?"

There it is—no, that's no Akaz, not even a wolf, though the size of one, and it runs not unlike a cartoon dog.... But that is no dog. For a body it has a jawless golden humanoid skull, its whole body like a great big Skull of Kaios. Four gnarled limbs end in wicked claws that clack upon the pavement. Has Blood Eagle induced the Skull to grow legs...?

Nope, says Akaz.

Whatever it is, I find myself filled with utter loathing for it, and unleash a salvo of Wargus-Fire bullets at it. To no avail: they fly back at me and the thing keeps running. I stand there stunned as Beth drives us down the lane. The Sovereign Shield granted to me by Akaz in my gullet sends the bullets back at this fucked-up golden skull-monster, and whatever sick sorta False Sovereign Shield it has sends them back to me, back and forth a dozen times a second, perfectly tracking our relative movements, until the thing runs around a corner and the intervening booths are blasted to burning smithereens.

What the fuck?

Next thing I know we're speeding in through the arch of the giant building. It's like a hangar of stone arches, the vast, dark ceiling vaulted overhead. Seems like the entire floor is just more bazaar. There's no one. Beth speeds down the widest aisle, crossing toward a far archway. I don't even know how we know where we're going, no wait, yes I do: if I focus on Akaz inside me, I can sense the telepathic intention he is shoving at her.

A number of Herax longboats enter through the opposite archway. I unload essential fire upon them, dropping them onto tents and booths. Fires start fast. The whoosh and crackle of burning wood, cloth, and inventory weaves a loud susurrus around us. Impossibly fast, it seems—oh, but there are also Givers all over the place, setting everything on fire. Splendid. So goddamn tired of trying to rein these guys in. Guys, some people might need some of this stuff? So maybe we could give it to them instead of burn it? But nah. This is a clusterfuck.

I fire at a cocky oncoming Herax ship and it crashes into our path, tumbling toward us through tents and booths, scattering blazing timbers and harpooneers. Beth veers out of its way and through a burning tent. I duck down as a tent-flap of burning canvas whips across the hatch. I shove it away. It catches on the fender and side mirror, trailing a banner of fire alongside us. Super.

We zoom out the other side of the enormous indoor bazaar. Scanning around us I see three-masted warships creeping around the building toward our right and left flanks, eerie Herax soldiers chanting: "We come as one! We come as one!" I curse the ring mount as it catches, again, again, annoying like a zipper that won't zip, but eventually I blast both ships out of the air. One of them, swarmed with crows, smashes into the side of a stone mansion.

Mansion? I look around. We're in some sort of posh district. Ahead, down a wide street, the evil Circus. Herax boats and ships swarm the air above it. Something else about that squatting stone pile gives me chills. The purr of a motorcycle engine breaks that grim reverie—here's Doomer, thank god. We make our way down the broad street toward the Circus of Burnt Skulls.

Down the middle of the street runs a row of stone columns, ten feet tall, supporting nothing. Crows caw and ravens croak on every gable and house corner. Echoes of Giver drums come rattling to us from all directions. Some sort of thrumming sound comes from the Circus. Halfway there, sculptures start to surmount the pillars: busts of tough-looking warrior-types. Champions from the damn Circus, I guess. That thrumming sound resolves into hundreds of Herax voices, circling above the arena, chanting incessantly: "We come as one! We come as one! We come as one!"

"I hate this place," I say aloud.

Not for long, says Akaz.

"You're optimistic."

If you say so. He snickers.

A plaza surrounds the Circus. Herax soldiers crowd the gates. Longboats and warships circle around overhead in multiple intricate interlocking patterns, effortless with their distributed hive-mind. The things these guys could accomplish if they weren't controlled by someone evil. Fuck that, the lives they could lead if they weren't controlled by *anyone*....

We roll into the plaza and idle. Around us gather dozens of drumming Givers and howling wolves, and then hundreds, then hundreds more. The Wilders have turned to wolves, all of them. Damned if I know what it means, but the gesture's eeriness gets to me. Glad I'm not fighting them.

May as well make the most of this. Wish we hadn't lost the damn microphone, the van's P.A. is louder than the megaphone. But the megaphone will have to do. I dig it up, and while I'm down there grab the kukri, tucking it into my belt. Beth and I look at each other for a long moment, surrounded by the rattle of cannibal drums, and kiss. Far too soon I force myself to pull away.

"Git 'em," she says, gently, as we say to our dog Akaz, or used to back on Earth, when encouraging him to, e.g., chase a stick. Funny, I feel Akaz within me stir in response, and he makes my body stand up through the hatch, quick as thinking.

I sound the megaphone siren for a few seconds and cut it. Then through it I holler simply: "Cannibal-King!"

All the Givers around pick it up immediately, chanting it over and over. The Wilders howl along in bone-chilling symphony.

The Herax stop cold, voices silent, boats all frozen in their ornate ballet. Then after a moment they all break into a new pattern, arching over us like a wave about to crest, uttering a new chant: "Goromath is Cannibal-King! Goromath is Cannibal-King!"

So I hit them with the M240, blasting masts off one by one from left to right with Akaz's perfect aim and mighty Wargus-Fire, dropping ten longboats into the plaza before the entire armada pulls away and resets back into its old formation far above the Circus. Givers and Wilders descend upon the smashed boats, setting them on fire, tearing apart everyone within.

A dozen nearby boats break off into a subformation, flying in low over the plaza to fling spears down at my warriors in the wrecks. I shoot a mast off at the base, dropping its longboat like a stone onto an already burning wreck. Crushing some of my own people. I try not to look, try not to think about it, tell myself reincarnation is real like Akaz says. Try not to think of the Herax, for that matter, and whatever goodness they might be capable of were it not for their awful masters, Goromath and Apraxos. No time to think about any of this, not with harpoons and javelins raining down. I keep firing. Another boat falls, and another, adding to the mayhem in the plaza. The subformation retreats, reuniting with the main group rotating over the Circus, but I don't stop. A burning longboat drops onto the boat below it, flipping it over by the mast. Herax bodies tumble to the arena floor. Then the sail tears free and both boats fall. The formation slowly disperses, retreats a bit, and reforms into a different pattern, higher up and harder to hit.

Where the hell is Blood Eagle? Couldn't his loyalists burn them all out of the sky with that geyser inferno cyclone? Even with most Givers gone Bad, his inner circle must still include dozens. The Herax start again with their tedious and creepy war-mantra, "We come as one! We come as one! We come as one!"

I'm sick of it. Through the megaphone I blurt, "Well, come on, then!"

They instantly stop. They continue circling over the Circus in their alternating rings, rigging creaking in the windy sky. Doomer revvs the engine of the Vincent.

The rifle's more magical, says Akaz in my head. *I think we can do more with it.*

A raft full of Givers and Wilders lands right behind us. They clear off in all directions, except for one Giver—Blood Eagle. He comes around to the passenger side window, and I drop down into the passenger seat.

"Well well," says Beth, "look who's back, baby."

"I will fly you on the raft," says Blood Eagle, "up closer to the Herax."

I realize there's no sign of the Spine of God. "Hey, where's the Skull?" I'm unable to hide my agitation.

"Back your vehicle onto the raft," he says to Beth.

I watch as she does so, without hesitation and without a word, feeling uncomfortable in my skin. She cranks the emergency brake, looks up as if coming out of a trance, looks at me, looks around startled. The raft rises up from the ground.

I feel the Akaz-fire flashing in my eye and find myself saying, "Be right back, baby." My rifle Victoria in hand, I stand up on the seat, leaning through the hatch. I clear my throat like I'm hawking phlegm and spit Wargus-Fire onto the barrel. Flames dance up and down its length. We rise, up, up, to the height of the bottom ring of the Herax formation. I lever a round into Victoria's chamber, take aim, squeeze the trigger, and magic fire erupts from her barrel. Recoil slams me against the inside edge of the hatch. "Oof!" A mast shatters into burning fragments and another boat falls into the Circus. I circle around and shoot down another. "Oof!"

Givers and Wilders stand on the other rafts, circling the Herax formation, taking turns to swoop in close and then away, never entering javelin-range for more than a moment. Givers burn sails. Wilders slay with bow and arrow. The Herax continually adjust their formation as ships are taken out of it, moving to restore symmetry.

Something strange below—that other fire-eyed wolf, sprinting toward Doomer and *leaping into his mouth*.... Doomer twitches his head like he's shaking off a punch, aims a pistol at a Herax boat, and shoots. Unmistakable Wargus-Fire blasts forth and punches out part of a long-boat's hull. It starts slowly sinking. "Yeah!" he hollers, and rides off.

"Another Akaz..." I say aloud.

Shush! says Akaz inside me. *Never mind that. Just make sure you steer the hell clear of them like I said.*

Giver drums echo cacophonously in the plaza. Without warning, hundreds of Givers and Wilder-wolves charge the front gate, crows and ravens flying over the wall. I wonder who the order came from, if anyone. Herax spears impale dozens. I can barely follow what's happening on the ground at the gate—explosions? How? My army starts pouring into the Circus. *Wait a minute, you schmucks, what more of a trap could there be than to run into a corral with no roof but a downpour of harpoons overhead?* I'm getting the megaphone when the raft starts sinking. *What the hell?* I look around and all the rafts are dropping smoothly to the ground, then unceremoniously discharging everyone aboard with a sharp tilt. We are allowed to drive off but not without a (in my opinion unfriendly) tilt-threat of our own. I can't see Blood Eagle anywhere. The rafts flash up out of sight, and there's a rending and cracking from above, followed by the sight of several Herax boats falling. The formation disperses again, slowly re-forming into something else.

By the time I have the megaphone, most of my little army, it seems, has made its way in through the gate or over the wall. I see the rafts, surrounded by cawing crows, soaring into the Circus laden with—trees? Looks like entire trees, just cut down. *But those rafts were just down here in the plaza....* A new chant arises among my warriors: "Wargus-Fire! Wargus-Fire!"

Get the hell in there, jackass, says Akaz in my head.

I sit down in the passenger seat. Beth and I look at each other. She knows what I'm thinking. "Still," I say, "what else are we going to do?"

She shrugs. "Shall we?"

I shrug. She drives the van up to the gate. Not a living Herax in sight. Beth makes our way in among the press of the crowd.

"I don't like this."

"I know, baby," says Beth. "Me neither. Looks like pretty much the textbook definition of a trap."

"Thank you." I then find myself saying, "Uh-oh," and popping up through the hatch, through no volition of my own. Akaz wants a direct view of the middle of the Circus: there's a massive blaze of light as a fire roars into life, entire pine trees piled upon burning Herax ships.

"Wargus-Fire!" chants my army. "Wargus-Fire!"

I feel Akaz's voice rumbling in my throat. I fling back my head and through me he roars: *The Fifth Sphere is mine once again! Can you feel it, Goromath? MINE! Prepare for your final defeat!*" And I find myself holding out my right hand—toward nothing in particular? No, here comes Blood Eagle, handing me both the Circomangkus and Token of Time Dilation, bowing, and backing obsequiously away.

"What gives?" I ask his retreating form.

He says nothing, and Akaz does not relinquish my body and will. With the Circomangkus I find myself setting all but one of the rafts swinging at random through the Herax formation, sowing constant distraction and tearing an occasional sail or line. I land the final raft before us. Beth looks at me. I'm able to shrug. She drives onto it and we rise up into the middle of the Herax formation. With my arms and aim, Akaz unleashes Victoria upon hulls and masts.

All too late I realize that at least ten longboats have gotten the idea to ram us, simultaneously, from ten different directions. Panicked, I activate the Token through fear and force of will. Everything seems to freeze around me. My heart races. Anxiety shivers my limbs. *What have I done?*

Yet somehow I sense that being possessed by Akaz will pro-tect me from its dangers.

Of course it will, doofus, says Akaz.

"Thanks," I say out loud. Looking around, I see the would-be ramming boats are marginally closer. Everything around me moves at a molasses crawl, while I move shakily but very fast, adrenaline spiking into my hands. One at a time I carefully shoot through the masts of the approach-ing longboats. Then I release the Token. Time resumes and the attacking boats all fall, fast, burning, most of them smashing into one another a few yards below us.

Pandemonium surrounds the conflagration: hundreds or perhaps thousands of Givers, Wilders, Digglies, and Deep Ones dance and revel around the titanic, leaping flames. From overhead rumbles the incessant chant: *We come as one! We come as one!* Herax boats dive and attack, and are welcomed with burning arrows and fireballs. Birds turn into attack-wolves and then into birds once more.

I want to go in the fire, says Akaz.

"What?"

But without an answer I can feel Akaz reach through me to command the Circomangkus, and I find us descending whether I like it or not. As soon as we land, a longboat dives at us, spears pouring down from it only to bounce back up into the deck or the bodies of their throwers. I shoot the boat down. It lands squarely on the crowd of revelers near the fire, smashing dozens of them. I would freeze in horror at this unintentional mass-murder of my allies, but Akaz simply takes control of my body and jumps it down from the van, Victoria in hand. Here's Doomer on the motorcycle.

"Hey," Akaz says to him through me, *"gimme the bike. You take the machine gun."*

"Rockin'!" he says.

"Beth," I find myself saying, *"let's go for a ride."*

"I don't have a Sovereign Shield," she says.

"Stick close," come the heedless words of Akaz from my mouth.

Akaz, you fucking asshole, if she gets hurt—

Relax, he says.

Beth gets on the bike and I hop on behind her. The driverless van lifts into the air. Doomer, evidently no longer possessed by that mysterious Other Akaz, uses the non-magical machine gun to shoot mundane holes through any Herax in range.

Beth drives us on her motorcycle through the crowd and up to the fire's edge. I hop off and clamber up into the conflagration. The intense heat feels delicious. I skip from burning timber to burning timber, joyously sure-footed with Akaz's superhuman agility, even as the limbs, trunks, and underlying shipwrecks shift perilously under my weight. Charred bodies grind between enormous embers. Wounded Herax, dragged from their boats overhead, tumble down and slam onto the fire. I see a pair of Wilders fling a Herax corpse onto the fire, its back hacked open like a rack of lamb, lungs flopping hideously. But the horror of mutilated corpses, burning underfoot and falling from above, cannot dim the ecstasy of the Wargus-Fire.

I find myself tossing Victoria to Beth: apparently Akaz has an idea. I grab ahold of the trunk of a small burning tree, wrench it out of the pile with Akaz's superhuman strength, and hurl it end over end to smash into a longboat. The boat flips, crew falling onto the fire, followed by tree and finally upside-down boat itself.

I hop down from the fire and get back on the motorcycle. Through me Akaz says, *"That should give the motherfuckers some strategic data to analyze,"* whatever the hell that means. *"Oh wait,"* he adds, looking up with my one eye at a large, ornate Herax ship, flying away toward the Herax Zone. *"That ship!"* Akaz makes my hand whack Beth on the shoulder and point past her cheek. *"Follow that ship! Go! Go!"*

With uncharacteristic obedience that I can only infer as more Akaz mind-control, Beth revvs the motorcycle and weaves us swiftly through the openings in the crowd, cutting around the edge and heading across the Circus to the far gate. The engine echoes thunderously in the tunnel. Then we're out among some truly picturesque ruins, haunting in the silver moonlight, me taking aim with Victoria and firing at the mast of the fancy ship. Wargus-Fire erupts from the barrel, the bike shudders from the recoil but Beth manages not to dump us. Something magical is protecting that ship, because instead of the mainmast exploding into burning fragments, sparks dance up and down it. I lever the rifle to shoot again, but though its mast seems physically intact, the ship swiftly glides to the ground, hull cracking, plowing up cobblestones, coming to rest on its side against a ruined wall. Beth pulls up close to it and we dismount. Dead and dying Herax lie scattered on the wreck and in its wake.

Up from the broken ship floats a robed and masked figure whom I know to be Minister Apraxos. I take aim at his center of mass, even knowing he has a Sovereign Shield.

"Ah, it's our Earth-boy!" he says, meaning me I assume, but he seems to be looking past me.

"Cannibal-King!" says some grubby teenage metalhead kid, suddenly at my elbow. *What the--?* I struggle to maintain my aim.

"I'm busy," I tell him.

"I need to talk to you!" he says. *What the hell? Who is this kid?* Holy shit, half his face is scarred. This is that kid I saw in the Vast Plain. This is teenage Aleck.

"Looks like you have the same dog we do," says Beth, in a bit of a daze.

I look. Back behind Young Aleck is that Other Akaz. *Oh no no no,* says Akaz in my head. My eye meets those of the Other Akaz, and in my head I can hear him think, *Fuck, fuck fuck fuck.*

"People are murdering each other in there!" says Young Aleck, pointing back at the Circus. "Your revolution is going genocidal!"

"Our dog's inside him right now," Beth says, dreamily. "Want to meet him?"

"Uh, don't do that," says the Other Akaz, backing away.

Akaz's jaws burst forth from my mouth, snarling, "What the hell are you doing here?"

"Oh, shit," says the Other Akaz. "What are *you* doing here?"

"You aren't supposed to be here yet!" says Akaz with his own mouth, his snout still sticking out between my jaws. "Get out of here!" I gag on the taste of his stinky, ashy face-fur.

Apraxos soars away. Beth fires after him. I swallow Akaz's face and try to regain my aim but the wizard's gone from view.

Oh no, says Akaz, *goddamn it, go get him!*

Now Young Aleck is grabbing at me. "Get away from me, kid!"

"You have to stop those maniacs in the Circus! They're eating people!"

"Oh, really?" I'm genuinely stunned that he could think this is news to me, or that he is helping the situation in any way.

"Yeah," full of himself, dripping with his own sarcasm, "you're the Cannibal-King, aren't you? What do you expect?"

Again, mind blown at the cluelessness of this kid. "Dammit! I made every goddamn one of them vow not to do that!" I stop short of adding a *Golly gee-whilikers!* He picks up on none of it. Chrissakes.

The weirdness of this circumstance apparently not yet being maxed out, however, up ride two more random-ass people on our fallen and feared-to-be-lost-forever Schwinn, a woman who looks uncannily like Beth except Black standing on the pedals, and precariously balanced on the seat a white-haired scar-faced dude holy shit *another* Aleck, maybe in his thirties. Good grief.

"Aleck," the Beth-looking woman says to the kid, "come on. This is much too risky."

"No no no," says the Other Akaz, continuing to backpedal, raising his voice as he gets further away. "This is bad! Get the hell out of here you jackasses, *now!*"

I stand staring, dazed, while Akaz within me has a panic attack.

An amplified voice booms: "Freeze! Reality Patrol!" Soldiers in black armor with silvery rifles appear all around us. Some of them mutter technical gibberish back and forth, and then one of them shrieks:

"Oh my God! They all have Weird Luck!"

"Hold your fire!" booms that amplified voice. Then there's a burst of static, and "—fire!"

Beams of light flash in all directions. The couple perched on our bicycle fall over, shouting. The Other Akaz, now a good distance down the block, screams something that I could swear sounds like "TRAIN WRECK!"

Doors and windows up and down the street fly open, each revealing a different scene: rooms and streets, rivers and mountains, bustling cities and storm-tossed oceans.

What the ever-lovin'—

—the Other Akaz flies through the air, from fifty yards away, and straight into my mouth. The impact knocks me flat and I skid painfully on my back across broken cobblestones. Blankness, then light exploding in jagged patterns in every direction, within, without, back and forward in time: fire, so much Wargus-Fire. I have no idea how Akaz was split in two, but he has reunited now, reunited in the kiln of my being, reunited as fire.

I take a deep breath and vomit a huge gout of flame across a full third of the Reality Patrolmen present, one two three four guys blazing afire, synthetic uniforms and gear melting to their burning flesh, their screams a quartet of distortion and static. As my fiery breath proceeds from right to left, from man to man, so too do I lean leftwards with the same movement, grabbing Beth in my arms as the stroke of fire peters out, bearing us both down to the cobblestone road, she landing with a thump, me inadvertently jamming the hilt of the kukri hard into my floating ribs. Ow. I cover as much of her body with my own as possible.

Beams of light flash crisscrossing over us, some maybe hitting me and bouncing off, I can't tell. From the ground I see the fallen thirtysomething Aleck, unconscious or dead, on top of his poor struggling wife and intertwined with our Schwinn. Right beside them, a little doorway opens up in space, through which I can see three white men sitting in a little white room, two in sinister black suits, one dressed I could swear like a character in a community theater Shakespeare play.

They jump to their feet and grab for Aleck's dazedly stirring body. Aleck's Beth, though, has extricated herself, and with the rage of the nearly-widowed she kicks one suit square in the side of the head, knocking him to the cobblestones.

As he falls I recognize him as my torturer, Agent Xax. *That* I did not expect.

Before he even lands, her other foot has come up heel-first toward the chin of the other suit, to be barely deflected and dodged. Not losing an iota of momentum, she launches off of his block, fulcruming her body around to launch a fist squarely into the face of old Polonius, dropping him cold. But Xax zaps up at her with something, and she falls, limp. He hops to his feet and angrily adjusts his tie. Then just like that they've dragged Aleck, his ass-kicking spouse, and our goddamn Schwinn through their doorway to who-knows-where and shut it.

Weird. And not good. I want our goddamn bicycle back.

Then a split second later, gunfire: Beth under me, our limbs tangled with each other and with Victoria the rifle, shooting her pistol at Reality Patrolmen; then from over-

head, manning the M240 on single fire, Doomer picking off
Patrolmen as well. In my mind I plead with Akaz for advice.
Nothing. He's there, but he seems dazed, stunned, catatonic. I
stay put, covering Beth with my body as best as I can manage
while trying not to block her view or impede her gun-arm.
Glancing to my right I see those four burned men on fire and
motionless. To my left, men are shooting their pale light-
beams up at Doomer and the van, or over at me and Beth.
My Sovereign Shield must work, then—yes, some of the men
stand there unmoving. Some of them fall. Fewer and fewer
shoot until, before I know it, none remain standing.

With the Circomangkus I bring the raft with Doomer
and the van to rest on the half-plowed cobblestone street
nearby. I look around but see no sign of that teenaged pest,
Young Aleck. Beth and I sit up and survey the surrounding
ruins. Through every doorway and window still standing,
up and down the block, lies a different scene: a daytime
forest, the crowd of a rock show, the immediately-recogniz-
able pre-Giuliani Times Square, and a hundred other places. Portals flicker open and shut of their own accord.

"One of these must be a way home," says Beth.

"My thoughts exactly." I look around desperately for it.

There's a crow on the handlebars of Beth's motorcycle. It
spreads its wings and flaps them, demanding our attention.
In Older Aleck's voice, it says: "So I think now's when you go
to the Herax Zone and take over."

"No," says Beth.

"I'm not taking anything over!"

"We quibble over terms," says Older Aleck through the
Crow Terminal. "Point is now you kill Apraxos to liberate

the gods, and kill Goromath to make the requisite power vacuum for Xax. Without them dead, though, all this is for nothing."

I understand little to none of this, and though I might agree eventually if I did understand it, when it comes to anyone giving me orders to kill I default to a starting position of, "No way." Before I can extrapolate beyond this, though, that golden skull-monster gallops past us, cackling eerily, and skids through a doorway out of this world. The door slams shut after it.

"What the—" says Beth.

"Don't ask," says the Crow Terminal.

Cannibal-King IV

We fly low. The Crow Terminal perches on the hood, leading the way. Beth and I hold hands in the front seat, me behind the wheel 'cause keeping my left hand on it helps me steer the raft. The Circomangkus only needs mental command, but I sometimes find myself twisting the steering wheel a little bit, like the unconscious body english of someone playing a video or pinball game. Doomer stands in the ring mount keeping watch with Akaz inside him. I'm nervous to be without a Sovereign Shield, but frankly relieved not to have that hound in my head; although Akaz is awake and talking now, he's clearly frazzled and I find his anxiety contagious. Doomer though doesn't give a fuck.

Beth and I huddle together against the chaos outside. Doors and windows fly open and shut to reveal fragments of any world anywhere. Every block has a building on fire. Screams and roars abound. Beings of all description fly in and out of gates, and I find myself rising unintentionally higher to get away from it all. Wilders fly alongside us in a swarm of birds, keeping their own distance from the cosmic havoc below. Others in myriad beast-forms crowd the remaining rafts arrayed around us, perched, squatting, or standing. I force myself to descend close enough to keep an eye on what's actually going on in the street. Dozens of Wilders still rampage through the madness, constantly metamorphosing back and forth from humanoid to any number of animals. Occasionally we pass over squads of Herax spearmen beset by Wilders—the Herax moving with uncanny, inhuman synchronized precision, clearly connected to one another by perfect telepathy like limbs of one body, but still unable to cope with the unpredictability of the earthbound Wilders' mammalian chaos. Wilders of the air look down with interest and often dive down to join in, others flying up to take their places. Doomer aims the MG over the side of the raft and shoots a few rounds now and then.

"Look," says Beth, pointing as an elk leaps into the air as some kind of crested eagle, lands on a raft, changes to man-shape and stays that way. Beside him a raven soars up and turns into a goat. A sparrow lands on our windshield wiper and remains a sparrow, flicking its gaze back and forth from us to the ground.

Another crow lands on our hood, switches to seven-foot bark-colored green-haired manlike form as he drops over the side of the van. He lands sure-footed on the very edge of the raft and stands there, indifferent to the precariousness of his position, leaning over to talk through my window.

"Greetings," he says. "I'm the Cook."

"Uh," says Beth.

I say, "Hi."

"Is Akaz here?"

"He's in him," I say, indicating Doomer.

"Ah," says the Cook. "Infinite thanks, my Lord, for bringing us this salvation." He gives me a little nod and stands up straight. Over the roof of the van he says, "Hoy, Akaz?"

Doomer's voice comes, "Yeah?"

"Our destination is the Herax Zone?"

"Fuck yeah," says Doomer.

The Cook howls like a wolf, so loud and languid it chills our bones despite our love of canine creatures. Then he ducks back down to peek in our window. "My Lord, you're aware the Bad Givers are eating everyone in sight? Souls and all."

"Yeah."

"Fucking assholes," says Beth.

"Shall we begin killing them?" asks the Cook.

"No!" says Akaz, through Doomer. "Not until the last Herax is dead!"

The Cook pops his head up, presumably to lock eyes with Doomer. Then he ducks back down and looks at me. "I revere Akaz, but am sworn to you."

"Um," I say. I look at Beth.

"What's Blood Eagle doing to rein 'em in?" she asks the Cook.

"Nothing. To the contrary, he has been telling all who will listen that you have repealed your commandment against soul-eating for the remainder of the battle."

"Fuck." I clench my jaws and grip the steering wheel. "Have you seen him recently?"

"He is below." The Cook points straight down.

"'Scuse me." I start to open the door. He sidesteps toward the front wheel so I don't knock him off the edge of the raft. I lean out from my seat to see the roofs passing fifty feet below, glimpsing down into streets and alleyways. Some sort of bat-winged crab-man, clutching a struggling Herax in its many claws, flies into a portal and vanishes. Several Givers huddle over a partly-eaten body, staring up at us as we pass over. Around the corner from them, a screaming woman bursts out of a doorway at a full run; a pair of Givers dive out of the building after her, grab her, drag her screaming and flailing back inside. "Hey!" I lower us quickly into their street. On our way down we pass by a window that looks like it opens into a blast furnace, and even with Akaz's protection the heat radiating from it feels uncomfortable. For a sec I think the interior of the building is on fire, but it's just a portal to a burning world.

"Jack, where are you going?" asks Beth.

Akaz's voice, bursting forth from Doomer's mouth, demands, "What the fuck are you doing? We have sorcerers to kill!"

I ignore them both and land us. "C'mon." I grab Victoria and disembark.

"I like it a lot better fifty feet up," Beth says, mad, sliding out after me.

I head toward the doorway that screaming runner got dragged into. Smeared trails of blood lead up to it from all directions. Within come the sounds of pleading, and screams, and ravenous devourment. "Givers! This is your King!" As I arrive the door slams shut of its own accord, flies open again to reveal dense jungle dimly lit by daylight filtering through canopy. From another direction a swarm of those shrieking bat-winged crab-things flies past, uncomfortably close overhead. They ignore us.

"Jack!" Beth catches up to me. "Let's get the fuck out of the street!"

"Yeah!" says Akaz/Doomer in assent from the van.

I look up and down the block. An upper-story window explodes outward, showering the street with what looks like a truckload of half-rotting food. From a doorway up at the next corner several green, thorny tentacles the size of tree trunks slither out and start creepily feeling the surfaces of flagstones and buildings. Into another doorway I see several Givers hurriedly dragging bodies in various degrees of completeness, some still moving. One especially disturbing carcass has its back splayed open, the lungs sticking out like bloody water wings. I raise my voice. "I bind you to the letter and spirit of your oath!" A couple of them glance at me indifferently. I spot Blood Eagle overseeing them.

I run up, Beth close behind. "Dude!" she says in understandable exasperation. Blood Eagle stands in the doorway, at the nexus of a bouquet of smears of blood.

"Blood Eagle! The fuck you doing?"

"Ah!" he greets me with uncharacteristic warmth. "Holding the door, as you see."

I gesture at the blood on the cobblestones, then at the darkness through the doorway. From inside come the sounds of vigorous raw cannibalism.

"Looks like you're collecting civilians for dinner," says Beth.

"Souls and all, for all we know," I add.

Blood Eagle laughs, once, an eerie and mirthless bark. "What the Givers of Fire and Flame choose to do is their own affair, each to his own preference. Now that the Herax are broken, and the Givers no longer need the Lesser or Greater Bindings to be lifted, I imagine many may grant themselves broad freedoms. And the Bindings will evaporate altogether and forevermore soon enough."

"How so." As much as I hate my absurd social position in this horrific world, as much as I supposedly hate hierarchy itself, I find myself seething at his insubordination.

"Apraxos will die," says Blood Eagle. "By your hand, presumably, no?"

That stings a bit. Then again, I could spite him and not kill Apraxos. Hell, Blood Eagle might be worse than Apraxos after all. I look at him. No, fuck that 'lesser of two evils' bullshit. They both die.

"And these guys aren't acting under your guidance?" asks Beth, on a whole other train of thought. "You didn't happen to point out to them that they don't need him anymore?"

Blood Eagle shrugs. "I merely hold this doorway open against the Storm of All Worlds." He points a forefinger to his temple. "The Skull of Kaios you so kindly granted me enables me to readily do so." He twists his spine and neck in a helical motion that would come across as funky on Earth.

"He has the fucking Spine of God stuck in his head and back."

"That's pretty much what that is," says Beth, "yeah."

I stare into one of Blood Eagle's eyes, trying to invoke the Power to Clear Men's Minds. "I don't suppose you'll give it back."

He feigns a flat smirk and gives a little shake of the head. "I have need of it still. In the Herax Zone."

Akaz lopes up, followed by a jogging, panting Doomer. A couple of crows land, hopping, behind them.

"'Sgoin' on," says Doomer.

"We gotta get to the Herax Zone," says Akaz. "Like now, before Apraxos fuckin' pulls something."

"Indeed," says Blood Eagle. He turns back to me. "Perhaps you'd offer me the convenience of the Circomangkus and your rafts?"

"Trade for the Skull?"

He does that little fake smile head shake thing again. It's unnerving in its false and forced affect, especially in his blood-covered face.

I level Victoria at him and lever her action. He taps the side of his head again. "The Skull grants the Sovereign Shield," he says.

Beth immediately shoves down Victoria's barrel.

"Fuck." I keep my finger away from the trigger.

Blood Eagle does a far more unnerving full-bodied gesture involving a quick roll of the spine while clutching at the air, followed by a double-throwing motion. I can see the blood magic energy flow up from the carnage, through Blood Eagle's body, and through the air at me. Invisible forces yank at the Circomangkus and Token; the Token's thread breaks, and it flies through the air into Blood Eagle's hand. He puts the little blue-green wafer in his mouth and vanishes in time. In the next instant our van is gone too, and the Circomangkus, and the rafts, and so are the sounds from within the building except for a few moans.

The door slams, reopens to allow those huge, spiky tentacles to emerge and grab for us. We run. The tentacles grow and grow, continuing to follow us for a terrifying distance down the street as we pass portals to beach sunsets, urban riots, arctic tundra blasting icy air at us, undersea scenes with water held inexplicably in cross-section in the doorway. Finally after a block and a half the tentacles run out of length or give up, and we find ourselves in a flagstone courtyard overlooking the river, facing the tall, ominous curtain wall surrounding the Herax Zone. We approach the river's edge and lean against the carven stone balustrade. Dark waters flow beneath us, rustling and chirping peacefully.

I count the towers in the fortress wall. Thirteen. Above each one hovers a translucent white sphere containing a human-shaped being made of flickering fire. To our right, centered in the long wall, a low but massive keep straddles the river. The river splits into eleven guarded gateways, every dram of water within the banks of River Oshta that flows through the city to the bay having thereby traveled between bars forged by the Herax. Crenelations atop the river keep bristle with Herax manning ballistae and bolt throwers. Five towers span the river, each warding the river-gateway to either side of it, each ornamented with a ten-foot floating sphere hovering above, incandescent with its imprisoned fire-spirit.

Also glowing, somewhere behind the fortress, some-where in the heart of the Herax Zone, is something huge and afire with the flying rafts swarming above it. There is not a Herax ship or boat to be seen over their walled private city, or anywhere else. I spot our van on one of the rafts.

I look to Beth, then Doomer, down at the two crows, and finally at Akaz. Turning back to Beth I say softly, "What the fuck we do?"

"This one's easy," says Akaz. "Everyone's just on clean-up at this point. This battle's over. But *you* gotta make sure fucking *Apraxos* doesn't escape to fucking Argentina or whatever."

"*This battle's over,*" says Beth, gesturing at the river fortress with her glock.

"Yeah watch," says Akaz, jumping into my mouth, levering Victoria, and shooting a tongue of fire from the rifle through the central ice sphere and the fire-spirit within it. "Now that we've reclaimed the Circus," he says through me, "and regained the power of the Fifth Sphere, a little Wargus-Fire is enough to crack that magic ice. Dig."

A fireball explodes inside the sphere. A dot of light, piercingly bright like the sun, slides leftward across the sphere?—no, the sphere is slowly rotating, the spirit inside pressing its fiery hands against the interior and turning it sideways. The dot reveals itself to be a bullet hole spitting fire, with a matching jet from the exit-hole opposite it; and the fire-spirit within, supercharged with Wargus-Fire, blasts through those quickly widening holes to incinerate the Herax guards and weapons atop the wall to either side of it. The jets of fire pour ever more hotly from the hands of the creature as it grows nearer its liberation, bathing the ice spheres on its right and left and melting holes in them as well. The centermost sphere gone forever, its blazing occupant descends abruptly into the tower directly beneath it. Every window and arrow-slit explodes with light and fire.

The fire-spirits to either side melt the rest of their way out of their spheres, exiting in a movement somewhere between clambering and flowing. They burn away the rest of the soldiers atop the river keep, and melt holes in the outermost pair of spheres. Then they descend into their respective towers, immolating them. The final pair of fire-spirits melt their way out and descend, completing the five-tower inferno. The walls of the keep crumble into the river, crushing the enchanted river-dominating gates; and the waters rush through, tumbling aside the rubble.

"Whoa," says Beth.

Akaz leaps out of my mouth, dropping me to my knees.

Beth crouches, arm around me. "Baby, you ok?"

"Just fuckin' exhausted," I say.

She kisses my temple.

Akaz stands watching intently downriver toward the bay. The riverwater looks troubled. After a moment I realize something is storming its way toward us through the water. Twenty yards away, Oshta bursts up out of the river and hovers over its surface. All three of her eyes shine bright white. She floats up to face Akaz, levitating above the now-rushing river. He stands on the balconied stone verge at the river's edge. They stare at one another.

After a time, Akaz says, "You're welcome."

"This did not need to happen this way."

"Fuck you!" says Akaz. "You'll get the rest of your power back when we kill Apraxos, meanwhile enjoy the liberation of your river source. Now get the fuck away from those of us who are actually doing shit!"

"You dare claim I do no work?" says Oshta. "I, who keep the last vestiges of compassion alive in this world? If my sphere cracks, all love is lost. I grant no thanks to you, not one iota, for destroying love and the capacity for love; and all the less for your pretense of doing so for my benefit."

"Then go tend your precious little sphere," says Akaz, "never mind about being able to set foot outside it for the first time in four hundred years. Go and contemplate to your heart's content the wonders of the Herax capacity for love or whatever."

She closes her blazing eyes, bows her head, and floats away over the river. From above the burning fortress, silhouetted against the sky, the raft with our van on it angles between two columns of smoke. It flies down and lands in the courtyard near us.

Akaz and the two crows—the Cook, and Older Aleck the Crow Terminal—immediately arrange themselves on the hood. Doomer jogs up and climbs aboard. "C'mon!" Akaz barks at us. Beth and I look at each other.

"May as well," she says.

"So long as Blood Eagle doesn't drop us from a height," I say.

"He wants the guns!" says Akaz. "And he needs gunners. He doesn't know how the fuck to shoot. He's not dropping any of you. C'mon!"

"How do you know this?" I ask.

With his paw, in an oddly human gesture, he points back and forth, back and forth, from his own head to the direction of the big glowing fire in the Herax Zone. "Connected. C'mon!"

We get on board, Beth taking the wheel, me in the ring mount, Doomer in the middle blabbering a little with excitement at Beth. I overhear him say something like, "This is some of the best splodey shit I ever been party to," followed by something monosyllabic from Beth in response.

He proceeds in that vein nonstop for a short while, Beth offering tolerant "Uh-huhs" at intervals.

Our van floats over the burning ruin of the river keep and into the Herax Zone. All the way around the Herax wall the fire spirits are freeing one another and destroying the towers beneath them. Within the Zone sprawl several hundred small, flat-roofed barracks, each sized perhaps for two or three dozen soldiers, a few with boats still docked on the roof and burning. Among these endless rows of barracks stand three huge stone buildings, on the scale of the Circus or the windowless monstrosity straddling the river: each with different architectural traits and style, but clearly of a family, designed by the same mad architect. One of them is surrounded by fires and fighting, Herax besieged within, Givers attacking on rafts and on foot. Parts of the building burn.

Our raft swiftly approaches and sets down in a plaza beside the burning palace, temple, whatever it is. Out from the base of this building emerges the river, through a series of archways with no metal gates barring them.

Blood Eagle alights beside us, alone on a raft, gesturing regally with the Spine of God. "One last task, Cannibal-King," he says. "Blast open that main door." He points to the iron-bound wooden drawbridge-style door dominating the front of the palace.

"Fuck you!" I swing the M240 at him.

He rattles the Spine of God. "Sovereign Shield."

"Heads up heads up heads up!" comes Akaz's voice, urgent and swiftly approaching. I turn to see him diving at my face. Reluctantly I open wide, and as Akaz vanishes into my gullet, here comes the surprisingly speedy and nimble bulk of an eight-foot giant of a man, sprinting straight this way. The crows split. The giant's massive limbs and torso are barely contained by an austere black uniform: this is the guy whose statue we saw earlier. I swing the machine gun to bear on him and fire a dozen rounds as he launches himself into the air at us. My bullets turn into a stream of superheated metal, trailing a comet's tail of fire—only to bounce off him, of course, and come straight back at me, to then get repelled by the Sovereign Shield of Akaz within me and fly back, and so on, streaks of molten metal and Wargus-Fire threading back and forth in a noisy, supersonic flicker.

"Goromath is sovereign!" he says, landing on the front of the van, crunching the hood with one boot, smashing his other through the windshield. Beth and Doomer ditch out the driver's side. General Goromath grabs the M240 in both hands. White-hot metal lances back and forth between us in a continuous stream, faster and faster the closer we get, whistling louder at a higher pitch, the glow illuminating Goromath's demonic grimace of absolute rage. The golden orb in his eye socket glistens with the reflection of the bright, flashing metal.

"You forget, Akaz!" he roars in my face. "Even without the Fifth Sphere, I am still a fire god!"

His hands blaze with light and heat and the machine gun glows as he wrenches it apart, molten metal dripping from the severed halves. I punch him in the face. It's like punching a tree. He grabs the ring mount with one hand and crunches a huge fistful of van roof in the other, unthinkable heat blasting from his hands to burn the paint off the surface of the van, ignite the entire interior, melt windshield, roof, ring mount. Beth, Doomer, and I are unharmed thanks to Akaz's protection, but pained and stunned from the wave of incredible heat nonetheless.

Amid the inferno of the van and everything in it, Goromath grabs me by the throat, threads of molten metal still filling the air between our faces. Gasoline ignites, ammunition explodes, but I barely perceive them through my transfixion. Goromath's one nonmetal eye stares into my one remaining eye, as if through this connection he could focus all that is wrong with his world (*how I wish / that the world / had just one throat / and my fingers were around it*) and eradicate it in one apocalyptic strangling swoop. An execution to correct the whole universe. (Destroy it, more like, no? *Whosoever destroys a single soul....*) In the back of my mind I wonder what would happen to this world if he *did* kill me. Would it vanish at once? Or am I now irrelevant to its continuous existence, less than a lost demiurge? If I even ever did have anything to do with it! How did I get hooked into entertaining such bullshit in the first place?

Regardless, it seems that Akaz by possessing me has granted me not only Sovereign Shield and fireball bullets, but superhuman strength and durability: Goromath's huge hands, strong as the jaws of a hippopotamus, hurt but barely harm my throat, neck, and shoulders.

In my hand I find my Grandfather's army bayonet, somehow completely unmarred from heat that is causing the van's steel to soften and sink. Protected by Akaz as well. I plunge it into Goromath's diaphragm to the hilt. His weight sags against me for a moment as he grunts with discomfort.

Whatever we're standing on, seat, floor, chassis, burns through. We fall through the van to the ground, boots crunching through remaining embers of the raft. As I fall through the red-hot, half-rended roof the back of my head bashes against the edge, denting it. I manage to keep my footing, but Goromath shakes me by the neck, smashing the side of my head against hot metal with a *clang*. "Ow!" I say, shoving the bayonet into his guts again. He stares me in the eye, drawing his snarling face closer to mine, the superfast white-hot liquid metal between our foreheads increasing in intensity until his forehead is pressed against mine, burning metal starting to press into my forehead with inhuman force despite Akaz's blessings still protecting me. Goromath's scream resounds in my ears. I wrench out the bayonet and shove it with all my might up under his chin. It seems to make it up through his tongue—as he wrenches himself upright, letting go of my neck with one hand, loosening his grip with the other, I glimpse into his screaming mouth, his impaled tongue, tip of the bayonet touching the palate but not penetrating to any depth. I shove but it won't go any deeper. He pulls back a fist to smash my face—

Then something slams him in the side of the head: Beth, unharmed, wielding Victoria, also unharmed, bashing Goromath with the rifle-butt in the side of the eye socket.

His golden Eye of Kaios pops out of his head and right into my hand. The dozen or so threads of gleaming molten metal that have been flashing back and forth between us for as long as I can remember simply pass through him and keep moving, blasting a dozen wide holes in his head and torso from front to back. I dance aside as he falls into the charred, burning wreckage of the van, almost losing the bayonet under his enormous oxen bulk but managing to wrench it free from the mangled remains of his head. The knife gleams, untarnished.

I look around. Doomer stands there giving me a little wave. My gaze meets Beth's. We stare. Then something funny happens. At first there's just a tingling in my chest. Then Akaz shoves his head halfway out through my mouth, making me retch. A vague twilight glow emerges from the lethal holes in Goromath's body, then arises in streamers of light like a softly luminous mist to float into Akaz's mouth. The effect on me is immediate and overwhelming, though surely only an echo of what is happening inside Akaz: a firestorm of death-magic energy from devouring the soul of a fellow god. This influx of cosmic power stuns us both; waves of disorientation resonate between his astral skull and my astral skull, contiguous in the Otherworld. I lose focus on the material plane, senses spiraling into kaleidoscopic cascades harmonizing with the pattern that underlies the multiverse.

My attention swims its way through the maelstrom down to this round thing in my hand. What is it? Point? Disc? Sphere? Hypersphere? I wrench off my eyepatch and shove this golden circle into my empty eye socket.

Binocular vision returns immediately, and I begin to weep at how much I missed it. Something unlocks within me. I've been partly dissociated ever since Xax began torturing me, not allowing myself to feel it, not facing the horror of Agent Xax burning my eyeball with cigarettes and then cutting it out. Sobs wrack my body.

Profound as this feeling is, I can't help but notice that I can not only see through the eyes of every remaining living Herax, but I can fully comprehend all that they see. There remain forty-seven Herax spearmen alive, almost all of them defending this building, the Palace-Temple of Goromath.

I hear Akaz's voice in my head, coldly stating two simple words:

Kill yourself.

He wouldn't magically force me to commit suicide—? No, he was not addressing me.

The last forty-seven Herax soldiers draw knives from their belts and stab themselves through the heart more or less simultaneously. My view through their eyes and into their minds fades almost as quickly as it arose.

I become aware of Beth grabbing my arm and shaking it. "Jack! Jack!"

I look her dazedly in the eyes, my two eyes staring into both of hers.

"You ok?"

"Yeah," I find myself saying without emotion. Then I'm walking toward the big drawbridge-door, Victoria in one hand *(when did I take it from Beth?)*, bayonet in the other, Beth and Doomer chasing after and trying to demand my attention.

I arrive at the door. Sheathe the bayonet at my belt. At my other hip hangs my Grandfather's kukri. Tucked also through my belt is my Grandfather's roofing hammer: a cast iron hatchet backed by a hammer-head with wooden grips riveted onto the sides. All three of these, plus Victoria, unharmed by the inferno at the van. I level Victoria at the huge, solid door and blast it into flaming debris.

Inside the hall, Herax corpses lie around everywhere with knives in their chests. I proceed through to the temple chamber, somehow knowing my way from Akaz's mind, thanks not only to his secret visits during Goromath's reign but also from ancient days long before, when it was a humble fane and the footprint of this huge building merely the layout of the surrounding gardens. No Palace-Temple, simply Kaios the Magician's altar to the Dragon of the Sun, when Akaz went simply as the Wolf of Kaios.

The Temple howls with wind. A bright light glares from the altar.

Atop the altar sits the mightiest Engine of Apraxos, a square cage a yard on a side with a glowing sphere within it; the Cage Around the Sun. Long ago, before the Great Breach, before even the Empire of the Eclipse, Apraxos trapped the Sun Dragon into its daily orbit. No longer able to walk among us as it did during Godtime, this engine enabled the advent of the Empire. For in this cage shines the Sun Dragon's heart.

Beside it stands Blood Eagle, brandishing the Spine of God. Levitating nearby, Apraxos. Hovering fanned out behind him, five other sorcerers, all focused on blasting hurricane-winds at the fifty Givers in the room, every one of whom is pinned against the walls with wind. I recognize one of these wizards as the very first of Apraxos's apprentices we met, with the invisible ship.

Blood Eagle wrenches a metal bar from the Cage Around the Sun, heats it red hot with fingers like blowtorches. He hurls it at the wizard I'd just recognized, spears him through the chest with a hot hissing that can be heard even over the roar of winds. The impaled wizard plummets to the floor, dead.

An adjacent sorcerer tries to blast Blood Eagle with a jet of wind, but the Sovereign Shield from the Skull of Kaios reflects it; the wizard is blown into a pillar, the impact stunning him just long enough to fall to the stone floor and crunch his bones.

I shoulder Victoria and shoot one of the sorcerers out of the air, blasting off both head and arm with an exploding fireball to the shoulder. Another sorcerer tries blasting me with a wind jet, shoves himself back but stops before smashing himself into anything. He, his final remaining comrade, and Apraxos take note that their team was just cut in half in a couple of seconds, and so start to fly out through a back door.

Imbued with power by Akaz, and still supercharged from eating Goromath's soul, I leap across the room and grab hold of Apraxos by the shoulders. He keeps moving, the toes of my boots dragging across the stone floor, but my weight holds him back and threatens to haul him down. Apraxos squawks in disapproval and sends lightning coursing through my body. It tickles. I pull him around and pound him once in the jaw. His mask flies off.

His face is hideous.

With a mortified screech, Apraxos flies away, followed by his last two wizard colleagues.

I look to Blood Eagle. He shoves the Spine of God back into his own astral body and focuses on the Altar, chanting, both astral hands shoved into the sides of his own head to grip the astral Skull of Kaios. Using the Skull to liberate the Sun from its binding spell.

"I'm not sure this is what we need to be doing right now," says Beth.

"No." I'm still high on Goromath's soul and dazed from psychological upheaval, but at this moment my hate for Blood Eagle eclipses everything. He played me like a pawn since the moment I landed in his world.

My rage burns strong enough for me to wrest my will back from Akaz. I clamber up beside Blood Eagle at the altar. He continues chanting, but shies away from me. The Givers take note and start to approach.

Uh, Jack, says Akaz within me.

I don't reply.

What are you doing?

I wrench the kukri from my belt and raise it to strike Blood Eagle. He sees what I'm up to almost quickly enough to get the Token of Time Dilation into his mouth—

—but I land the heavy blade square to the crown of his head, then backhand it to his right eye socket, then forehand it to his left jaw hinge, each strike breaking bone; then backhand uppercut to the floating ribs, then a mirror image of that strike but forehand to his ribs on the other side. Then a chop to each hip, a stab to each eye, and finishing with a strike straight through his sternum and heart.

Akaz, making the best of my mutiny, sucks down Blood Eagle's soul. Its power burns as mightily as Goromath's,

for with his ritual Blood Eagle had just wrested control of
the First Sphere from Apraxos. Whatever that means...?
All I know is Blood Eagle had sufficient demigodhood in
his moment of death that the blast from his soul puts me
over the edge.

I cannot tell what is my will, and what is Akaz. I am barely
able to notice Doomer or even Beth, who both speak to me
with some animation. I think my body has become wreathed
and haloed in fire, death magic energy overflowing forth
from me. Not really understanding the meaning of what I
am doing, I wrest the cage and the Heart of the Sun up from
its position atop the altar. I carry it out the front gate of the
Palace-Temple, and despite it being half as big as me I wind
up, shout "Hup!" and hurl it half a mile. It flies over the wall
of the Herax Zone. I see it tumble into the middle of the Circus. Unable to see through the walls I know nonetheless that
I landed it right in the Wargus-Fire. A blaze of light brightens
the sky, a blast of smoke erupts up from the Circus, rising,
cooling, widening into the form of a mushroom. I watch as it
continues to erupt, adding more and more volume of smoke,
spreading the cap of the mushroom out into a broader and
broader canopy, soon covering the entire city and beyond.
Flying sparks and flashes of illumination in the rising column of cloud give the unmistakable impression that I have
just transformed the Circus into an erupting volcano.

I'm dimly aware of Akaz in the back of my mind, *Get after Apraxos before he pulls something,* but I want my goddamn Skull of Kaios back. Beth and Doomer still seem to
be talking to me and they follow me back inside the Pal-

ace-Temple. The Givers are all gone. Where? Crouching at Blood Eagle's body I try to stick my astral hands in to grab the Skull. No dice. I string the Token around my neck and take back the Circomangkus. With a couple of chops from the kukri I sever Blood Eagle's head. I wrap it in a makeshift bag made from a section of curtain with its corners tied together and carry it on my belt.

I hold the Token in my hand and look closely at it. Beth and Doomer are trying to get my attention, I think. I put it in my mouth.

It tastes like stinky ocean. My heart pounds painfully. Debilitating anxiety besets me at once. My mind races like it has never raced before.

But with the world more or less stopped, it is a smallish matter to hop on a flying raft, catch up with Apraxos, and haul him aboard. The eyes in his gruesome face look genuinely terrified, and they somehow follow me despite the rest of his body being frozen in time. I can hear his voice normally as I fly us back into the Palace-Temple. He pleads with me not to kill him, imploring me to have mercy.

I hit him in the head with the hatchet, again, again, twenty times more, till what is left lacks any coherence. No one would ever know, from looking at what remains, whether he were beautiful or ugly.

Then I spit out the Token and collapse.

The soul of mighty Apraxos flows into Akaz within me, to be consumed in the firestorm of devourment. Some huge portion of this magical energy flows by contagion into my body—the third demigod I've fed upon tonight. Any physical depletion from the Token more than vanishes: I am on fire, inside and out, limbs rigid with lightning, mind over-whelmed into confusion and madness.

And I am in this state when the little alien space ship, the size of a truck and bristling with guns, materializes in the Temple and those two guys in suits come out, Agent Xax and whoever his equally-soon-to-be-dead partner is.

Bababadalgharagh

Akaz leaps out of my mouth and stands there, barking furiously at Xax. The fires in me and on me go out. With Akaz gone from within me, some of the souleater madness also lifts from my mind, allowing the outer world to seep into my awareness: the twisted body of Apraxos pinned under my knees, head-remnants scattered and splashed across the raft. The other rafts hovering in a semicircle to either side. Beth and Doomer, each to a raft, shooting after the two remaining mages of Apraxos as they fly away, Beth with Victoria, Doomer with a pistol in each hand. In the corner of my eye I could swear I see Agent Xax's suited accomplice sidestep into the doorway of their invisible ship, then back out, and the doorway vanish—

Before I am quite back, though, Xax teleports right in front of me and punches me in the face. I feel him groping at me—then he holds aloft Blood Eagle's head in victory. Grinning widely, he levels a gun at my head, and in that instant it crosses my mind that with neither the Skull of Kaios on my person nor Akaz possessing me, I have no Sovereign Shield. Unless the Eye of Kaios grants such a thing...?

We'll find that out another time, preferably in a nice, safe experiment with Nerf projectiles, because Akaz dives into my mouth and the deafening crack of Xax's gun is followed by the whistle of a bullet whining back and forth between us. Dazed from Akaz repossessing me, still stunned from Xax's fist in my face, still cosmically disoriented from the souls of gods, I do my best to kick the head of Blood Eagle out of Xax's grasp. Xax teleports back out of reach. The bullet follows him, still maintaining perfect connection between us, its pitch lowering with the increased distance. He shoves Blood Eagle's head under his jacket and it vanishes without leaving a lump.

"How the fuck—?" I ask.

Still smiling, Xax turns and gestures in the air. Nothing happens. He frowns at his accomplice.

"Max, the ship!"

'Max' makes the same gesture. Nothing happens. He shrugs.

A massive tremor rolls through the ground, knocking me and Xax prone. Max somehow keeps his footing while I bash both elbows. Xax's pistol flies from his hand. He and I fall at different speeds and angles, giving a weird trajectory to the bullet zipping back and forth between our mirror-shields. It cracks into a flagstone and ricochets away. I reach for Xax's pistol with no particular plan in mind except to deny him it, but he gestures and it flies right back into his grip. He levels it at me.

I respond with an exasperated *what the fuck you think that's gonna accomplish?* gesture, suddenly aware though that Beth's doomed if, in the heat of the moment, she fires upon him to save me. I dare not call to her in warning nor even look to see if she sees us, lest I draw his attention to her and she becomes his target—but I cannot help but glance her way. She's staring at the un-smoky patch of sky past Mt. Kaios. My gaze follows hers and from the corner of my eye I see Xax turn to follow mine.

The sun soars low over the horizon, approaches swiftly, and falls to earth beyond the mountain.

There's a flash across the horizon, silhouetting the mountain, soon followed by a deafening thunderclap and a tremor worse than the last one. Even Max falls down this time.

Flattened, wind knocked from me, I dimly reflect that I might be happier up on a raft just in case. I get to my feet, calling over the raft Beth is on—a little fast, causing her to stumble and almost fall, but not quite pulling it out from under her—

I start to say "Sorry," but only manage "Sor—!" before another tremor knocks me back to my knees, distracting me from managing Beth's raft. The ground shakes, up and down then side to side, bashing flagstones against my knees and pulling the ground away, dropping me just in time to duck under the approaching edge of Beth's raft. Dazed, I bring the raft to a stop right over me, earthquake bouncing me up and down between it and the ground a couple of times before I slide it aside and clamber aboard, half-dragged by Beth.

Mt. Kaios erupts.

The peak explodes, sending stones and boulders flying into the sky and in all directions. Out from it bursts a coiling sphere of blazing light and absolute blackness, chaotic tendrils of both brightness and dark writhing in and among each other like scores of copulating titan worms made of fire and night. These amorphous titans, the Sun Dragon and the Earth Dragon, confuse the eye and disturb the mind. The maddening sphere of light and darkness soars into the sky, trailing a thick column of smoke, sparks, and fire.

The Great Stone Face carved into the mountain nods out over the city, fire blazing from its eyes. The near side of the mountain blasts open as Shamash slams his way out through it, far larger than when we saw him before, his body aglow like flowing lava contained in bipedal form, broken chains trailing from shackles at his wrists and elbows. His hair and beard of living fire form a halo surrounding the Great Stone Face of Kaios, now affixed to his face as a mask, as if in parody of his former captor, Apraxos. Rocks and boulders from the shattered mountain start falling in the Herax Zone, smashing barracks, so I fly us the hell out of there. Shamash roars in triumph behind his stone mask, the thirteen fire-spirits orbiting him in ecstatic circles. His massive voice echoes across the city as we flee.

Beth and I cling to each other on our raft, vaguely aware of the other rafts trailing behind us, captivated by the city below shattering from earthquake. As we reach the cliff at the edge of the bay, we behold the waters swiftly receding to reveal the weed-choked submerged half of the city. Its slimy buildings and streets crack with the shaking of the earth. Atop an inexplicably intact tower stands a giant man with the head of a heron. Not far from him, a huge, many-spired building slick with green ooze both collapses and erupts, its towers crumbling outward as the ground pushes its way up through it, a titanic, green-gray mound of earth rising through its walls to shrug them aside.

The mound stands erect. Spreads enormous bat-wings. *Fat Man awakens and arises.*

It turns to look at us with its incomprehensible, many-eyed head, gesturing at us in intricate patterns with the innumerable feelers covering the front of its grotesque face. Almost subsonic resonances eerily emanate from it in an otherworldly garble of sounds and syllables, sound waves so massive that they vibrate the raft beneath us and press the air from our lungs. As the mountainous being spreads its dragonlike arms, reaching toward us with a claw that wavers like the boughs of an elm, these words force themselves into my mind:

I awaken from dream and arise from death. You have slain the Binder, who summoned me to this world and trapped me under the sunken city. Along with his skull, his spell is broken, rendering me free to return to the stars and beyond the stars.

Akaz jumps out of my mouth and nods at the obese thing. It bows its massive head in response.

Ah, Destroyer, it says. *You must be pleased to have finally achieved your revenge. If you wish a boon of me before I depart your world, ask it.*

"Nah," says Akaz.

Then your mortal vessel, perhaps, it says, its many eyes boring into me.

"Uh," I say.

"Return us to Earth!" says Beth.

Akaz and I look at her.

You could not survive my methods, says the giant being, *but the Witch-Queen of Gomothrax can send you safely to your home.* It stretches an arm toward the far end of the bay and seems to gesture. *Proceed hence, and I will follow, to ensure she grants your request.*

Across the bay we soar, not far above the waves, Beth and Akaz and I leading the way. Two crows, the Cook and the Crow Terminal, perch at the front edge of the raft and lean into the wind. Doomer sits alone on a raft just behind us looking deeply shaken. I can't blame him; I know I'm deeply shaken. Beth's deeply shaken. Even Akaz is still frazzled and twitchy from his overdose of godsoul.

The dark bay stretches around us for miles, jagged black hills biting the horizon in every direction. Directly across from us looms the silhouette of a huge, intricate castle, flanked by massive bridges that cross the narrow mouth of the bay. "That's Gomothrax."

"You trust this Witch-Queen?" asks Beth. "She was in your game as, what, someone with interdimensional powers?"

"She wasn't in my game at all. I never even figured out what was in Gomothrax. It was just a name on the map."

The rest of the rafts follow behind us, empty, like trays skimming along an invisible luncheonette counter, the unthinkably huge, gelatinous mass of Fat Man shambling after, his almost-translucent form backlit by the twin volcanoes of the Circus and Mt. Kaios together devouring the city of Melkhaios in fire and molten stone. The glowing body of Shamash dances in the ruins, Salamandrines flitting around him.

The rafts are not all empty. Something stands silhouetted upon the hindmost—

—Two man-shapes. Xax and Max.

I flip their raft over but they vanish, Xax grabbing Max
by the lapel, and reappear on the next-closest raft. I flip that
one over but Xax teleports them again, this time all the way
onto Doomer's raft right behind us. Doomer shouts and
jumps in surprise and nearly falls off.

I swipe the edge of the nearest empty raft through the
space occupied by Xax and Max, but Xax somehow senses
it without having to see it and blinks his way onto our raft
right in front of us. He lets go of Max's lapel and grabs two
guns out of nowhere, placing one against my forehead and
the other at Beth's.

I have my Grandfather's bayonet at his throat.

"Jack!" says Beth, "Jack, Jack!" and I realize we're speeding right at the side of the castle. We've crossed the bay far
faster than I expected. This place looms gigantic, more like
a town all built on top of itself than what I'd call a 'fortress.' A
bizarre accumulation of different architectural styles, most
of them ornate and exquisite, somehow impossibly harmo-
nious in their relation to one another despite no apparent
coherence or plan to their arrangement. To either side, it
sprouts great wings of stone bridges, stretching across the
narrow mouth of the bay to steep cliff promontories on either side.

Close at hand, as Beth observed, we are just about to
slam into a wide stone balcony with carven balustrade. In-
stinctually I flip the raft nearly upright and bring it to a sud-

den stop, causing us all to fall flat on it, or rather against it, except for Akaz, who remains effortlessly perpendicular regardless of gravity or laws of motion. Then before we slide off into the drink, I flip the raft back and tilt it to dump me, Beth, and Doomer onto the balcony. Akaz hops nimbly across. Before Xax and Max can follow us I shove the raft right the hell out from under them and they fall. With superhuman agility Max springs off the departing raft, grabs hold of the railing, and launches himself onto the balcony, landing on his feet. I have the point of my bayonet pinned to his tie at the solar plexus, but he holds up one finger in a distinctly non-combative peremptory gesture.

"Hold it," he says simply.

The Cook flaps down into humanoid form, gray and lanky like an ambulatory sapling, but Max makes an equally mollifying gesture at him as well, which the Wilder pauses to consider.

Xax appears out of nowhere, again with one gun at my head and another at Beth's.

"Before I finalize formally taking the reins," says Xax, "as God-King of the World of Kaios, I wish to thank you, Waghalter, for creating a world with such mighty magicks in it."

"Fuck you, Xax," says Akaz.

"Stay your hand, little God-Dog," says Xax. "I've got the drop on your precious Earthlings, and if you so much as flinch I'll blast their heads off. Now where was I."

"What's with the villain speech?" Beth asks me.

"I know," I say, "right?"

"It's not any fun," Xax continues, "unless you understand. You have to know why, so you truly *suffer*. That's how I like it. So. Once I take command of Shamash, and Great Cthulhu here," nodding at the tentacle-faced Fat Man standing waist-deep in the bay—at the suggestion of being 'commanded' it unleashes an uncanny telepathic squeal of scorn and disbelief—"and the other remaining god-things, this will prove to be the perfect staging ground for my conquest of your Earth. As has been my plan all along." He grins hugely.

"What," I say.

"The fuck," says Beth.

Older Aleck steps through a doorway onto the balcony, even shaggier and shabbier in person than in the Vast Plain.

"Hey," he says, with a little wave. "It's me. Aleck. You know, from in the bird." He nods at the Crow Terminal.

"Hi," I say.

"Hi," says Beth.

"You're all welcome here in Gomothrax," says Aleck, "except for this asshole." He nods at Xax.

"I'll get to you in a moment, Old Woad," says Xax.

Out of the sky plummets the writhing sphere of the inter-mingled, copulating Sun Dragon and Earth Dragon. It crashes into the middle of the bay, causing a momentary tremor—

Then a translucent sphere, like a luminous soap bubble, surrounds the entirety of Gomothrax, all the way out to the tips of the promontories marking the mouth of the bay. The citadel stops shaking.

The world outside does not stop shaking. The dragons' impact sends a ring-shaped tidal wave in all directions. When it reaches us it splashes against our surrounding sphere, covering our view entirely, even cresting over the top to send a sheet of water down the far side.

When the waters recede from the face of the sphere, we see the bay roiled by tumultuous chaotic waves—not the mighty but regular ripples I would expect (not that I know enough about fluid dynamics to reasonably expect anything), but strange, jagged walls of waterfall radiating out at random angles from the site where the Dragons landed.

I can't quite make sense of what I'm seeing, until the Dragons burst up from the bay again, launching their coruscating sphere of light and darkness up into the sky to arc overhead and descend again somewhere out over the ocean behind Gomothrax. In the wake of their eruption from the bay arises not only a massive column of water, but enormous sheets of stone, miles across and a mile thick—

—and then it dawns on me that the world I invented for my old D&D game—the world which had been projected into my unconscious mind as a boy?—was a hollow sphere, its interior surface inhabited by drow and dero and innumerable other underearth "monsters," its crust as little as one mile thick.

Now I comprehend what I'm seeing, what's causing those weird waves, those walls of waterfall: the Hollow World is breaking apart, fragments tilting this way and that, and the bay is pouring down through the cracks.

We watch as the entire shell of the planet shatters into a vast archipelago, hundreds of islands floating in space like a spherical array of Roger Dean Yes album covers. Great Cthulhu tumbles down and away into darkness.

Inside our sphere of protection Gomothrax floats free: citadel, bridges, promontories clipped from the Isle of

Kaios, even a hemispherical segment of bay-water below us, without the slightest hint of tremor.

"Like I was saying," Older Aleck says, "all of you are welcome but this guy." And some invisible force flings Xax's guns from his hands out over the balcony.

"Wha—!" says Xax.

Without missing a beat, I stab at Xax with my Grandfather's bayonet—but he's gone, teleported behind Max.

Xax is already pulling another pistol from somewhere inside his jacket. Max, however, elbows him in the face, stunning him enough to drop his gun. Aleck, quicker than I'd expect, shoves his hand under Xax's suit-jacket—

—up to the shoulder.

Then pulls out a glittering golden Skull, which he pitches out over the balcony.

"No!" shrieks Xax, grasping at the air after it.

"Fetch," says Aleck.

Max shoves Xax over the balcony. Moments later, far below, wet Xax floats away out through the protective bubble and into the aether.

Aleck turns to me and Beth. "Thanks for your help." He offers his hand. I dazedly shake it. "Trapping Xax here saved your Earth probably, and you all played key roles."

"Indeed," adds Max.

"What the fuck," says Beth, shaking Aleck's hand listlessly. "Destroyed this whole world though?"

"The fuck," I agree.

"It's not destroyed," says Aleck, gesturing at the spherical archipelago, Sun Dragon and Earth Dragon still coiling wildly at its center. "And this cataclysm had to happen anyway. It's part of this world's cosmic myth-cycle. We just piggybacked on it to trap Xax here."

"Myth-cycle?" I scoff. "You're ok destroying a world because of its myth-cycle?"

"Don't blame me, man," says Aleck, and I realize what he's going to say a split second before he does: "You made this world, not me."

Beth and I look at each other, clearly unconvinced: *Looking forward to discussing this with you in private.*

Aleck holds out to me the gory bundle containing Blood Eagle's head. "Here you go," he says. "Got this out of Xax's pocket for you."

I hesitantly take it from him. I can feel the Skull of Kaios resonating within it. "The Skull is in here," I say. "But you threw it over the edge...."

"That was fake," says Aleck. "Plastic. Heh. Hahaha!"

"Man," says Doomer, "I could use some fuckin' brisket."

"Tell me about it," says Akaz.

"Yes," says Max.

Beth and I stare at Max.

"I told you we had allies in unexpected places," says Aleck.

"I'm not at liberty to discuss my role here," says Max.

Beth and I look at each other.

"Oh yeah," says Doomer, "this is our old pal Max. I keep forgetting where you guys are in your timeline."

"The Witch-Queen of Gomothrax can get you to California if you want," says Aleck. "Let's eat first, though."

They head in. Beth and I take each other by the hand, pause in the greenish glow coming through the ornate marble archway, then follow slowly after them.

Epilogue in the Ruins of the Palace-Temple

AGENT XAX sits on a plain stone throne much too big for him. The great seat rests on a section of stone floor a few yards across, which floats unsupported in empty space.

In every direction float islands of all sizes, some as small as Xax's plinth, others miles long. The near ones hold ruined buildings of Melkhaios. The rest of the planet lies scattered around in a massive archipelago of floating islands, retaining a roughly spherical configuration.

Xax broods, holding a gold-looking Skull, tapping it arhythmically in agitation. It sounds plastic.

XAX: If it hadn't been for those accursed Earthlings.

A featureless white sphere nine inches across appears from nowhere and hovers beside him. Xax jumps, startled.

XAX: Shit, don't do that!

SPHERE: *(in a mellifluous voice)* Apologies, Lord.

XAX: From now on, appear over there a few yards *(he gestures vaguely)* and announce yourself before flying up.

SPHERE: Understood.

Pause while Xax stares at the sphere.

XAX: Well?!

SPHERE: Report: we have confirmed that interdimensional contact is blocked from anywhere in the discernable vicinity of any of this world's remnants. All known portals or permeabilities are gone without trace. The Archive of Thoth is gone. The *Sign of the God-Dog* is gone. There are no other planets in this universe; the stars are small lights several miles overhead. There is no sign of your ship. No known exit seems possible from this pocket dimension or, as such places are often known, 'snowglobe world.'

XAX: Fuck.

He scowls down into the False Skull's eye sockets.

XAX: Anything else?

The hovering white sphere drops the Spine of Kaios out of nowhere into Xax's lap.

SPHERE: This may be of some interest. I detected indications of other related items scattered among the other islands as well. Nearly two hundred pieces.

Xax hefts the divine relic Spine and the cheap plastic Skull.

XAX: Hmm.

He affixes the top of the Spine to the base of the plastic False Skull. They click into place.

XAX: Hmm.

He sits there brooding with his bony golden scepter.

November 1, 2013—October 31, 2015
Berkeley, Calif.

continued in

the Jack Waghalter adventures

TALES FROM THE CALIFORNIA ARCHIPELAGO

and

CANNIBAL-KING OF EARTH

About the Author

Andrew M. Reichart is also the author of the novel *Wallflower Assassin*, which takes place long after the *City of the Watcher* trilogy and features some of the same characters. His short fiction has appeared in *Tales from Fiddler's Green*, the zine *Weird Luck Tales*, and several volumes of the annual *Spoon Knife* anthology. With Nick Walker he cowrites the webcomic *Weird Luck*, which is illustrated by Mike Bennewitz. He lives in California with his wife and a couple of dogs.